THE UTTERLY UNACCEPTABLE ATROCITY OF ISABELLE MARSDEN

THE UTTERLY UNACCEPTABLE ATROCITY OF ISABELLE MARSDEN

A NOVEL

NAN SANDERS POKERWINSKI

SHE WRITES PRESS

Published in 2026 by
She Writes Press, an imprint of The Stable Book Group

32 Court Street, Suite 2109
Brooklyn, NY 11201
https://shewritespress.com
The Library of Congress Control Number is available upon request.
ISBN: 979-8-89636-096-4
eISBN: 979-8-89636-097-1

Interior Designer: Kiran Spees

Printed in the United States

To Ray, the most creative (and sometimes crazy, but in a good way) person I know.

Thank you for encouraging and inspiring me with your energy, ideas, and outside-the-box approaches to problems and projects.

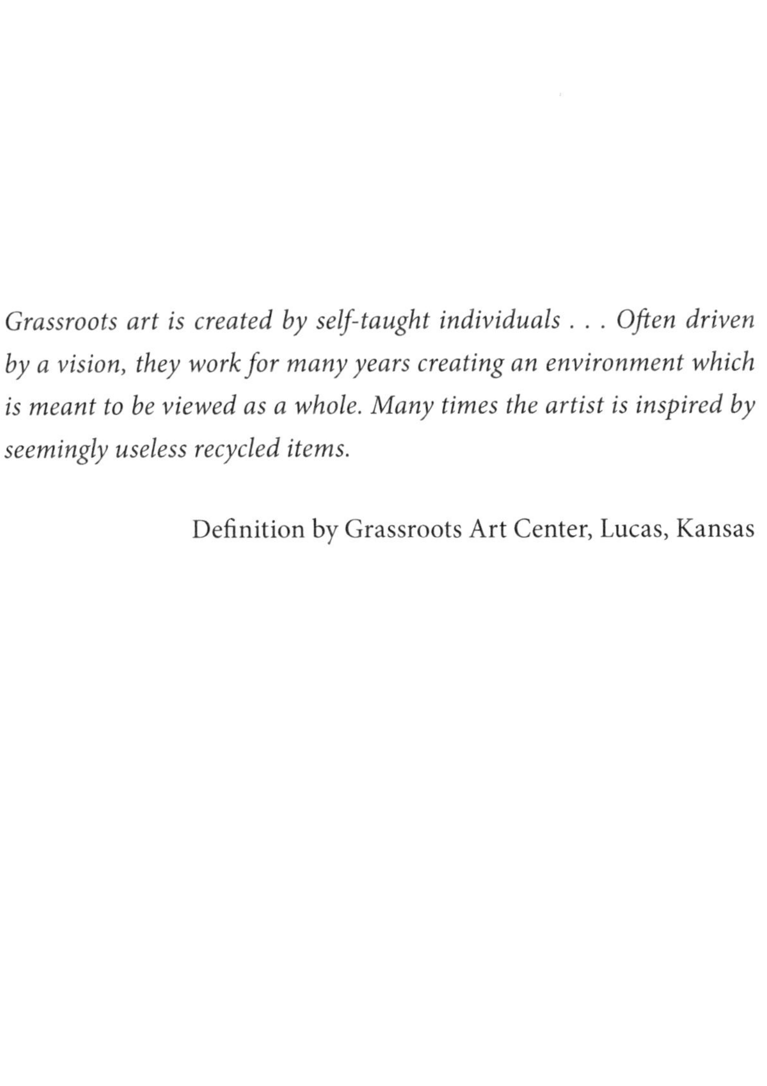

Grassroots art is created by self-taught individuals . . . Often driven by a vision, they work for many years creating an environment which is meant to be viewed as a whole. Many times the artist is inspired by seemingly useless recycled items.

Definition by Grassroots Art Center, Lucas, Kansas

CONTENTS

CAST OF CHARACTERS

LUCY BAILEY – Belle's mentor and first boss at the Magnus hotel chain

BELLE (ISABELLE MARSDEN) – the main character, former event planner who moves from Chicago to Kansas to heal from a traumatic experience

ROSCOE BOX (aka the Penitentiary Poet) – Soulstice gang member who works at federal penitentiary and writes poetry

COOGAN – roadside zoo owner and exotic animal dealer

DESHAWN – Soulstice gang member, waiter, tenor in community choir, and history buff

SAMUEL PERRY DINSMOOR – eccentric artist who created the Garden of Eden in Lucas

MRS. DUMAS – Belle's landlady

EZRA – librarian and nephew of Belle's neighbor Mitchell

MRS. GLICK – Belle's second-grade teacher

TYREE GUYTON – unconventional Detroit artist and creator of the Heidelberg Project

GRANDPA JAKE – Belle's deceased paternal grandfather

MARCUS JAMISON – Belle's second boss at the Magnus hotel chain

JAX – Soulstice gang member and roadside zoo volunteer who's fond of neon hair and nail colors and creative snack foods

LAKSHMI – Soulstice gang member who works at the roadside zoo

ARTHUR MACADAMS – Parks and Recreation director for the city of Lawrence

MAE (aka Aquamaureen) – Soulstice gang member who dresses all in shades of blue-green, loves crossword puzzles, and seems ditzy but knows a thing or two

DANA MARSDEN – Belle's late mother

GREG MARSDEN – Belle's father

SHELLEY MARSDEN – Belle's stepmother

MIRANDA – Belle's best and most trusted friend since elementary school

ROGER MORTON – Lawrence city manager and good friend of Steve Schwann

MITCHELL MULDOON – Belle's next-door neighbor, a retired custodian with a green thumb and Ezra's uncle

NICK – Miranda's fiancé

OZZY – young fox, a recent addition to Coogan's roadside zoo

BEN PARK – Belle's college boyfriend

OLIVE PICKLE – Soulstice gang member who's gaunt but cheerful

POLLY – gift-shop manager at the Garden of Eden in Lucas

MRS. PRUITT – Belle's nosy neighbor across the street

REBA – artist who creates unconventional quilts, wall hangings incorporating roadkill, and other unusual works and Soulstice gang member

RIP – Mitchell's dear, departed dog

STEVE SCHWANN – Lawrence city zoning department head and Belle's adversary

URSULA – Ezra's former romantic interest in Nebraska

WALLACE – young wallaby and Reba's sidekick

ZEBULON – Soulstice gang member with a flair for costumes

– 1 –
THE ARTISTE

A bit wild for Kansas, wasn't it?

Not that Belle had anything to compare it to—she'd never been to a quilt show before, never paid much attention at all to quilts—but there was something distinctly *off* about the counterpane that hung before her like a curtain on a rod. At first glance, its design looked traditional, like the one titled "Sunbonnet Sue" hanging beside it. But closer inspection revealed stitched blocks depicting ferocious animals escaping from cages and running like hell off the edges of the quilt.

Definitely unconventional.

Unconventional made Belle woozy. As did the woman standing next to her—a little too close for Belle's comfort. The woman looked like *she* might have escaped from an animal pen, with that untamable tangle of hair and the way she rocked back and forth, low to the ground, on her footpads.

"Ooooooo," the woman intoned, her voice ranging from chirp to coo as she spoke to no one in particular.

Belle sidled away. She was in no mood to engage with anything more than quilts. The woman gave Belle a sideways, slantwise look and sidled in the same direction. While normally that would've been enough to make Belle turn and flee, she considered her reason for visiting the quilt show in the first place. To try something new. Besides, the strange quilt held her spellbound.

A sound like "Hmmmmmm" escaped Belle's lips. It wasn't so much a comment on the quilt as her reflexive response to any overture from a stranger: a signal that though she was responding, she wasn't inviting intimacy. Then she hiccupped—a nervous tic that annoyed her no end.

"Well, how do you dooooooooooo," the woman said, drawing out the last word in a downward glissando while turning her head and studying Belle in the same manner as she had the quilt: with an expression that was half scowl, half squint. The woman's tawny eyes had an animal quality, too—feline, but not in a suspicious or sneaky way. More lioness than housecat. Unconventional for sure. *Artsy.*

What on earth was Belle doing here—at a quilt show, of all places—exchanging nonsensical sounds with this unconventional (artsy or just plain crazy?) woman?

It was like this: Lulled by last night's bourbon—just a nip to toast her new life—and exhausted from the 450-mile drive, Belle had slept deeply, dreamlessly, and awakened with enough energy to spend the morning unpacking moving boxes. Then to reward her industry, she'd driven to the coffee shop she'd glimpsed on her first drive through the leafy college town that was to be her refuge for the next six months. On the way she'd seen the signs: Quilt Show—Central United Methodist Church. She'd never been to a quilt show, never had any inclination to go to one, but how very Kansas. Perhaps it would offer a perspective on her new surroundings. And how comforting. Belle was no artist herself—far from it—yet she had always found solace in other people's artistry. And solace was what she desperately needed in the wake of that wretched experience with Jamison, her former boss.

But solace wasn't exactly what she found when she followed the arrows and ended up here, beside this peculiar woman, staring at this peculiar quilt.

Except for the two women's voices and the shush of feet on the wooden floor and occasional murmurs of appreciation from other quilt-show goers, few sounds circulated through the church activity-room-turned-gallery. Color was the predominant sensory stimulus. Not on Belle, of course. She wore the usual: jeans and a tank top the same shade of gray as her eyes. The woman beside her was a different story, dressed in Southwestern shades of turquoise, terra-cotta, and gold and sporting a crocheted, Rastafarian-style hat that barely contained her fuzzy mane. Around the room, quilts in Sunburst, Log Cabin, Flying Geese, and the ubiquitous Sunbonnet Sue designs hung hem-to-hem with splashy abstracts.

"Mmmmmm, this one's unusual," Belle said aloud, to fill the awkward pause. "Seems unconventional. Don't quite know what to make of it."

Bird-lion woman laughed, a trill. "Neither do I," she said. "And *I* made it." Then cutting her cat-eyes toward Belle, added, "I'm Reba. And if you ask me if I like country music, you'll be automatically disqualified from new best friend status."

Belle hesitated, pinching her lower lip between her teeth, then reached out to shake Reba's extended hand. "I'm Isabelle . . . but you can call me Belle. Nice to meet you, Re—*Whoa!* What the devil . . . ?"

"Oh, how rude of me." Reba turned face-on, revealing a denim sling around her shoulders—the kind made for carrying babies—from which protruded a doglike snout, two furry ears, and a pair of feet that looked like oversized clown versions of a rabbit's feet. "Meet Wallace. He's a wallaby. Or wallababy, if you will. We were just heading home for iced tea. You could come along."

Just days before, Isabelle Marsden, age thirty-four and seven months, known to friends as Belle, was on her way to a new life. Alone. No husband, no kids, no pets. Never had the husband and kids; pets, not since childhood. She knew her destination—a randomly selected Kansas town—but nothing more of what lay ahead. Everything she'd known was behind her in Chicago: job (intolerable, courtesy of Jamison), home (if you could call it that: a studio that was little more than a place to sleep and eat cereal and takeout), friends (mostly from work, except for Miranda, her bestie from grade school through college and careers).

A fuchsia stripe on her GPS showed her route, a line so straight the disembodied voice she called Sabrina had no reason to speak up. On either side of the road, acres of densely planted corn: monoculture monotony. And on the radio—until the signal faded out—McCoy Tyner's jazzy piano, broadcast from the Chicago public radio station Belle had supported with semiannual pledges. She had the T-shirts, tote bags, and mugs to prove it, all tightly packed with the rest of her belongings in the back of her Chevy Spark.

She'd driven through countryside like this on her way to college in Indiana, oh, so long ago. How different she was then: eager to engage with the world and its interesting people. Now, all she wanted was a haven—a place to retreat, regroup, reassess, regain control, and use her rational mind to figure out how the hell to get herself back on track.

On the short walk to Reba's house—just a few blocks from the Methodist church—Belle's mind was a jumble. *It's not like me to follow a stranger home. Much less some boho Salsa-farian who carries around a kangaroo. Wallaby. Wallababy. Whatever. Shouldn't I really get back to unpacking? What difference would it make to this stranger if I just thank her for the invitation but turn around and go back to my car? I'm not here to make friends; I'm here to hole up and decide what's next. To heal. I don't need other people for that, least of all crazy ones.*

And yet she could not bring herself to stop. It would be rude. Besides, there was something in Reba's exuberance and unconventionality that cheered her the way Miranda's always did.

Color outside the lines, Belle. That's what Miranda had inscribed in the grown-up coloring book she'd slipped into a box of leftover miscellany while helping Belle pack. "Salmagundi," Miranda had scrawled in her loopy script on the label she'd stuck sideways on the box. Belle would've stuck the label on straight and detailed the box's contents on it, but she'd been so exhausted that last day before the move, she'd let Miranda take over. When she'd seen the label and started to protest, Miranda had hushed her: "C'mon, Belle. It'll be like a surprise package."

Belle was not a surprise-me kind of person. Not. At. All. Surprises made her queasy, but she'd trusted Miranda on that one, as she trusted Miranda on so many things.

"Well, here it is," Reba announced, jarring Belle out of her ruminations.

Reba's house struck Belle as the architectural equivalent of its inhabitant. A patchwork of iris, daffodils, tulips, and hyacinths crowded a sidewalk that led to a weathered porch festooned with Tibetan prayer flags. Old bowling balls encrusted with mosaic tiles and faux jewels crowned a stone retaining wall out front and stood like sentries on either side of the porch steps.

Reba started up the steps and motioned for Belle to follow. Belle remained rooted in place, wishing she could blend in with the flowers and disappear. She took a step forward and then two steps back when she caught sight of the front door, decorated with swirls of blue and green that spiraled around a doorknob painted to resemble an eyeball.

"How . . . unusual," Belle said.

Reba looked over her shoulder and raised an eyebrow. "Think so?" She pushed open the door with one hand.

Unlocked. But of course it would be. The eyeball held Belle's gaze until she shook her head to break the spell.

"Well, come on in." Reba bustled inside, slipped off the Snugli, and deposited Wallace on the floor. Wallace blinked and sniffed the air. Then he sprang onto a window seat strewn with pillows in colors suggestive of Mumbai.

Belle crept up the steps and edged a toe toward the threshold. Drew it back. *What am I doing here? Seriously, this is crazy. And whatever else I may be, I am not crazy.*

"Just make yourself comfortable while I get the tea," Reba said, heading into the kitchen. With a skeptical look toward Belle, Wallace bounded off the window seat and hopped after Reba.

Belle leaned into the open doorway. As her eyes adjusted to the dimmer light, two impulses tugged at her. One, to explore the room and its strange contents. The other, to pivot on her heel and run the hell away from any more surprises.

Color outside the lines, Belle.

She gave the doorknob one last furtive glance and slid past it into the room but left the door ajar in case she felt the need to escape in a hurry. With each tentative step toward the window seat, a new peculiarity snagged her attention. On one wall hung an object—an assemblage she guessed you'd call it—made from porcupine quills, feathers, beads, and a scaly, shell-like thing that looked like the carapace of an oversized insect. *Armadillo?* Belle never had seen such a creature in real life but recalled encyclopedia pictures from childhood. She suppressed a shiver.

Another wall was covered floor to ceiling with masks—skulls, birds, Buddhas, demons—all beaded, bejeweled, and embellished with bits of colored glass and mirror. On a side table, a collection of animal bones sat alongside a spread of cookies, donuts, and an entire layer cake that, close-up, turned out not to be actual food but crocheted and papier-mâché likenesses.

Strange was not an adequate word for this place. Creepy? A little. Intriguing? That too. Belle's insides mirrored her thoughts: A current skittered through her belly, circled around, and coursed through again; her chest thumped.

Or was that thumping coming from Wallace, bouncing into the room behind Reba, who carried a tray laden with glasses of iced tea and a plate of cookies? (Real? In this place, who knew?)

"So," Reba said. "I see my creations haven't scared you away—yet. Some people are put off by the roadkill, but I say, 'It's there for the taking and a whole lot cheaper than ordering from Dick Blick.'"

Belle peered through slitted eyes at the armadillo shell and back at Reba. "I'm not sure I—"

"Dick Blick? The art supply place? You're not an *artiste*?"

"Hardly! I almost flunked kindergarten because I couldn't draw a stick figure. And then in second grade . . ."

Reba set the refreshments on the coffee table and plunked herself onto the window seat. "Second grade was a long time ago. Besides, there's more to art than drawing," she said, lingering mid-sentence over the word *art*.

The interruption took Belle aback; she swallowed an indignant *hmph* but didn't think it worthy of comment.

Wallace nibbled Reba's ankles until she hauled him up beside her. Then, patting a pillow-free space on her other side, she looked at Belle with an intensity that turned her feline eyes to glittering amber.

"Sit yourself down here, woman, and tell me about *your* talents. Or as I like to call them, your gifts."

Her gifts. What, exactly, would those be? Organization? She was good at that—so good she'd made a living at it back in Chicago, as a closet organizer and event planner. That seemed like more of a skill, though, not a true talent or *gift*. Certainly not on a par with drawing or painting or even making wall hangings from parts of dead animals, and not something she cared to disclose to new acquaintances. Once people knew you were an orderly type, they expected you to organize every disordered thing that came along. Then there you were, doing the drudge work while everyone around you lived it up. What's more, she had no interest in doing anything that would remind her of her previous life—and Jamison. What he'd put her through: the indignities, the shame. As if anyone could ever truly forget something like that.

Belle kept thinking. She'd been told she was a good listener. Again, big deal, gift-wise. What else, what else? At thirty-four-plus, surely she had cultivated one or two talents.

"Mmmmmm, well, I guess I—" Belle began, stalling for time.

"Oh, good lord!" Reba leapt from the window seat with such force the ice in the glasses on the coffee table rattled, and her Rastacap flew off her head. "Him again! I was sure he was out of town, and we could breathe easy for a few days. Wallace! *Allez!*"

Wide-eyed, Belle looked from Reba to Wallace to Reba to Wallace as the two scrambled, Reba running to the front window for a better view of the red-bearded man striding up her front walk, Wallace—as if following a practiced routine—making a beeline for a doorway in an alcove off the living room.

"Belle! Get him downstairs!" Reba hissed. "*Please?*"

Without thinking, Belle shot from the window seat, scooped Wallace into her arms, flung open the door before him, and clattered down a rickety wooden stairway into a basement dark as a snake hole. Depositing Wallace on the floor, she sprinted back up the stairs to slam the door and scurried back down just moments before Reba's voice wafted through the floorboards.

"Mr. Coooooogan! What a surprise. And yet, I must have known someone was coming to visit. Look—I was just about to have an iced tea, and something impelled me to pour a second glass and set out a plate of cookies."

In the dark of the cellar, Belle groped for a light switch, but her fingers found only stone walls draped with . . .

Cobwebs? Are you kidding me? What kind of horror movie cliché have I stumbled into?

Wary of making any noise that might attract the visitor's attention, Belle lowered herself onto the bottom step and stared into the blackness, trying to make out the cellar's contents. Given the weirdness she'd already encountered above ground, she could only imagine what might be stored beneath. Cauldrons? Shrunken heads?

A furry snout nuzzled Belle's kneecap. She gathered Wallace up and held him on her lap like a toddler, stroking the top of his head. His jittery heartbeat slowed, and so did hers. And then, against all odds, both Belle and wallababy dozed off.

At first, the pounding was a drumbeat in a convoluted dream. Grotesque figures danced around leaping flames as Belle tried to herd a troupe of capybaras. Then she roused and realized the sound was Reba beating on the basement door.

"Hey—you okay down there? The coast is clear now, you can come up."

Clutching Wallace to her chest, Belle grabbled up the stairs and fumbled to open the door. The afternoon light dazzled her so, she could hardly make out Reba standing with arms outstretched, a glass of iced tea in one hand, a fresh plate of cookies in the other.

"Sorry for the delay," Reba said. "Had to get rid of that pest. He's been sneaking around ever since he got a tip that I might have been responsible for a little—shall we say—mischief at his roadside zoo."

"Were you?" Belle surprised herself with the bold question. Normally, she'd have waited for an explanation and if none came, just wondered silently.

Reba turned to lead the way back to the living room. "Of course. But not in the way he thinks."

Weary all at once despite the basement nap, Belle sank onto the window seat and leaned against a pillow. She wasn't sure she wanted to know more, but she had a feeling she was going to hear the story whether or not she fed Reba prompts. "So, you . . ."

"I liberated Wallace from that prison camp, yes. But Coogan has no clue about that—I made it look like Wallace dug his way out. Coogan thinks I stole his armadillo to use in one of my creations. Of course, I would never! That creature got out on his own and then had the misfortune of crossing the highway at the wrong moment. I merely gathered and memorialized his remains. But the more Coogan comes poking around here, the more it complicates life for Wallace and me. I can only take him out in public when I'm sure Coogan is away, which, fortunately for everyone, is most of the time." Reba chugged half her glass of tea. "Enough about us, though! We were talking about you when we were so abruptly interrupted. You must be new in town. I've never seen you around before."

"Total newbie." Belle reached for a cookie. "Mmmmm, I could use one of these right about now. So, yeah, I just moved here and—oh! What kind of cookie is this?" She held it up and scrutinized the green flecks running through it.

"Zucchini jalapeño. Grew them myself. Not the cookies, the squash and peppers. I'm not much for chocolate chip or oatmeal. So anyway, what brings you here to the Kansas Capital of Kookdom and Quirkdom? Got a job at the college?"

Belle took a tentative bite of the cookie. "Nothing like that. I guess you could say I went for a spin and landed here. That's the short version. The longer version is—longer."

– 2 –
THE PUZZLER

Belle didn't need dishes; she'd brought her Crate & Barrel plates, bowls, and mugs—the chip-resistant, stackable dinnerware set—along from Chicago. So why was she fondling this blue china cup on the yard sale table? And why was she poking around a yard sale, anyway?

She hadn't planned to go exploring. She'd planned to spend a quiet morning at her new home. *Retreat. Regroup.* That's what she had planned, especially after the somewhat bizarre encounter with Reba and Wallace the day before. But after another morning of unpacking boxes in her little stone rental house, with its smell like old books and face powder, she found herself restless. Couldn't hurt to go for a drive, get some fresh air, get to know her surroundings. She wouldn't have to stop anywhere, wouldn't have to talk to anyone, just have a look around.

Yet somehow, after driving through a landscape of silty ponds, fields flat as pool tables, and trees that in lusher settings would barely qualify as shrubs, she'd ended up in a place called Tonganoxie, where the yard sale, like the quilt show, drew her interest. It seemed *so very Kansas*. Her curiosity got the best of her. Couldn't hurt to just look, right?

She glanced at her phone to check the time. Against her better judgment, Belle had agreed to meet Reba for coffee at four, at which time Reba promised to elaborate on the circumstances under which Wallace had become her roommate. But that was still a few hours off, and Tonganoxie was probably only twenty minutes away. Her attention returned to the cup in her hand. Totally impractical. For one thing, her fingers barely fit into the space between handle and cup. For another, it was delicate china. And blue? Not her color.

Yet she couldn't put the cup down.

"Like it? It was my mother's." The voice came from a woman slumped like a half-empty sack of chicken feed in an aluminum lawn chair beneath a shade tree.

"Your mother's?" Belle would never sell anything of *her* mother's. She had so few mementos as it was: faded snapshots of the two of them at Disney World when Belle was eight; her mother's favorite turquoise-and-silver earrings; a pair of crocheted gloves the exact size of Belle's own hands; the rings her father had given her the day of her mother's funeral fifteen years ago. She wore the rings often and cared for the other artifacts like a curator, swaddling them in tissue paper, storing them in archival boxes. On the trip down from Chicago, the collection had occupied the passenger seat like a long-time companion. "You sure you want to sell it?"

Another glance at the hapless woman made Belle regret the question. Of course the woman wanted to sell the cup and everything else on the tables, which looked to be just about everything she owned.

"Ain't that why it's there?" the woman snorted, sounding like a scornful barnyard animal. She gave a look that Belle couldn't read. Disdain? Indignation? Had Belle offended her?

Summoning skills she'd honed in a job where smoothing ruffled feathers often was required, Belle tried to find common ground. "Are you moving? I've just moved myself, and I did a lot of load-lightening as well."

"Moving—that's a good one. Don't I wish." The woman swiped

a hand across her forehead and rubbed it on her shapeless polyester pants, then nodded toward a Ford Escort parked in the driveway, its battered grille a grimace of dejection. "Gotta get that thing running, and that takes money. Which I ain't got at the moment."

Belle set the cup down and picked up a flowered plate with a chip the size of a thumbprint on its edge. She didn't need any dishes, but something about the woman's desperation struck a chord. No amount of money could make up for what the woman was losing, for what she'd perhaps already lost. But maybe, just maybe, a little cash would help get her on the road to someplace better. A quest Belle could identify with. Pulling her wallet from her purse, Belle turned back to the woman. "Got any boxes and newspaper? I'll take all the dishes you have. And that lamp over there. And how much for the little end table?"

Parked in front of One World Café in downtown Lawrence, fifteen minutes early for her coffee date with Reba, Belle rolled down the windows and watched people passing on the sidewalk. A young man with tattoo sleeves on both arms and nickel-sized plugs in his earlobes pushed a toddler in a stroller. A large woman carrying a guitar and sporting a purple hat with a feather plume ambled over to a sidewalk bench, took a seat, and belted out a bluesy tune. A trio of young women with identical straight, side-parted hairstyles and Pi Beta Phi T-shirts fiddled with their phones and stopped to snap selfies in front of a street sculpture of a taco with legs.

Belle watched them all with more detachment than interest. Her eyes drifted over a planter spilling in an artful way with begonias, sweet potato vines, and ornamental grasses to the street scene beyond: a main street filled with boutiques, galleries, restaurants, and a few old-school businesses like the hardware store and barbershop. Not one vacant storefront that she could see. And flowers, flowers everywhere. This was a community that kept up appearances. Exactly the kind of agreeable, colorful, yet orderly place she'd hoped to find.

But wait—this guy jaywalking right behind her car—that wasn't exactly orderly, was it? Or even necessary, with that crosswalk just a few steps away. In profile, the man's face—the angle of his jaw—looked familiar, but not in a comforting way. Familiar like . . . *Jamison*? Here? Right behind her car? Was that possible? Her colon contorted. Then the man turned his head to check for traffic before darting across the street. No, of course it wasn't Jamison. Just some other guy who thought rules didn't apply to him.

Jamison. Her former boss was the last thing she wanted to be reminded of now. Yes, *thing*, not person, that's how she thought of him, when she thought of him, which she'd almost stopped doing, what with all the driving, house-hunting, and unpacking. Now he'd intruded again. Oh, he was good at that.

Her heart hammered. She took a deep breath—*in through the nose for a count of five, out through the mouth for a count of seven*—just the way Miranda had taught her. Inhaaaaale. Exhaaaaaaale. Again. Again. She focused on the begonias—*pretty flowers, pretty flowers*—anything to take her mind off that creep Jamison. The drubbing in her chest softened to a steady lub-dub.

Just beyond the planter, in a throng of shoppers crossing the street—*properly, in the crosswalk*—was an eightyish woman dressed entirely in aqua: aqua muumuu, aqua anklets peeking out of aqua canvas flats, aqua headband holding her braided and coiled white hair off her face. It wasn't just the woman's outfit that captured Belle's attention, though, it was the way she moved across the street, taking a few quick steps, stopping and looking all around with jerky head motions, then a few more steps, another round of darting glances and so on. Watching her was like watching a squirrel with a nervous disorder. Was she lost? Afraid someone was following her? Afflicted with a medical condition?

The woman stopped in front of the café, looked all around again, then pushed open the door and walked inside. Belle checked the time. Reba should be arriving soon, might as well go in and get a table.

Inside the café, the aquafied woman stood in front of the pastry case, regarding it in her herky-jerky way. Belle walked over, debating whether to offer help or just mind her own business. Just then Reba swept in wearing the denim sling with Wallace tucked inside.

"Oh, I see you two have already met," she said, taking her place in line behind Belle and the older woman. "Guess you don't need me to make introductions."

Belle and the woman looked at each other, then at Reba, their expressions slowly shifting from blank to bemused.

Belle spoke first: "Actually, we—"

"—haven't," the older woman finished. "Who's she?"

"This is Belle, Mae. I told you about her, remember?" Reba shifted the Snugli; Wallace raised his head, eyed Belle with a glimmer of recognition, settled back in.

The woman stared at Belle in an unfocused way. "I guess."

"Belle, this is Mae, or Aquamaureen, as Roscoe calls her."

"Roscoe?" Belle was still absorbing Reba, Wallace, and Aquamaureen. Now there was another character in this weirdo cast?

"Yes, Roscoe, the Penitentiary Poet. You'll meet him soon enough." Reba winked at Mae, whose face flushed as she dropped her head. "Oh, Belle, don't worry," Reba said, apparently catching the flicker in Belle's eyes. "He's not *in* prison, he works at the prison. Leavenworth. And he writes poetry on the side. Mostly the left side, politically."

Mae's head snapped up. "Bravo for that."

Once their drinks arrived—café con leche for Reba, Earl Grey tea for Mae, chai for Belle—the women found a table by the front windows. The aromas of freshly ground coffee beans and just-baked pastries—the same in coffee shops everywhere—gave Belle a sensation of fullness from belly to heart. She'd done a stint as a barista between her organizing jobs, and that time had been a happy, uncomplicated one.

"How'd you and the *Times* make out today, Mae?" Reba asked as she shrugged out of the Snugli and set the sling and the now-sleeping wallababy on the extra chair.

Mae made a face. "Twenty-seven down tripped me up. Ten-letter word for sinister. Starts with M."

Reba counted to ten on her fingers. "Well, I sure as hell don't know. I'm a visual, not a verbal."

The espresso machine—a high-end La Marzocco, Belle had noticed—hissed and gurgled in the background. Crockery clattered as departing customers deposited their cups and plates in a bin near the door.

"Hmmmmmm . . ." Belle was trying to say something, but no actual words came out. She could feel Reba and Mae waiting for her to go on. She hiccupped, but softly enough she hoped they didn't hear it in the coffee shop din. "Mmmmmmaybe 'malevolent'?"

Mae registered surprise with widened eyes and a single head snap. "I do believe you've nailed it, Belle." She reached into her muumuu pocket, pulled out a rumpled scrap of newsprint, and smoothed it on the tabletop. The morning's *New York Times* crossword puzzle was almost completely filled in with letters precisely printed in peacock blue ink. Mae took out the matching pen and wrote M-A-L-E-V-O-L-E-N-T in one string of spaces, then quickly filled in the rest of the puzzle. "You've done me a great service, Belle," she said. "I must repay you with a favor."

Belle held up two hands, palms out, as if pushing the suggestion away. "Oh, no, that's not necessary. It was nothing."

Mae twitched and blinked a rapid succession of eye flutters. "You mustn't refuse my reciprocation, Belle. That's a form of rejection."

Really? That was a new one on Belle. She thought she knew how to interact with people—she'd done it all the time in her event-planning job, and she'd had some pretty unusual clients. Yet her social skills seemed entirely inept in this setting. What *were* the rules here?

"All right, then," Belle said in a tone intended as kind. "But I can't think of any favor I need right now. Could we put it in escrow?"

The suggestion mollified Mae. The blinking and twitching stopped, and she beamed.

"Okay, let's get down to the business at hand," Reba said. Wallace roused like the dormouse at the Mad Hatter's tea party and stuck his nose into Reba's cup.

There was business? Belle had presumed this was a social date, a chance to continue the disjointed conversation from her visit to Reba's house. She waited for Reba to explain.

"The parade is only a month away. We need to get costumes and instruments ready and help Roscoe plan the after-party. So much to do." Reba tipped her cup to let Wallace lap up the last of her drink. "We're hoping you'll help us out, Belle, being new in town. It'll be a way to get involved in the community, make new friends."

Oh no, oh, no!

Belle reflexively raised her hands to make the pushing-away gesture again—she hated getting roped into things, and she'd vowed not to get involved in anything during her time here. *Recoup, regroup, heal.* Remembering Mae's reaction, though, and not wanting to offend, she dropped her hands back to her lap.

"Parade? Party? What's the occasion?" The only summer parades Belle could think of—Memorial Day, Fourth of July, Labor Day—would not take place in a month. Did Lawrence have some special festival or celebration?

Reba reared back and peered at Belle as if she were a newly discovered species of organism. "Soulstice, Belle. The summer solstice celebration. You've not heard of it? No matter. The thing is, it's gotten bigger every year. We started it as a lark—just a bunch of us dressing up like suns and sunflowers and sunglasses and watermelons and parading around my neighborhood. But then it caught on, and now damn near the whole town turns out in costume, with drums and dancers and acrobats and every kind of street performer you can imagine. Since *we* started it, it's fallen on us to keep the thing organized. And this year's the tenth anniversary, so it's kind of a really big deal."

Belle nodded. "Okaaay . . . so . . . ?"

Pulling his nose out of Reba's café con leche, Wallace knocked the cup onto the tile floor. Cup and tile collided with a clink, but nothing shattered. Without missing a beat, Reba swooped down and picked up the cup.

"Well, as you may have noticed, organization is not my forte," she continued. "Mae's either." She nodded at Mae, who covered her face and peeked over her fingers like a bashful child. "As for the rest of our friends . . . they're *our* friends. What does that tell you?" Reba stopped and looked at Belle, her eyes pleading.

Belle had to sit on her hands to keep from doing the back-off thing again. Damn. She was sure she hadn't told Reba about her organizational abilities—she was always so careful to keep quiet about those tendencies around people she'd just met.

She extracted her hands from beneath her seat and with an apologetic smile, gave a helpless, palms-up shrug.

"Afraid that's not my thing either, Reba," she lied. That was all she needed to say, right? Now she could just finish her chai, wish Reba and Mae well, and head home, entanglement-free, to figure out what to do with all that yard sale crap in her trunk.

Yet something tugged at her—a sensation so physical she thought Wallace was nibbling at her T-shirt. But no, the tug came from *inside*. With Miranda so far away and nothing definite to do with her time, Belle was as empty as the little stone fortress of a house she'd chosen for her refuge. The parade and party—whatever they were—could fill some time and take her mind off all those things she was trying not to think about. Would that qualify as coloring outside the lines? Surely it would.

"Okay," Belle said, finally. "I'll help if I can." Then before she could stop herself: "Costumes and instruments—that actually sounds fun."

Belle flipped open the Chevy's hatch and unloaded her yard-sale purchases onto her front lawn, trying to be as unobtrusive as possible. Just like the neighborhood itself, a wallflower sitting on the sidelines here in North Lawrence, on the *other* side of the river, far from the historic district's prissy Victorians and even farther from the suburbs that sprawled west of town. Its chief landmarks were railroad tracks, a grain elevator, and Johnny's, a onetime gin joint turned tavern with the slogan "Longest runnin' tap in town."

The scrape of metal on hardened earth told Belle the old guy next door was poking around his petunias again. She'd seen him from her living room window the day she moved in, over there fussing with the hard-packed soil where he somehow managed to convince flowers to grow. When he'd looked up, Belle had wiggled three fingers in a feeble wave, then ducked beneath her windowsill. Now here he was again, and Belle was just as determined to avoid interaction. She kept her eyes trained on her boxes, lamp, and table, but the man shuffled over anyway.

"Hey there, Miss . . . Ma'am . . . Miss, let me give you a hand with those."

Belle raised her hands, palms out. "Oh, thanks, but that's really not . . ." She remembered Mae's admonition and dropped her arms to her side. "Well, all right, I guess I could use some help. Thanks."

The man hoisted the end table onto his shoulder, grabbed the lamp with his free hand, and marched toward Belle's front steps as she fumbled with her house key.

"Keeping your door locked, that's a good thing," the man huffed from under the tabletop. "Not that we've had any trouble around here lately—we watch out for each other. But still, you being a single lady. Or so I presume."

"Ummm," was all Belle said. Not about to reveal personal details to some old dude in overalls, even if he was her neighbor. No, sir. She stationed herself by the open door as the man deposited the table and lamp in the living room. On his way back out for the boxes, he stopped and extended a hand.

"Name's Mitchell. Mitchell Muldoon. Some people call me Mitch, but I don't like it much. Mitchell's the name my mama give me, and I reckon that's what she meant for me to be called."

Belle shook the man's hand. It was sandpapery, like his voice, and his grip was strong.

"Isabelle Marsden. You can call me Belle—my mother did."

"Well, all right, then, Miss Belle. I can remember that 'cause you kinda look like a bell—the ringing kind—the way your hair flares out there at the bottom."

Belle fingered the ends of her hair, short and wispy around her face, longer in back. It never behaved the way she wanted, always stuck out in the wrong places. Overdue for a trim, it was even more unruly in the Kansas humidity.

Mitchell turned back toward the living room, looked out the window, and winced. "Didn't realize you could see my place so good from here. Got a little overgrowed lately, but my nephew's coming down from Nebraska pretty soon to give me a hand. Maybe then it won't be such an eyesore for you to be looking at."

Belle waved a hand as if making the scene disappear. "Not to worry, Mitchell. All I see when I look out that window are your pretty petunias."

Mitchell brightened and turned away from the window. "Let's get them boxes in here so I can get back to scratching that dang dirt."

Once the boxes were inside and Mitchell had left, Belle busied herself unwrapping the secondhand dishes.

Just what I needed—more boxes to unpack. But that woman was so . . . down and out, and no one else was buying anything.

Belle stacked the chipped dishes in an empty bottom cabinet and arranged the unchipped ones in a glass-fronted cupboard built into one corner of her kitchen. The mishmash of colors and patterns was not at all her style, but the delirious mixture made her smile. *Salmagundi.*

When she came to the blue china cup—the one that belonged to the yard sale woman's mother—she stroked its surface and placed it alone on its own shelf, wishing it had belonged to *her* mother. She mentally inventoried her "Mom-entos" again: the photos, earrings, gloves. She held out her right hand and gazed at the rings she'd worn most every day since her mother's funeral. The memory floated through her mind like the weighty scent of lilies she associated with that day.

After the funeral, after the graveside service, after friends and relatives had gone home, after the remains of the casseroles had been stashed in the fridge, the extra sheet cakes and pans of lasagna stacked in the freezer, Belle and her dad had sat side by side on the living room sofa, surrounded by potted plants and floral arrangements that gave the room an earthy, flowery, leafy, greenhousy smell.

"It doesn't feel right without her here," her dad said. "But at the same time, it's where I feel closest to her."

"I know. So you think you'll stay here?" Belle could hardly get those words out. She couldn't bear the thought of her childhood home in Des Plaines disappearing the way her mother had, the thought of her father in any other setting. This home was safety, shelter. Her family was safety, shelter. Had been. Now that was shattered. And though she was no longer a child, she was desperate for something to hold onto.

Her father didn't answer right away. He stared out the window, then straight into Belle's eyes. "I want to say yes, honey. I know how much this house means to you—and me—and I'm not about to make any sudden changes. But I have to be honest, Isabelle. I don't know what's ahead for me." He paused, took a breath, and exhaled as if deflating. "I do know this—I'm always here for you, whether I'm *here* or somewhere else."

He wrapped his arms around her and rocked her like a child. The antique wall clock—the one whose ticking always steadied Belle—counted off five minutes, ten. Then he said, "Wait here." He stood and walked down the hall. A door opened and closed with a click. Belle waited, her eyes traveling around the room to the paintings her mother had bought at art fairs—scenes of sunlit fields and farms. Happy, colorful, hopeful scenes, free of foreboding.

Her father returned with a small velvet box and handed it to Belle. "Open it."

Inside, her mother's wedding band and diamond solitaire gleamed against the satin lining.

"She always planned to give you these when you married. She used to say she'd hit me up for a bigger rock then." He smiled and wiped his eyes with a knuckle. "But our love doesn't depend on whether you get married or on anything you do or don't do. Our love is always with you, and I want you to have these rings now as a reminder."

With that, he slipped the ruby ring off his right pinkie—the ring he'd worn as long as Belle could remember—and laid it beside her mother's rings in the box.

"This one was Grandpa Jake's. He gave it to me when I left for college—when I went 'off into the world,' as he put it. I'm giving it to you now to remind you that you mean the world to me, and you can always count on me, no matter what."

And she had counted on him. Until a year later, when he married Shelley and moved to Phoenix. Oh, he was still "there for her"—*just a phone call away*, he'd insisted. *A three-hour hop on the plane.* But with their marriage, Shelley became the center of his world, a whole new world that Belle wasn't part of. They might even have kids together—Shelley was young enough. Belle didn't begrudge them their happiness, but not wanting to intrude, she stopped confiding in her dad and let the miles between them create a deeper distance.

The buzz of Belle's phone on the countertop scrambled her thoughts. Relieved to see the familiar face on the screen, she answered right away.

"Miranda! Is it ever good to hear from you. About time you checked in."

The woman on the other end of the line laughed, throaty and full. "I wanted to give you time to get your bearings. You *are* still there, aren't you? Not on your way back to Chicago?"

"Oh, I'm still in Kansas, all right." Belle looked around the kitchen, taking in the scuffed cabinets, the shallow sink with gooseneck faucet, the kaleidoscope of dishes she'd just stacked in the corner cupboard. "You made the ground rules, and you know I'm good at following rules. I'll stick it out here for six months like you said, and then see what's next."

"Good girl. So how's it going? Met any interesting people?"

Belle carried the phone into the bedroom and flopped onto the inflatable bed she was using until . . . until what? The bed sighed beneath her. "Interesting? You could say that. There's this one woman who carries around a wallaby and makes art out of roadkill, and another one who's twitchy and dresses all in aqua, and an old guy next door who's growing petunias in concrete. Oh, and I think I'm going to be in a parade."

There was silence on Miranda's end. Then a voice too soft to be coming from Miranda. "Belle? Either you're making this up, or you're already coloring way outside the lines."

Belle laughed, and her laugh sounded more like Miranda's.

"You know, in this place, I'm not even sure there *are* lines."

- 3 -
THE MADMAN

Belle stared through the glass at the figure below. She'd seen dead people before, sure, at funerals, badly made up as if they'd been cast in a community theater production. But the spectacle she regarded now looked like something that would flash on the screen at an unexpected moment in a horror movie. What did it have to do with the Soulstice Parade? Why on earth had Reba sent her here?

"You've got to get yourself over to Lucas," Reba had insisted after Belle agreed to help with costumes. "It's the Grassroots Art Capital of Kansas. It'll get you in a creative frame of mind."

What Reba failed to mention was that Lucas was even better known as home to the Garden of Eden, a collection of concrete sculptures created in the early 1900s by local eccentric Samuel Perry Dinsmoor. Open to the public. Visitors could amble through the grounds under the crude, hard stares of Civil War soldiers, Indians, angels, babies, vultures, turkeys, maidens, and monsters, all perched atop the intertwining branches of concrete trees. It was a menagerie of masonry. Like gargoyles on cathedrals, the sculptures seemed to look down on visitors who passed through as they toured the property and its two main buildings: Dinsmoor's home—a handsome two-story structure made of stone logs—and a pyramid-like mausoleum in which, per his instructions, Dinsmoor's remains were on display for all eternity.

If Reba had failed to warn Belle about the weirdness she'd encounter in Lucas, the black-and-white sign in front of the Dinsmoor place offered a hint:

THE GARDEN OF EDEN
OPEN DAILY
10 AM TO 5 PM

GUIDED TOURS OF THE CABIN HOME & GROUNDS ARE GIVEN DURING OPEN HOURS DAILY. BY TAKING THE TOUR, YOU WILL FULFILL S. P. DINSMOOR'S WISH. EXPERIENCE THE CABIN HOME. HEAR HIS STORIES ABOUT THE SCULPTURES. SEE HIM IN HIS COFFIN. YOUR CONTRIBUTIONS HELP SUPPORT THE PRESERVATION OF THIS UNIQUE SITE.

Unique. Well, that was one way to put it. Staring through the glass at the blackened skeleton dressed in Dinsmoor's Sunday best, Belle cringed and covered her mouth with both hands. Yet she couldn't look away. Minutes passed. Then, her eyes still riveted on the glass-topped coffin as if she expected old Dinsmoor to pop up and holler *Boo!*, Belle backed out the door into sunshine.

After the crypt and its contents, the sculptures didn't seem nearly as sinister as they had at first. They weren't what she'd call attractive, but she could see something strangely compelling in the statues' stances and expressions and the juxtaposition of figures. Now that she'd come face to face with Dinsmoor—or what was left of him—she was curious to know what had driven him to devote years to creating this colossal monstrosity. Was it celebrated in his time, or did Dinsmoor alone see the worth of his creation and endure the humiliation of the townspeople of Lucas?

As Belle walked through the grounds, she couldn't make sense of some images and their references to the populist politics of a bygone era. The female figures, though, she understood. She lingered beneath each one, studying its posture and countenance. Standing strong, gazing into the distance, some figures were unabashedly naked, but not in a provocative way. It was as if they all felt right in their weathered concrete skins. Had Belle ever felt right in her skin? Maybe once, long ago. Before Jamison. Before she absorbed the shame that should have been his.

One statue held Belle spellbound. Draped in a long striped dress that resembled an American flag, and holding a lamp aloft like the Statue of Liberty, the woman loomed over an eight-legged, open-mouthed creature. Was she riding the beast or slaying it? Or was it attacking *her*? Belle chose to believe the woman was in control, precarious as her position appeared.

The chatters and whirrs of a flock of starlings settling into a cedar tree broke the spell. Belle moved on to discover an elaborate gateway she'd somehow missed when she'd first arrived. Beneath a scaffold with the words GARDEN OF EDEN formed in concrete, Adam and Eve stood at the entry to a vine-draped arbor. In her outstretched hand, Eve held an apple. From the tangle of vines, a serpent coiled down to taste the forbidden fruit. At first glance, the scene looked idyllic, inviting. A scent like mock orange filled the air, prompting Belle to look around for the source. Then she glanced up and flinched at the sight of a shifty-eyed, smiling demon holding up one hand in a jaunty wave. Of course. There always was some kind of evil lurking in every haven, wasn't there?

"Whadja think of the place?" a bright voice from behind the gift shop cash register asked.

Startled, Belle turned to find that the woman who owned the voice looked ordinary as a cornfield. Doughy shape filling out her calico dress, overpermed hair, glasses a decade or two out of date. Could this cheerful, *normal* woman really work in a place like this?

Or was the weirdness of Dinsmoor's garden—glass-covered coffin, statues in trees—warping Belle's perceptions?

"Well . . ." Belle ventured, "It's certainly unlike anything I've ever seen before."

"Yessiree," the woman said with a tinge of . . . was that pride in her voice? "Folks come to Lucas from all over the world just to see our Garden of Eden." She flipped pages in a looseleaf guest book that sat on the counter. "Look here—here's a bunch from Japan who came on a tour bus last week. And right here's a couple from France who was here yesterday. As if they don't have enough art to look at in that big museum you hear so much about. The Loove or whatever they call it." She chuckled and pushed the book closer to Belle.

Belle studied the pages and nodded politely, then turned to take in the rest of the shop with its racks of postcards, booklets, and such. A stack of slim pamphlets caught her eye: *Pictorial History of the Cabin Home in Garden of Eden, Lucas, Kansas.*

"I'll take one of these." Belle laid the booklet on the counter and spun a postcard rack around. "And one of these," she said, plunking down a reproduction of a card Dinsmoor had sold to tourists. In the photo on the front, a very alive Dinsmoor stood in the crypt, looking down on his dead self in the coffin.

Maybe if she stared long enough at that image, Belle would begin to understand this madman and his creation. Maybe it would even put her in—as Reba put it—a creative frame of mind.

– 4 –
THE TENOR

Exhausted from the trip to Lucas, Belle stumbled into her house through the side door, paused in the kitchen to gulp a glass of water, and headed for the bedroom. She slipped out of her clothes and into an oversized T-shirt and collapsed onto the air bed. Most nights since her arrival eleven days earlier, Belle had writhed and wrestled the mattress, seeking a comfortable niche. Tonight, she was out within minutes of clicking off the yard sale lamp, a twisty, angular thing crafted from Popsicle sticks.

It wasn't just the six-hour round trip that had worn Belle out. The encounter with Dinsmoor and his handiwork had taxed her brain and whole being as she struggled to understand what it had to do with Soulstice, let alone her concept of art. Living in Chicago, she'd spent many a lunch hour at the Art Institute, if only to escape the drudgery of work—and that despicable business with Jamison.

She gravitated to soothing images: Monet's water lilies, O'Keeffe's swath of open sky above a field of symmetrical clouds, Cézanne's bounty of fruit and wine, Renoir's soft-focus girls in flowered hats. The weirdest it got was Picasso's cubed and jumbled body parts. Certainly no corpses with their petrified progeny skulking and shooting and sawing and pointing, always pointing, overhead. Was that even art? And if not, what *was* it?

Belle had turned the questions over and over in her mind the whole drive back to Lawrence, until she could no longer think of anything but sleep.

Now, in her little stone cottage, on her makeshift bed, she slept. Deeply, deeply, deeply. And then, a shift in consciousness. Not an arousal exactly, but an awakening into a different body in a different place.

Standing high above the ground, looking out on treetops, Belle waited for the wobbly, woozy sensation that always overtook her when she climbed even a kitchen stepladder. It didn't come. Her feet seemed rooted to her perch; her body, though heavy, perfectly balanced. And firm. Not in the resilient way of toned muscles, but in a stony, solid way.

At once, she knew what and where she was. She had become one of Dinsmoor's creations, one of those strong, unashamed women, fully at ease in her rough skin, surveying her world with a confident gaze. Yet stuck in one place.

And then, she was back in her bed, rolling over to peek at the clock: 10 a.m. When was the last time she'd slept that late? High school?

She arched her back and reached out her arms and legs in a languid motion that made her think of pulling taffy. Pulling taffy? Where did *that* come from? Had she ever in her life pulled taffy? She wasn't sure, but she could taste it now, sugary and stretchy, softening in her mouth.

Another glance at the clock reminded her she was supposed to meet Reba at 11:00 to kick around parade costume ideas. She bounded out of bed with an energy that astonished her. Usually, Belle bumbled around for at least half an hour after rising, groping for the coffee grinder and beans, waiting, dazed, for that first head-clearing cup.

Not this morning. Perky as if she'd drunk a whole pot of French press, Belle skipped the coffee-making ritual and simply splashed a little tepid water on her face before pulling on her standby jeans and one of many nearly identical tank tops whose color palette ranged from ashy to dusty to slate. Gray, gray, and gray.

She was halfway out the door when an impulse sent her back inside to root through her bottom dresser drawer. From beneath a pile of still more tank tops in noncommittal colors, she unearthed a filmy bit of fabric. To call it a scarf was to understate its magnificence. Certainly it was long and drapey and meant to be worn about the neck or tossed over a shoulder. But it was no mere scrap of chiffon or cotton. Handmade in India, its spider-webby background was covered with cloud-like spirals of silky thread in shades of violet, turquoise, and chartreuse.

A gift from Miranda. At the time, Belle had thought it totally impractical—ridiculous, even. She'd kept it—only because it was from Miranda—instead of immediately donating it, as she did most unsuitable gifts. Yet she knew she'd never wear it.

Only now, she knew she would.

A stone turret loomed overhead. A pair of massive wooden doors shielded the entrance. Could this gothic edifice, so out-of-place in its neighborhood of bungalows, really be where Reba intended to meet? They'd agreed on One World Café, but just as Belle was getting into her car, Reba had texted a hasty, "Change of venue: Castle Tea Room."

A sign on the window, CASTLE TEA ROOM, LUNCHEON SERVED DAILY AT 11 AM, TEA AT 4 PM, assured Belle she was in the right place. She climbed the stone steps, strained to pull open one door, and stepped into a setting that brought to mind feathered hats and finger sandwiches. Crystal pendants dripped from chandeliers; velvet draperies and Persian carpets soft-pedaled what little sound dared intrude on the decorum. A faint scent of asparagus wafted from the dining rooms.

The hostess—silk-sheathed, with blond hair sleeked into a

bun—eyed Belle's tank top, jeans, and scarf. "You must be joining the two ladies in the parlor."

Belle had only to glance at the other lunching ladies they passed on the way to the parlor to see how the hostess had made the connection. All the other women wore flower-splashed summer frocks and held their teacups and wine glasses in French-tipped fingers. Their laughter tinkled like wind chimes—not the resonant, Gregorian-tuned ones Belle admired in gift shops, but the shards-of-glass kind. In the parlor, Reba and Mae, in their usual Rasta-salsa and aqua outfits, sprawled over notebooks and sheaves of paper at a small table.

"No wallababy?" Belle asked, slipping into a chair that looked like it was made for a pixie.

Reba swept papers aside to make room. "Roscoe's walla-watching today. Things have been heating up with Coogan, so I've been keeping Wallace under wraps. We'll get to that, but first I want to hear about your trip to Lucas. You did go like I told you to, didn't you?"

"Right. Lucas. About that . . ." Belle reached into her purse and pulled out the postcard of the dual Dinsmoors in the crypt. "I really don't see how a dried-up dead guy and his creepy concrete friends have anything to do with the Soulstice parade. He's already giving me the weirdest dreams."

"Well, Belle," Reba said, flipping through a stack of papers, "they *could* be weird, or they could be simply intriguing. Inspiring, even."

Belle considered that suggestion—and pondered what might have inspired Reba's unconventional quilt, roadkill assemblages, faux foods, and other creations. But before she could ask, Mae jumped into the conversation.

"Did you see the mosaics and rocks too?" she asked, her eyes riveted on the edge of the tablecloth she fiddled with. "The Ed Root thingies and the Florence Deeble faces? And the Garden of Isis? There's so much more to Lucas than the Garden of Eden."

"I did," Belle said. Indeed, at the gift-shop woman's urging, she had ventured beyond Dinsmoor's garden to discover the jauntier sculptures that retired farmer Ed Root had assembled decades ago from broken china, bottles, doorknobs, marbles, mirrors, and Model T rims. She'd toured Mri-Pilar's house, wallpapered with Mylar and decorated with jewel-encrusted mannequins, religious icons, dolls, Slinkys, and assemblages that made Reba's art seem positively mainstream. She'd strolled through Florence Deeble's backyard fantasyland of concrete mountains, streams, cacti, and Mt. Rushmore-ish tribute to Lucas notables. And she'd concluded Lucas had more than one kook among its former and current residents, even if they hadn't all built their own mausoleums.

"Like I said," she went on, "I don't see how this all relates . . ."

"Mmm-hmm," Reba said absently, looking at Belle but focused on some internal scene. She picked up a notebook and began thumbing through it just as a waiter appeared and placed an index-card-sized menu in front of each of the women.

"May I start you ladies off with a beverage while you're looking over the selections?" A smile expanded across his face, and tossing a headful of microbraids, he winked at Mae.

"Let's all have the iced pomegranate green tea," Reba suggested. Belle nodded; Mae murmured assent, eyeing the waiter as he walked away.

Feigning shock, Belle turned to Mae and teased, "Looks like you two have something going on."

Mae flushed and patted the silver bobby pins that secured her braids to the top of her head. Chandelier light reflected off the pins and made glittery patterns on the wallpaper.

"Oh, that's just DeShawn," Reba said. "He and Mae sing in the community choir—fine tenor, he is—and he helps her out with odd jobs. Very odd, from the sound of it, though I wouldn't know for sure.

DeShawn and Roscoe are the only people she'll allow in her house. I've never even seen the inside of it."

"Nothing to see," Mae said, fingering the tablecloth again. "Do you realize this is *punto tagliato* cutwork? Don't you dare spill any of that pomegranate Kool-Aid on it. Somebody's grandmother probably made this cloth."

"So you sing in a choir, Mae," Belle said. "You're just full of surprises, aren't you? And I'm guessing you do needlework too."

Mae dropped the tablecloth and twiddled her fingers in the air.

"Acupuncture, yes. How'd you know?"

Belle's forehead pulsated. *Now I know how Alice felt at the Mad Hatter's tea party. Can't anyone have a normal conversation around here?*

As if to answer that question, Reba held up the notebook. "My friends, we have an agenda today, so let's get on with it. Costumes. We still have the sunflower masks from the last two years, and we can make flower crowns and garlands like we always do."

The throb in Belle's head became a fizzy tingle. "That sounds nice. But you know, I'm picturing lots of gold lamé and some kind of inflatable headpieces. And what would you think of making bra tops out of zinnias?"

Reba and Mae exchanged raised-eyebrow looks and slowly nodded in unison.

"Inflatable. Wow, that's a new one," Reba said. "I mean, we've done papier-mâché to death. So sure, inflatable. Why not? Why the *hell* not?" She laid her notebook down. "Listen, Belle, I know it's a drive, but get your ass back to Lucas first chance you get. That place is stirring up something in you."

– 5 –
THE NEBRASKAN

Curled up on the secondhand futon she'd snagged at another yard sale, Belle scrolled through Google search results: "Caring for a Wallaby," "The Complete Wallaby Care Guide," "The Not-So-Sweet Side of Raising a Wallaby."

"Guess I'd better get up to speed if you're going to be bunking with me for a while, buddy."

Wallace, hopping around Belle's living room, turned to look at her as if signaling agreement, then bounded off to sniff her bookcase.

Reba had blindsided Belle with the request as they were leaving the tearoom after lunch the day before. "Oh, hey, Roscoe has to go back to work at the Pen, and I've got no one else to watch Wallace until he's off again. Do you think yoooooou . . ."

Reba lapsed into those bird sounds when she was being solicitous, Belle had noticed. This time, Belle didn't even bother with the palms-out protest gesture, knowing by now that Reba had a way of dissolving her resistance.

"He's pretty easy to have around," Reba had assured her. "I'll fill you in on the basics when I drop him off." And so she had. But "the basics," à la Reba, left Belle with more questions than answers.

"He's not a fussy eater—just some hay and fresh grass, a little produce if you've got it. He likes to sleep with a pillow. Oh, and he understands English, but French is his first language. So if he seems confused, *parle en français.* Okay, gotta run. Call me if you have questions."

Hence, the Google search:

Since wallabies are small they can be kept indoors and allowed to run around in a wallaby-safe environment and then kept in a secure, large enclosure or small bedroom when unsupervised. They can live outside in warm months or year-round if they have a doghouse with supplemental heat to retreat to.

You may have heard horror stories about wallabies attacking humans and doing some serious damage, but what these stories fail to mention is that these are wild wallabies. A lot of animals in the wild can be dangerous. It's just natural animal instinct to protect themselves. Pet wallabies on the other hand are just lovely. When you combine the fact that they are friendly, devoted, incredibly cute, and affectionate, having wallabies as pets is more than worth it.

As she read, Belle absently stroked Wallace, who'd bounced up beside her and sat with his nose pressed against the window behind the futon.

A rapping at the front door jolted Belle out of her reading reverie. As she rose to answer the knock, Wallace reflexively headed into the kitchen, searching for a basement door.

Mitchell, Belle's petunia-tending neighbor, stood grinning through the front door windowpane. Belle opened the door, and the old man held out a crumpled paper bag.

"I seen your dog looking out the window and thought he'd like a treat. These doggie biscuits was for my little Rip, but I had to have him put down about a month ago. Old age, you know. Broke my heart. Anyway, these ain't doing me any good."

Belle took the bag. "I'm sorry about Rip, Mitchell. How kind of you to share these."

A rustling sound came from the kitchen. Mitchell craned to see over Belle's shoulder. She leaned sideways to block the view. Mitchell leaned the other way and raised his eyebrows.

It was hopeless. No keeping secrets from this curious old coot. Belle made a palms-up gesture of surrender. "All right, Mitchell. Here's the deal: That, um . . . animal you saw? That was Wallace. He's not really mine—I'm keeping him for a friend—and he's actually not a dog."

Another rustle. Then the clatter and shatter of something crashing to the floor.

Mitchell bobbed his head, still angling for a glimpse of whatever was causing the commotion. "Okaaaay. I get it. The landlady don't allow you to have a dog—I know she can be a witch about them things—so that furry critter you got there ain't a dog, and it ain't yours. Uh-huh. Just making sure we got our stories straight here. You oughta know, though, some of the neighbors might rat you out to your landlady if your dog gets too yippy. Some of 'em used to complain about Rip's barking."

"He's really not . . ."

"That's okay, Miss Belle. I gotcha covered. If you ever need me to dog-sit or anything—you know, I just miss that little Rip so much, I wouldn't mind another furry feller around now and then."

Mitchell rubbernecked over Belle's shoulder once more. Belle put a hand on his elbow and gently steered him onto the porch.

"I think we're good here for now, Mitchell, but I'll let you know." Then seeing his face cloud, she pointed to a bare patch about the size of a bathtub on the lawn. "Hey, Mitchell, I was wondering if you could suggest something to grow there. You're so good at coaxing beauty out of this stubborn soil."

The corners of Mitchell's mouth twitched upward ever so slightly.

Then his eyebrows bunched together like dueling caterpillars. "Wish I could, Miss Belle. That there patch has been bare as a baby's bee-hind long as I can remember. I don't think nothin'll grow there. You might oughta get yourself a nice lawn decoration at one of them yard sales—a wishing well or a windmill or some such thing."

He ambled away with an over-the-shoulder wave.

Yard sales, Belle thought. *Exactly.* Only it wasn't wishing wells or windmills that came to mind. She turned and walked into the kitchen. Wallace, licking honey from a spoon he'd knocked off the table along with the coffee cup Belle had left there, watched wide-eyed as she picked up the pieces and laid them on the counter. Then, turning toward him and reaching for the doorknob: "Wallace, *restez içi*! I have work to do."

Belle labored over the bare spot in the front yard with a rusty rake she had found in her landlady's so-called shed—a ramshackle structure at the back of the property. The sun beat down on the unshaded worksite, but Belle ignored the heat until sweat streamed into her eyes. Crouching on the ground to rest and wipe her brow, she startled at the sight of two blue-jeaned legs beside her.

"Oh, sorry! Didn't mean to scare you." A male voice. Not Mitchell's twangy rasp, but a mellower baritone.

Belle followed the legs upward—and upward—this fellow was tall, over six feet, she guessed. And bony. All crooked angles and pointy parts. His face, too, once she reached it. Sharp chin, jawbones, cheekbones. A smile that softened all the edges but, like the rest of him, was off-kilter. A shock of black hair tumbled across his forehead, almost obscuring eyes that didn't quite match in size or shape. The hodgepodge of features made it hard to guess his age. Not young, but not old. Middle-ish, Belle guessed. Mid-thirties, like her?

"I'm Ezra, Mitchell's nephew." The tall man jerked a thumb

toward the neighbor's house. "Just came down from Nebraska to help him out for a bit. And I happen to know you're Belle—Uncle Mitchell's been telling me about you."

"Oh, really?" Belle wasn't sure why the comment made her hands clench and her spine stiffen. Remembering her manners, she forced out a "Nice to meet you, Ezra. I do recall Mitchell saying you were coming, but he didn't tell me you'd arrived already."

"Got in late last night, and I'm just now getting up and moving." He stretched his long arms skyward. "Well, I don't mean to interrupt your, um . . . work—which looks mighty ambitious, by the way—but I was concerned about you being out here in the sun. The heat can creep up on you. Sunstroke, you know. Maybe I could get you something cold to drink?"

"Oh!" Belle sat back and looked blearily around as if waking from a long sleep. "Yes. Something to drink. Why don't I get us both something?" Immediately regretting what might have sounded like an invitation, she added, "You can wait over there in the shade. I'll just be a minute."

In the kitchen, Belle took out tall glasses and fumbled to fill them with ice cubes and tea from a pitcher in the fridge. She sipped from one, and her head began to clear. Only then did she notice the silence, the absolute quiet of the house. No scuffles, no thumps, no clatters.

"Wallace? *Où es-tu?* C'mon, Wallace, no games. Where *are* you?"

Not a sound. Belle searched room to room, peering under tables, rummaging through closets and cabinets. No sign of the wallaby anywhere. Then, behind a pile of still-packed boxes in the back room, she saw it: a torn screen flapping against the window frame.

"Omigod! Wallace!" Belle raced through the house and out the side door, nearly crashing into Ezra, who'd heard the ruckus and started inside to see what was wrong.

"Wallace is missing," Belle exhaled between ragged breaths.

"Your dog?"

"He's not a . . . oh, never mind, yes, my dog. We've got to find him. I mean *I've* got to find him. I didn't mean to . . ."

Ezra laid a hand on Belle's shoulder. She tried not to flinch. *Not every touch is* that *kind of touch. Not every man is Jamison.*

"Come on," he said, trying to catch her wildly darting eyes. "I'll drive you around the neighborhood. He probably hasn't gone far."

Without another thought except the urgency of finding Wallace, Belle crawled into the passenger seat of the Jeep parked in Mitchell's driveway, and the two took off. They crept down streets and cut through alleys, squinting into gardens and onto porches. Squirrels scampered across lawns and vaulted up trees. A rabbit nibbled grass beside a fence.

"What kind of dog are we looking for, exactly?" Ezra asked, steering the Jeep into the parking lot of Johnny's tavern to turn around and search the neighborhood again.

Belle sighed. "Okay, here's the thing, Ezra. He's *not* a dog. Wallace is a . . ."

"Wallaby?"

Belle's mouth fell open, and she shot him a look. "How'd you know?"

Ezra pointed to an overturned garbage can beside the bar's back door.

"He's right there."

With Wallace safely stowed in the Jeep's rear cargo space, Ezra headed back to Belle's house. He tapped his fingers on the steering wheel in time with the radio—some old-timey, swingy, cowboyish tune—then paused and glanced at Belle. "Any idea how he got out?"

"Torn screen," Belle said. "In a room I don't use that much, so I hadn't noticed."

"I can fix that for you."

Belle bristled. "Thanks, but I'm perfectly capable." She wasn't, actually. Her experience with hand tools was pretty much limited to hanging a picture in her old apartment. She had no idea how to fix a screen, but surely there was a YouTube video.

"Of course you are! What I meant to say is, I'd be happy to *help* you. Sometimes an extra set of hands is, you know, handy." Ezra grinned, his features tilting in ways that made his face even more lopsided.

Mae's admonition replayed in her mind: *Refusal equals rejection.* With Ezra's peculiar looks, he'd probably experienced more than his share of that. She didn't want to encourage him, but brushing him off seemed downright cruel.

"All right," she said, returning his smile. "I accept your offer."

Ezra's grin evened out as it spread. "I'll just go next door and get some things. Come along if you want."

Belle herded Wallace inside and stashed him in her bedroom after checking to make sure its screens were intact. A breeze swept through the house, bringing the dusty, summery scent of petunias.

Ezra led the way across the brittle grass of Belle's side yard, through an arch-shaped trellis to Mitchell's lawn, and into his uncle's garage. Belle followed, once again asking herself why on earth she was tagging along with a friendly stranger.

The garage's side door hung slantwise on its hinges and creaked when Ezra tugged it open.

"One more thing on my Ezzy-do list," he said. "I'll get to it before summer's up."

Belle peered into the murk beyond. Old gallon cans, their labels obscured with dried paint, towered against one wall. Well-worn shovels and hoes leaned at oddball angles. A stack of toolboxes teetered beside a well-worn workbench.

Ezra rummaged through the workbench, toolbox drawers, and dingy corners and came up with tacks, hand tools, and a roll of screening, which he tossed into a rusty wheelbarrow with an emphatic thump.

"Look at all this stuff! Mitchell hasn't used most of it in years and probably never will. If you ever have a need for any of it, help yourself. Consider it your right-at-home Home Depot."

Back at Belle's, Ezra unloaded the supplies and crossed his arms. "We could just patch that hole, of course, but to be on the safe side, I think we'd better replace the whole screen."

Belle nodded. Safe sounded good. *Safe and sound. Safety first. Better safe than sorry. In safe hands.*

Hands. She noticed Ezra's—their surprising symmetry, their certainty as he set to work removing the screen from the window, prying off molding, measuring and cutting screening. She thought of other hands, hands she'd just as soon forget. Jamison's hands. A shudder ran beneath her breastbone. She stared at the ground and focused on the sounds of Ezra at work until they blotted out the ugly images.

"Here," Ezra said, "you can take over now." He handed her a small hammer and a package of tacks.

Belle took them from his hands, feigning assurance. "Okay, I'll just . . . um . . ."

"Mind if I stretch while you tack?"

Yoga? Now? It seemed an odd request, but whatever. "Sure, if you want to," Belle said. Then catching on, "Oh, stretch the *screen*? Yes, thanks."

They worked their way around the frame, Ezra stretching the screening taut, Belle hammering in tacks every couple of inches. After an awkward minute or two, they eased into a compatible rhythm. Belle's breathing slowed and deepened.

"I noticed the Chicago skyline bumper sticker on your car," Ezra said as they worked. "Is that where you moved here from?"

Yes would be a safe enough answer. But then what? How much more did she want to say? Ezra seemed nice, and he *was* Mitchell's nephew. Still, she'd just met him.

"Mmmmmm . . . that's right," she finally answered. "Very observant. Just like my friend Miranda—she notices every detail. She's a writer. Are you?"

"Would-be. I was headed that direction in college, but I ended up a librarian, tending other people's books. What about you?"

"Oh, I read a lot of books." Belle avoided meeting the gaze she felt Ezra training on her.

"I mean, what did you do in Chicago, and what brought you here?"

Those questions again. She'd managed to avoid giving Reba more than sketchy answers. She wasn't about to give Ezra any more.

"Oh, this and that—in Chicago—but it was time for a change. You get to a point in life, you know."

"I do. I might be getting there myself."

The screen repaired, Belle started inside to free Wallace from confinement. "But don't go away—quite yet," she told Ezra. She returned a few minutes later with a fistful of cash. "Let me pay you for the supplies—and the expertise."

Ezra made the pushing-away gesture Belle knew so well. "No, no! It was an act of neighborly altruism. We had all that stuff lying around, and what else would I have been doing this afternoon—sitting in front of the blaring TV with Uncle Mitchell? I mean, I love the guy, but sometimes . . ."

"I get that," Belle said, laughing. "It was like that with my Grandpa Jake, too, with stinky cigars to boot."

"I'll tell you what you *can* do, though." Ezra's sideways smile returned. "You can make me dinner sometime. Uncle Mitchell's not much of a cook, and no matter how often I straighten up the library's cookbook section, I never seem to absorb any skills through osmosis."

Belle shook her head. "Sorry, cooking isn't my strong suit either." True enough, but even if she'd studied at Le Cordon Bleu, she wasn't sure she wanted to commit an entire evening to entertaining this fellow. Still, she *was* awfully hungry, and Ezra had been awfully helpful.

"Why don't I order a pizza—my treat," she suggested.

"Deal," Ezra said. "I'll grab a couple of beers next door. You like Free State Stormchaser? I always pick up a six-pack whenever I'm down here."

"Haven't made its acquaintance yet," Belle said. "But now's as good a time as any."

A series of thuds came from the living room. "Uh-oh. Wallace again," Belle said. "He's been nosing around my books—I think he's trying to teach himself to read, and it wouldn't surprise me if he manages to do it."

Ezra laughed. "There again, I can help. I run the kiddies' story hour at the library—Bookin' with Mr. E." He backed out the door as if fearing Belle would disappear if he turned away. "Back in a flash."

Once Belle's books were reshelved, the pizza was delivered, the beers were cracked open, and Wallace was occupied with a bowl of greens, Belle and Ezra scooted up to the kitchen table and grabbed pizza slices. Ezra raised his bottle in a toast.

"To friendly neighbors and neighborly friends."

Belle clinked her bottle against his and said, "*À votre santé.*" Wallace glanced up but kept chewing. Belle took a big swig of Stormchaser and her head went twizzly. How long had it been since she'd eaten anything? And how long had she spent in the blazing sun? She gripped a table leg to steady herself, hiding her hand so Ezra wouldn't notice.

"So, about moving here. You were saying . . ." Ezra looked at Belle with raised eyebrows.

"Was I?" Belle was sure she hadn't said anything of the sort—or meant to. But now, beery and bleary, she didn't see the harm. *Just a little small talk.*

"Mmmmmm, well . . . I needed to leave Chicago because—mmmmmm, well, *because*. But I had no idea where I wanted to go. East Coast, too snooty." Belle tipped her head back and stuck her nose in the air. "West Coast, too kooky." She made circling motions around her ear. "So Miranda—she's the writer friend I told you about—she came up with this totally crazy idea and somehow talked me into it. I think bourbon was involved."

Belle paused and pulled a string of mozzarella from her pizza slice, stretching it like Silly Putty and rolling it into a ball before popping it into her mouth.

Ezra tossed a mushroom to Wallace.

Belle swallowed, took another long draught from her bottle, and continued. "So anywaaay, we pinned a US map to my kitchen wall. I closed my eyes. Miranda spun me around and around—I was soooo dizzy—and she put a pushpin in my hand and pointed me in the right direction and told me to stick the pin wherever I 'felt guided' to stick it. It was all a little *woo-woo* for me, but like I said, some reeeally good bourbon was involved. Also," her tone turned serious, "I *trust* Miranda."

Ezra nodded, his expression earnest. "Sometimes woo-woo is just the thing. And bourbon. And trust. So you stuck the pin in Lawrence?"

"Actually no. I stuck it in a potholder hanging from a hook beside the map." Belle giggled. "But then Miranda readjusted my position and . . ."

"And then you stuck it in Lawrence."

"Um, no." Belle peeled back the label of her beer bottle as if expecting to find a message. "I stuck it in Lecompton—you know, just down the river from here? But there's only like six hundred people living there, and we'd agreed that if the town I hit was under two thousand, I could opt for the nearest larger town. Lawrence was it. Next thing I knew, we'd packed up all my stuff and I was driving down the interstate. The deal was, I'd stay here for six months and figure out what to do next. I've been here a couple weeks now and have no clearer idea than when I got here, but I've still got five and a half months to go."

Ezra reached for another slice of pizza. "You know what strikes me funny—besides this whole story, that is? You vetoed California because it's too kooky, but you ended up in a place with a fair share of wackos, from what I've seen."

Belle picked at the bottle label. Images of Reba's house, the Garden of Eden, Mae's aquamaureen ensembles and twitchy, darting gait flashed through her mind. "Yes, well, I realize that—now. At the time I had no idea. I thought it was just a pleasant college town where I could live a quiet, undemanding life until I'm ready to move on. Of course, it didn't take long to discover the kookiness. But you know what? Now that I'm in the midst of it, it's kind of . . . okay."

She reached down and scratched Wallace behind his ears. He seemed to nod but perhaps was only angling for a better scratch. She could see why Mitchell missed his furry companion; she was already getting attached to this wayward wallaby in a way she hadn't bonded with an animal since Purrceval, the marmalade tabby she'd adopted from a shelter as a kid.

Watching Belle with the wallaby, Ezra edged closer. "I can tell. But don't you ever miss the big city? Your friends? Your job?"

At the word "job," Belle's daydreamy expression twisted into a grimace, and she shook her head as if dislodging thoughts.

"I'm sorry. Did I say something wrong?" Ezra straightened and slid his chair back from the table.

"Not really, no," Belle said. "It's just—hard to talk about. But that's no excuse, I guess."

Ezra sat silently, head cocked.

Belle took a long breath and slowly released it. "So, I'm sure you've heard of Hashtag Me Too."

"I have."

"Well," Belle said, "Me Too."

– 6 –
THE SOULSTICE GANG

Belle scuffed across the yard, uncut grass tickling through the sides of her sandals, Wallace hopping behind. Destination: Mitchell's garage, with its bounty of treasures for the taking—or so Ezra had assured her the day before.

A mob of hummingbirds whirred with purpose around the feeder that hung from Mitchell's back porch roof. Belle, too, whirred with purpose this morning, driven by thoughts of Dinsmoor's garden of oddities. Combined with her collection of chipped yard-sale china and the shattered remains of Wallace's mishaps, those thoughts had given her an idea for filling the empty space in her front yard.

She pushed against the garage's side door. It refused to budge. She pushed harder. Still nothing. Trickles of sweat sluiced down her cheeks. Wallace nudged her calf.

"I know, I know, pal. Be patient just a minute more. I'll get this." She glanced around. No sign of Ezra in the yard.

Good. Wouldn't want him to see me struggle. Although I could use a hand.

Wallace nudged her again, more insistently this time.

"All right, all right!" Belle scanned the ground for something solid to push the door with. Then it dawned on her: It was a pull-open door, not a push-open door.

"*Voilà*, Wallace!" she crowed as she *pulled* the door open.

Once her eyes adjusted to the dim light, she surveyed the garage's motley and mysterious contents. In addition to the toolbox tower, the teetering paint cans, and the fleet of aged garden tools she'd seen when she visited with Ezra, she saw hand tools, buckets, and near-petrified garden hoses scattered about. Even a department store mannequin, halved at the waist like a magician's assistant, occupying a cobwebbed corner.

And there, slumped against an aluminum lawn chair in a way that reminded her of the yard-sale lady, just the thing she'd come for. She'd noticed it on her previous visit but paid it little mind. Now, the sack of concrete was precisely what she was after. She sidled inside and poked at the bag.

Probably solid as a rock after sitting out here for who knows how long.

But no! At her touch, the bag shifted and slumped lower. She hoisted it up and dumped it into the wheelbarrow Ezra had used to transport the screen-fixing stuff.

"And I'll take this," she said aloud, throwing a dented bucket in with the concrete, "and this . . . and this . . ." A hammer and a hardened hose thudded into the wheelbarrow, along with the only hoe that looked like it might not fall apart at first touch.

The wheelbarrow's handles felt like callused hands in her own ungloved fingers as Belle rolled it out the door and bumped over the lawn, every hillock and furrow emphasizing her purpose.

A stack of chipped china sat on Belle's back stoop, where she had deposited it on her way to the garage. She loaded up the dishes with the concrete and tools and aimed the wheelbarrow toward the bare patch out front.

Wallace, spellbound by a bumblebee poking its way around a dandelion, snapped out of his trance and followed.

"Oh, no you don't, *mon ami*," Belle said. "Not the front yard. We need to keep you out of sight for now." She opened the screen door to let Wallace inside. "Try not to break anything else, huh?"

Unable to read the directions on the crumpled sack, Belle began mixing the gray powder with water she coaxed from the hose, guessing at proportions. A little more powder, a little more water, *scrape, scrape* to mix it all together.

Once the mixture looked like the blend she'd seen pouring down a chute from a revolving drum on the back of a truck when workers installed new sidewalks in her family's suburban Chicago neighborhood, she stopped mixing, grabbed the hammer, and set to smashing chipped china into ever smaller bits.

How surprisingly good that felt! Destruction driven by the urge to create.

Hours passed, lunchtime came and went unnoticed, and still Belle toiled, pouring and smoothing and pressing in shards. What started out as a stepping stone now filled an inner tube–sized space and had begun to inch upward around the edges. The mismatched colors made her think of Mitchell's garden: implausible yet appealing.

Hey, she thought, *I'm growing something too.*

Reba held a gold spangled T-shirt up to Belle's chest.

"Look what this does for your eyes! They're actually glittering like . . . like . . . glitter."

Belle squinted into the three-way mirror and cocked her head. "Really? Hmmm . . . I don't . . ."

Reba's invitation to meet at the resale shop on Main Street had lured Belle away from the front-yard *objet* she been toiling over for the past several days. Maybe she'd find more dishes and doodads to add to her ever-growing assemblage. Modeling outlandish outfits wasn't in her plans, but she was humoring her new friend.

She turned one way, then the other, still looking askance at her reflection. "But, isn't this . . . I mean, I'm not really into gaudy."

Reba grabbed a purple tie-dyed scarf with her free hand and tossed it at Belle. "Indeed you're not, and we've got to do something about that before the Soulstice party. You can't be showing up in one of your usual—forgive me—*drab* outfits. It's *Soulstice*, Belle, a celebration of this glorious season. Let's use our imaginations, shall we? I know you've got an imagination—you came up with that fabulous idea for the inflatable headpieces, didn't you? And I couldn't help but notice that remarkable work-in-progress in your front yard when I stopped by your house to pick up Wallace."

Belle draped the scarf around her neck and struck a dramatic pose, just to satisfy Reba. Her eyes darted right and left. *Please don't let anyone see me doing this.*

"All right. But only for the party."

Wallace poked his head out of the Snugli strapped to Reba's chest and gave Belle a look she interpreted as approving. Though Belle missed his company, it was a relief not to be responsible for him—or anything or anyone. She'd thought it best not to mention his little escapade to Reba and had simply answered "No trouble at all" when Reba asked how things had gone.

Reba and wallababy darted around the store gathering armloads of flowy, filmy, glitzy things, which Reba heaped on a table beside the full-length mirror and proceeded to drape on Belle. Belle stood with arms outstretched as Reba layered on embroidered vests, silken sashes, and ropes of beads. Shoppers steered their carts around the two women, smiling and offering opinions. "Looks good!" "More bling." "Here, try these shoes."

To Belle's amazement, they weren't mocking her; they were *admiring* her. And she was—kind of—loving it.

With Belle fully bedecked and bedazzled, Reba stood back to look her over.

"Hmmmm, almost there. Something's still not quite right."

Belle twirled in front of the mirror, stopped, and made a face. "It's my hair, isn't it? It's so droopy. I've never been able to do much with it, and this humidity doesn't help."

"Hold on! I know what we need." Reba dashed down an aisle and returned with a shaggy wig interlaced with feathers.

Belle reached out gingerly, as if the furry, feathered thing might bite. When it didn't, she plunked the wig on her head, turned to face the mirror . . . and burst out laughing. "I look like Steven Tyler." Shaking her head wildly, she grabbed a candlestick from a nearby display and pretended to sing into it.

"There are worse things, Belle," Reba said. "Steven Tyler is quite attractive—in a certain androgynous way."

Belle gyrated and pranced up and down an aisle, then stopped short. "But promise I only have to wear this to the party, not in the parade. My head would roast."

Reba's phone rang, a snippet of Bob Marley's "Stir It Up." She glanced at the screen, then held the phone in her palm like an offering as she spoke into it.

"Hey Roscoe, what's up?" Then in a stage-whispered aside to Belle: "Probably wants to read me a line from a new poem. He's working on a series about roadkill."

The phone mumbled. Reba swung it up to her ear. "What's that? I can barely hear you—where are you, next to a highway? . . . City hall. City hall?? What are you doing there? . . . Uh-huh, uh-huh. Crap. All right, we'll deal with it. Listen, Roscoe, round up everyone you can, and let's meet in the park at noon. We've got to put our heads together."

She ended the call and turned to Belle. "Bad news. We've been turned down for a parade permit. Never had a problem before—it's always been automatic. I don't know what's going on, but I'm not about to cancel the parade. We've already started making the headpieces. And besides, it's a *tradition*."

Belle began stripping off garments and jewelry and tossing everything into a cart. "Let me just pay for this stuff and throw it in my car. Then we'll walk to the park. Walking's better than driving for thinking."

Reba gripped Belle's hands in hers. "Yoooooou are a truuuuuue friend. And it's a good thing because you might be the only one who can get us out of this jam."

Belle gave her a quizzical look and stifled another urge to hold out her palms in protest.

Elms and oaks arched over the sidewalk that led from downtown to South Park. Grateful for the shade, Belle and Reba walked the three blocks, the soles of their sandals slapping the pavement. Overhead, blue jays jeered and chucked, gliding from branch to branch, pestering squirrels. The heat was not as stifling today. Filled with scents of heliotrope and mowed-this-morning grass, the air enveloped the women like one of Belle's new thrift-store scarves.

Belle glanced at the wallaby napping in his Snugli. "I'm still not clear on how you're sometimes so bold about carrying Wallace around in public and other times we have to keep him under wraps," she said.

"It all depends on Coogan's comings and goings," Reba said. Wallace woke and reached for a strand of her hair. "When he's in town, we play it safe. When he's away, we can relax."

Belle pondered the information for a moment. "But how do you know?"

"Early warning system." Reba winked, extracted her hair from Wallace's paw, and shifted the Snugli, all in one move. "A while back,

Coogan advertised for a helper at his roadside zoo. The place is an abomination, you understand, but until we can get it shut down, we figured we could at least infiltrate it and give the critters better care while gathering intel."

Belle had that dizzy sensation she often got when Reba imparted information: sort of knowing what Reba was talking about, but sensing key details had been left out. "Who's 'we'?" she asked.

The silvery roof of the park's gazebo came into view, glinting in the noonday sun. Beneath it, a handful of colorfully dressed women and men—ages ranging from late teens to beyond eighty—sprawled on benches.

"'We' is *them*," Reba said, making a sweeping gesture toward the gazebo. "Mae, Roscoe, DeShawn, and the rest of the gang. But it's really Lakshmi who does the heavy lifting—literally and figuratively. She took the zoo job, and she alerts me when Coogan's going out of town. Which, fortunately, is quite a bit—he's always off somewhere buying or selling animals, which is why he needed a helper for day-to-day stuff."

Reba waved at the gazebo group. They all waved back, except for Mae, who was absorbed in counting petals on a sunflower she clutched like a child with a treasured toy. *Surely must've come from a florist*, Belle surmised. The local sunflower fields were still at least a couple of months away from peak bloom, Mae had informed her, apropos of nothing.

"Of course, we have occasional slip-ups and close calls," Reba continued. "Like that first day you were at my house when Coogan showed up. Lakshmi was out sick, and Coogan slid back into town earlier than we expected. But for the most part, the system works."

"Well, that's good. But I still don't get why Coogan comes snooping around your place if he doesn't suspect you of taking Wallace. Does he think you've stolen more animals for your art, like he thinks you did with the armadillo?" Belle slowed her pace, hoping to get her confusion cleared up before they reached the gazebo. Fragmented conversations were the norm with Reba, but Belle craved closure.

"I keep forgetting you're new here," Reba said, matching her pace to Belle's. "See, shutting down the zoo was a plank in my platform."

"Your . . . platform?" *Here we go again. More confusing by the minute.*

"When I ran for City Council in the last election. I lost—by a narrow margin—to a bigshot real estate agent with a bad comb-over, but Coogan's still pissed. So every so often he drops by unannounced on the pretense of buying medicinal herbs. Luckily, with that red hair and beard, I can usually see him coming."

Belle stopped in her tracks and threw up her hands. "Wait a minute—medicinal herbs?"

"Oh yeah, I grow and sell them. You didn't think that big garden in my backyard was only for zucchini and jalapeños, did you? Coogan buys them to treat his animals, not because he's into natural products, but because he's too cheap to buy pharmaceuticals. But I'm wise to him. I know he's really popping in to try and catch me growing and selling illegal substances—hallucinogens and such."

The way Belle's head spun, she wondered if *she* was on some psychedelic trip. She wasn't sure she wanted to know the answer to the next question, but it slipped out anyway. "But you don't, right? Grow and sell that kind of thing."

"Not currently, no." Reba started walking again. "I did, but I cleaned up my garden and greenhouse before my campaign, just so my opponent couldn't dig up that dirt, so to speak. Since then I've stuck with the legal medicinals, but Coogan is convinced I'm involved in something shady. Which I am, but it's not what he thinks."

Laughter and some kind of strange music drifted over from the gazebo. Clarinet, strings, accordion, tuba—Belle had a knack for picking out instrument sounds, thanks to a music appreciation class in college.

"Don't you worry that Coogan might have his own surveillance system?" she asked. "You know, friends who might tell him if they spot you with Wallace?"

Reba hooted. "Coooooogan? Friends? Get real. The man's alienated everyone in town."

They reached the gazebo, and a round of heys, howdys, and holas greeted them over the music. Someone switched it off, and Reba introduced Belle to everyone she hadn't already met: Lakshmi, whose honey-toned face was shaded by an enormous straw hat decorated with marigolds and plastic zoo animals; Zebulon, heavily tattooed and multiply pierced; Jax, a youthful individual of ambiguous gender with chartreuse-tinted hair cut in an asymmetrical style; a gaunt but cheerful fiftyish woman Reba introduced as Olive Pickle; an assortment of other folks whose personalities seemed as vivid and unconventional as their boho garb; and finally, Roscoe, fortyish like Reba, stocky and scrappy-looking with his brush cut, tight black T-shirt, and camouflage cargo pants.

"So you're the fabled Penitentiary Poet," Belle said. He was shorter than she'd expected and reminded her of the ragamuffin character Sluggo from the *Nancy* comics Grandpa Jake used to read to her. It was hard to imagine Roscoe writing poetry, yet Reba had insisted he was quite accomplished, published in *Ploughshares*, *Prairie Schooner*, and *Poetry* magazine. Whatever that meant. Belle didn't read poetry and recognized the names of literary journals only from hearing Miranda mention them. Still, it all sounded impressive.

"And you're the fabled Belle." Was Roscoe smiling or smirking? Belle wasn't sure, but it looked more like the former. "Reba and Mae have talked of no one and nothing else since you hit town."

Belle dropped her head, aware of everyone's eyes on her. "Oh, please," she finally said. "I'm just delighted to meet you all." Though as she said it, she considered whether "delighted" was the right word. Maybe something more along the lines of "wary." She'd had diverse friends in Chicago, but they were more homogeneous in their diversity—all young urban professionals who drove fuel-efficient cars, frequented museums, and listened to NPR. These friends of Reba and Mae's were so *diversely* diverse.

Looking over the crew, Belle pictured them as a circus troupe or performers in an avant-garde production in some back-alley theater. Instead, they were at a midday meeting in Middle America, like a bunch of Rotarians. Go figure. She had to wonder how they'd all found one another. It wasn't as if the whole town was full of—what to call them? Eccentrics? Nonconformists? No, she knew it wasn't. She'd seen plenty of *regular* people shopping at Kroger and eating at Applebee's, where she sometimes stopped for the triple chocolate meltdown when only sugar and fat would appease her. Yet there did seem to be a particularly high concentration of unconventional types in these parts. Well, at least they were friendly. And so doggone exuberant.

Jax reached into a backpack, pulled out a dozen lumpy, grainy, cupcake-shaped things, and passed them around. Some sort of healthy snack, apparently. "Made them this morning."

The memory of Reba's zucchini-jalapeño cookies—strangely tasty—emboldened Belle to take one. She decided not to ask what was in it.

"There's kombucha in the Thermos," Zebulon said, "but we'll have to use a communal cup."

Several voices confirmed that was not a problem. Roscoe unscrewed the Thermos cap, filled it with the fizzy drink, took a gulp, and passed the cup to Belle. She sipped and offered the cup to Mae, who seemed unsure how to manage both petal-counting and kombucha consumption.

Even snacking is unconventional with this bunch, Belle observed to herself as she reached for seconds of Jax's treat.

Reba stepped into the center of the gazebo and turned in a slow circle as she addressed the crowd. "Well, folks, it's groovy to be gathered here on this magnificent day, and many thanks to Jax and Zebulon for the refreshments. But we have matters to discuss, so let's get to it. Now, as you may have heard, we've been denied a parade permit. All I can figure is, it might have something to do with that episode of, ahem, spontaneous disrobement on Mass Ave. last year."

Roscoe shook a finger at Mae. "Aquamaureen, shame on you!"

Mae flushed scarlet and turned her face away.

"He's joking, Mae," Reba said. "We all know it wasn't you. It was just a few hopped-up college kids that got carried away toward the end of the parade. And anyway, those body parts they exposed were nothing you don't see on Netflix these days. But then, our parade is supposed to be G-rated, so I guess some people got a little uptight about it."

"Is there an appeal process?" asked Jax. "I'll file whatever papers we need to file."

"Much appreciated, Jax, but it has to be an in-person appeal, and for that we need to present our most dignified—ahem, *conventional*—representative."

Everyone turned toward Belle.

Oh no, oh no, here it comes. Belle mentally rehearsed gracious refusals. *Don't get involved. Protect yourself. Retreat, regroup, recoup.*

Reba's eyes pleaded. "Will yoooooou?"

Belle looked around the circle. Like Reba's zucchini-jalapeño cookies and Jax's lumpy *whatevers*, these people took some getting used to, but once you acquired a taste, they were irresistible. What's more, Belle reminded herself, she excelled at getting things done.

She met their eyes, and against her better judgment flashed her most respectable, *normal* smile.

"Well . . . okay. But just this once."

– 7 –
THE ATROCITY

In the driveway of the house on the other side of Mitchell's, a little girl sprayed a hose at the back of a minivan. Belle waved as she walked by, but the girl was too intent on her task to notice.

Belle had taken to strolling around her neighborhood in the late afternoon, checking out people's flowers and lawn ornaments, waving if the neighbors looked friendly. Walking always helped her collect her thoughts, and she especially needed to do that now, as she considered her approach for the meeting she'd just scheduled for the next morning with the director of Parks and Rec, the department that granted—or denied—parade permits.

She'd just started around the block when the hose girl caught her attention. The girl sprayed and sprayed and sprayed, not soaping or scrubbing, just hosing as if it were the most essential undertaking. As she sprayed, she hopped from one foot to the other.

Hose, hose, hose, hop, hop. Belle had the feeling that if she came back an hour later, the girl might still be there, hose-hopping. Had Belle ever been that intent on anything? That *committed*?

She moved on. The next yard boasted the only sidewalk on the block. Well, "boasted" wasn't quite the right word. Instead of being weeded and swept as befitted its status, the walkway was overgrown and barely visible. Why bother when it led only from one driveway to the next?

Another yard, another house. Not run down, exactly, but not cared for, with an unmown lawn that was mostly crabgrass. From inside came piano music—ragtime—too *live* to be coming from a recording, yet too tuneful to be coming from a house like that. Through the front window, Belle caught a glimpse of a man playing an upright piano in what appeared to be his underwear, gently rolling from side to side, flabby flesh heaving over the top of white jockey shorts. Well, who *would* put on pants or mow their lawn if they could make music like that? Then again, maybe Kansas wasn't as normal as everyone assumed.

Belle rambled on around the block. Some yards were immaculate, with color-coordinated blooms filling flower beds and spilling from window boxes and hanging baskets; other yards served as catchalls for broken toys, upended trash cans, and whatnot.

Curious now to see how her little cottage fit into the neighborhood scheme, she rounded the corner and was startled to find her landlady standing in her front yard, hands on hips, staring at Belle's concrete creation, which had expanded to the width and length of a double mattress in a matter of days.

"Mrs. Dumas!" Belle rushed over. "I wasn't expecting you. Won't you come in for some tea?"

The older woman scowled, her salon-styled do shifting downward on her scalp, her red nails pattering against her broomstick skirt. "Miss Marsden, this is not a social call. I've been informed that you are keeping some sort of canine in this rental. May I remind you of the terms of your lease? No dogs. No cats. No exceptions."

"Oh, Mrs. Dumas!" Belle said. "I think there's been a misunderstanding. I have no dog. No animals at all. If anyone thinks they saw one, they are mistaken. Please, come inside and look around. You'll see." Belle made an expansive gesture meant to look inviting.

"That won't be necessary, Miss Marsden. I will take your word for it this time. But consider yourself warned. If I receive any more reports of dogs or cats on the premises, I will have no choice but to evict you."

Belle laid a gentle hand on her landlady's arm. "You needn't worry, Mrs. Dumas. I love this house. I wouldn't dream of violating the terms of our agreement."

Mrs. Dumas smoothed her blouse, a puckery thing that required no smoothing, and tossed her head. "Yes, well that's not all. There's the matter of this . . . atrocity." She pointed the chiseled nail of her index finger at Belle's creation. "What in heaven's name is going on here?"

Belle looked at the assemblage. What had seemed so entrancing as she was piecing it together now looked like a godawful mess as she pictured it through her landlady's eyes. But then, hadn't Dinsmoor's garden started out the same way? Hadn't it taken some time to become what it became—whatever that was? Wasn't that the way art progressed?

Feeling at once foolish and strangely emboldened, Belle straightened her spine and drew herself up to her full height—a good three inches taller than Mrs. Dumas. "This, Mrs. Dumas, is a work of *art* in progress. I realize it may not look like much right now, but I assure you, it will be an asset to the neighborhood when it's finished and complemented with floral designs. Assemblages like this are all the rage in the better neighborhoods of Chicago, you know."

Mrs. Dumas sniffed, then stood back and took another look at the mishmash of concrete and broken crockery. "Chicago? Really? Well, I guess I can see that it . . . might. But make no mistake, Miss Marsden. If this turns into an eyesore, I'll have you out of here so fast your head will spin, and I'll hold you financially responsible for cleaning up the mess."

A surprising serenity came over Belle. As Mrs. Dumas minced across the yard, buckled herself into her car, and drove away, Belle simply smiled.

Once her landlady was out of sight, Belle hustled to Mitchell's garage, filled the wheelbarrow with supplies and tools, and returned to the front yard freshly inspired. A few hours of daylight remained, enough to try out the ideas that had flowed through her imagination within moments of the confrontation with Mrs. Dumas.

Dog, indeed! Belle laughed to herself. *If only Wallace could hear that.* She laughed aloud. *Atrocity! We'll show her atrocity.*

She collected a few more pieces of china from the kitchen and took them out to the yard, where she got busy smashing them. Hammering, sending chips flying, delighting in the sound of shattering porcelain. Then she mixed a thick batch of concrete and began sculpting free-form shapes around the edges of her so-called atrocity, embellishing each one with ceramic slivers and a few unusual stones she'd picked up on her neighborhood promenade. Designs seemed to spring from her fingers: spirals, stars, handprints. Then in a flash of genius, a wallaby's head on a dog's body.

Who knows? Maybe some neighborhoods would *see this kind of thing as an asset. Maybe that thing I told Mrs. Dumas wasn't a complete fabrication.*

Belle worked until darkness obscured her vision and she had to call it a night. With a final caress to the work she'd just completed, she packed everything back into the wheelbarrow and carted it to the garage.

Back in the house, Belle collapsed onto the futon. Exhausted as she was, her mind still raced. Sleep would not come soon. She sprang from the futon and rummaged through a drawer until she found the colored pencils Miranda had stashed in the salmagundi box, along with a pad of drawing paper Reba had brought over, "in case your trips to Lucas inspire you to sketch."

Ignoring her own claims that she couldn't draw even a stick figure, Belle rendered her imaginings onto the page. She drew towers and fanciful animals. An armadillo with a cupcake for a hat. A porcupine with marshmallows impaled like shish kebabs on each quill. And people. Reba with her Rastacap; Mae all in aqua; Ezra with a bottle of Stormchaser in one hand and a children's book in the other. Herself—no, that's where she hit a wall, her imagination depleted for the night. Or was it only that she couldn't imagine herself any other way than she'd always seen herself: featureless and bland?

Morning came too soon, but Belle was ready for it. Up at dawn, she laid out her clothes for the city hall meeting: casual khaki skirt (respectable, but not too citified), her dressiest T-shirt, peep-toe flats. Hitting all the right notes. She took her time applying makeup, trying to remember the last time she'd bothered to put on mascara and lipstick. She fussed and fussed with her hair. As usual, it refused to obey. She eyed the thrift-store wig. No, definitely not the look she was after. Not *normal*. The spider-webby Indian scarf hung on a hook on the back of her bedroom door. Belle grabbed it and wound it around her head, hoping the effect was more stylish than hippie-chickish.

On the drive to city hall, she tried to focus on the case she would make to the functionary in charge of permits. She was good at this sort of thing, practiced in convincing reluctant establishment owners to lend their venues to offbeat events. Piece of cake. *Cake*. Her thoughts drifted from her Parks and Rec spiel back to the drawings she'd made last night. An armadillo with a cupcake hat? Had that really happened? *Me, Belle? Drawing?* From there, her mind replayed the past night's dreams, another curious conglomeration of images: Dinsmoor's solid women, the circus-troupe gang from the park, sunflowers, scarves, prickly and scaly creatures.

The Parks and Recreation Department was on the second floor of city hall. Belle took the stairs, counting on physical activity to settle her nerves, and arrived at the reception desk right on time, though breathless and damp.

"Isabelle Marsden. Appointment with Mr.—um, MacKenzie?"

"It's MacAdams." The woman behind the desk could've passed for a sister or close cousin of Mrs. Dumas. She spat the words and seemed to be looking at the tip of her nose as she addressed Belle. "You're with the parade people, right? He's expecting you." Had her nose squinched at the words "parade people"?

"That's right. The Soulstice *Foundation.*" What prompted Belle to create a phony foundation on the spot, she couldn't have said, but it worked some voodoo on the receptionist. Her face softened into something not quite a smile, yet not a sneer, and she gestured toward an open doorway.

"Please, go right on in, Ms. Marsden."

Arthur MacAdams had an expansive face, sandy hair overdue for a trim, and an affable air that reminded Belle of her favorite uncle Gary. Not at all the buttoned-up bureaucrat she'd expected. But then, this was Parks and Rec. It made sense that its director would be laid-back, even playful perhaps. Belle relaxed a tad and launched into the pitch she'd practiced—or tried to—on the drive over.

"Mister MacMmmm . . . Adams, I'm new in town, but already I feel like I belong. And do you know why? It's because this remarkable group of people—the Soulstice Foundation—has welcomed me and encouraged me to use my skills to benefit the community, as they do. In return, I'm committed to helping them see their projects succeed." Well, *committed* wasn't exactly true, but he didn't have to know that. "Right now, their main objective is the annual Soulstice parade. Now, being new here, I've never witnessed this event, but from what I hear—and not just from the organizers but from everyone I talk to in town—"

She was making things up again, but it was working. MacAdams, chin in hand, gave her his full attention.

"—well, everyone just raves about the parade. They say summer can't get underway until we've had the parade. And so this matter of the permit denial is, frankly, perplexing."

Belle sat back and mimicked the director's body language, resting her chin on her fist and fixing her gaze on his. He shuffled a few papers, pulled out the permit application, stamped with DENIED in inch-high red letters, and looked it over.

Belle waited. Her eyes swept around the room. The décor was Basic Administrator. On a shelf behind the director's desk, silver-framed photos of an attractive woman and three children—two boys and a girl—showed the family in beach and mountain settings as the kids advanced from toddlerhood to middle grades. A baseball glove and trophies suggested Little League coaching on the side, and a vase of fresh anemones told her someone—MacAdams himself?—was a gardener.

MacAdams took his time studying the application. With little else to investigate in the room, Belle stared out the window. Masses of treetops stretched into the distance like banks of green clouds. She envisioned the parade route, stepping off from South Park; heading north on Massachusetts Avenue, the main street through the heart of town; skirting the Kaw River before turning back toward town; and ending up at Watson Park, where music, dancing, and games would fill the rest of the day.

Even with all her organizing experience, she couldn't have planned a more entertaining event. And the amazing thing was, no one had *planned* it at all. It had just evolved over the years, from a neighborhood celebration to a citywide event that drew visitors from all over Kansas and neighboring states.

"Well, Ms. Marsden . . ." MacAdams flashed an avuncular smile. "I can't deny the Soulstice parade is something of an institution. My wife and I have enjoyed attending it, and so have our kids. But it's the *kids* we must consider here. Now, last year, there was . . ." He looked down at his stack of papers, and his ears reddened. "Well, there was some *nudity*, Ms. Marsden. We just can't have that kind of thing at a family event."

Belle leaned forward to communicate goodwill, but then wondered if the move came off as inappropriately intimate, given the subject matter. She slid back in her chair and stiffened her spine.

"I couldn't agree more, Mr. MacAdams," she said. "And the whole Soulstice Foundation is right on the same page with us. The instigators of that unfortunate incident were not our members, we're quite sure, and we're willing to do everything we can to prevent anything like that from happening again. Of course, we can't control what spectators will do, but we'll have all our parade participants sign pledges of modest and exemplary behavior."

Pledges of modest and exemplary behavior? Hoo-boy, that was a good one. She could imagine how Reba and Roscoe would mock her for that. But if it got the parade ungrounded, then whatever, right?

"And you would enforce these pledges how?" MacAdams asked, not in a combative way.

"Well . . ." *Think fast, think fast!* "We'll have parade marshals stationed throughout the marchers, and they'll nip any unsavory behavior in the bud."

Oh god, Reba and Roscoe are going to kill me.

MacAdams twirled a pen, swiveled in his chair, gazed out the window. "You know, Ms. Marsden, I was really hoping we could work this out."

Belle held her breath. Was a "but . . ." about to follow? And if it did, should she keep pleading the case, or would that seem grasping and pathetic? What more could she say to convince him?

MacAdams turned back to Belle, grinning. "And you've convinced me we can." He scratched out the red-lettered DENIED on the application and scrawled GRANTED across the top. Then standing, he reached out to shake Belle's hand.

"See you at the parade."

A celebratory lunch with Reba seemed in order, but the positive energy Belle's accomplishment generated in her made her rush home instead, change clothes, and get back to work on her—her what? Even in her own mind, she didn't know what to call it. It wasn't exactly a sculpture, but it wasn't *not* a sculpture. It resembled a mosaic, but not simply a mosaic. "Work of art" sounded too pretentious, "creation" too generic. She liked to think of it as something organic, growing and evolving, the way the Soulstice parade had. A garden, like Dinsmoor's Garden of Eden and Florence Deeble's rock garden.

Belle's Garden. No, wait—in homage to francophone Wallace, make that *Belle Jardin*.

She had just wheeled out her tools and supplies—now stashed in her own backyard shed—and was mixing a fresh batch of concrete when Ezra loped over.

"Thought you could use these." He held out two books: a glossy coffee-table-sized volume and a slim paperback. "I've been poking around the public library in my spare time—busman's holiday, you know—and I found these. I figured they might give you some inspiration and guidance. I see you're starting to build upward, and this one's got instructions on how to keep things from collapsing." He held out the paperback, and Belle read the title, *Making Concrete Garden Ornaments*. "Now, I know what you're doing here is not exactly a garden ornament," Ezra continued.

"Oh, but I just realized it kind of *is*," Belle said. "Your timing could not be more perfect. What's the other one?"

Ezra squatted on the ground beside her and opened the larger book. "You'll love this one. It's called *Fantasy Worlds*, and it's all about places like the Garden of Eden. You've been there, right? Well, it's in this book, along with all the other famous ones. You know, Watts Towers, the Bottle Castle, Paradise Garden, Thunder Mountain."

Belle wrinkled her forehead. "There are other places? Other

people who've made these things?" She stopped stirring concrete and stared at the pages as Ezra leafed through the book.

Spires and turrets, colored glass and seashells, miniature villages, and full-size houses decorated from foundation to rooftop. Fantastic animals and frightful faces. Rocket ships, whirligigs, windows made from old TV screens—the wildly imaginative gewgaws went on and on.

"I had no idea," Belle said. "Is there a name for these things?"

"Lots of different names. Outsider art, folk environments. The name I like best is visionary art because people who make these things are obviously guided by something only they can see. Just like you, most of them have no formal training as artists—they just get inspired and let their inspiration take them where it will. It's like they've been visited by some otherworldly muse. Is that how it is for you?"

Sunlight reflected off chips of pottery and illuminated the spirals and stars Belle had fashioned the night before. Images from the far-out dreams she'd been having swam through her consciousness. She thought about the parade costume ideas that had sprung from who-knows-where.

"It wouldn't have occurred to me to put it that way, but yes, I guess it is."

Ezra's expression turned serious, as serious as it was capable of looking, given the comical asymmetry of his face. "Then you've been given a rare gift, Belle. Use it well."

Despite the midday heat, Belle shivered.

"Hey!" Ezra lightened his tone. "It's lunchtime. Want to go grab a burger or something?"

Belle turned toward Ezra but looked through him into the middle distance. "Lunch. No. No thanks, I mean. I just mixed up this concrete, and . . ." She turned away and stirred the slurry.

"Okay, then. Maybe another time. I'll just set these books on your stoop, all right?"

"Mmmmmm," Belle said, already far away from the stoop, books, Ezra, and all the rest of the world except *Belle Jardin*.

– 8 –
THE VOICE

Belle had bills to pay, dishes to wash, laundry to launder. Reba, elated at the news of the permit victory, wanted her to stop by for another costume consultation. But the morning after the Parks and Rec meeting, Belle had other plans.

She packed a lunch and travel snacks, filled a Thermos with chilled tea, and set off for Lucas. What she intended to do there, she wasn't entirely sure. She just felt a need—no, more like a magnetic pull—to go, to inhabit the worlds of Dinsmoor and Deeble and Ed Root and Mri-Pilar. To commune with their creative spirits and perhaps, if she could be so bold as to assume she was worthy, absorb some of their genius. If that's what it was. She still wasn't sure if those so-called visionary artists were muse-guided geniuses or misguided kooks.

As she drove, she mulled over what she'd read in the library books before drifting off to dream-riddled sleep the night before. In a chapter titled "Concrete Folk Environments: A Source of Inspiration," the author of the garden ornament book had written this:

> *These are creative people on a mission . . . Some create out of a work ethic to be useful and to make something to give back to mankind, while others are motivated by divine inspiration, however personally translated.*

And this:

> *Often the builders were harassed and labeled social outcasts, or at the very least, creative eccentrics. But when all was said and done, in the best-case scenarios, members of the community began to see the value and uniqueness of the artist's work, and made the effort to preserve it for public enjoyment.*

So other communities *did* embrace these crazy creations, as Lucas apparently had. Interesting, but still no definitive answers to the questions Belle kept turning over in her head like one of those koans Miranda was always talking about: Where is the line between creativity and madness? Is there even a clear boundary? Does one shade into the other in a fluid, ever-moving dance? And if you find yourself caught up in that dance, how do you know which side you're on?

Deep in thought, Belle hardly noticed the passing landscape. Farmhouses, silos, wind turbines, and limestone fenceposts passed as blurs, and the three-hour drive seemed more like minutes. Once she reached Lucas, her first stop was Dinsmoor's Cabin Home gift shop, where the perm-headed woman—Polly, according to her nametag—again sat behind the register, a scent of Avon perfume emanating from her.

Belle paid the eight-dollar admission fee and started out the door, but had a thought and turned back. "Can I get a season pass? Or do you have memberships, maybe?" She was thinking of the Chicago museums with their yearlong free admission, gift-shop discounts, and special events for members.

Polly peered through her owlish 1980s eyeglasses—the frames a pearly coral shade that matched the teeny flowers on her print dress. She looked concerned.

"Well, now, dear, that's a new one on me. I'm not sure I've ever had anyone ask about that. Most folks just come the one time and see what there is to see, and that's it for them. But you're wanting to come regular-like? Just how often, do you figure?"

That was the question, wasn't it? If you'd asked Belle even a week earlier, she'd have said once was enough for her too. But now? Who could say how often she'd have the urge to make another pilgrimage?

"Once a week?" Belle smiled her most amicable, *normal* smile.

Maybe she shouldn't have asked for a discount. This place might need every eight-dollar admission fee it could get. She hadn't seen another soul on the Garden of Eden grounds when she drove up, and the gift shop and Cabin Home were empty too, except for Belle and Polly Perm.

"Goodness!" Polly said. "That would add up over time, wouldn't it? Let's just say twenty bucks, and you can keep coming back as long as I'm here. And I'm not planning on going anywhere anytime soon." She laughed from deep inside the folds of calico, flesh jiggling all over, and sputtered out, "If ever!"

Belle wandered around the grounds, noticing details she'd missed on her first visit. One figure in particular caught her attention. Atop the mausoleum, a winged woman leaned with outstretched arms over a ledge. An angel? Belle thought so at first but then noticed the figure's wings were long and pointy and stuck straight out from her body like the wings of a bird or an insect in flight. Nothing like the arched angel wings Belle remembered from pictures on the walls of her Sunday school classroom.

As the air pulsated with summer insect sounds, Belle imagined the woman as part of the stridulating, squeaking, buzzing chorus.

Another winged woman, arms and wings extended like the first one, soared above a collection of creepy characters: a bloodied, lifeless body watched over by a half-naked woman, her arm raised as in a benediction; a scaly gargoyle with broken fangs bared in a pantomimed roar that Belle could almost hear.

High upon a concrete branch, a single arm pointed in another direction, as if directing viewers away from the gruesome scene below.

"Looking for something?"

The woman's voice startled Belle. *Polly?* No. Polly's voice was flat and nasally. This voice was like music. Belle turned to see who was speaking to her. The grounds were as empty as when she first arrived. She scanned the Cabin Home's porch and balcony, checked out the walkway around the mausoleum, peered behind tree trunks—living and concrete. No one there.

"You will find it," the voice said.

"Find what?" Belle felt ridiculous talking to a disembodied voice. Maybe it wasn't even talking to her.

". . . or it will find you."

"Who are you?" Belle asked. "*Where* are you?" She waited for a reply but none came. Overhead, the gargoyle's grimace threatened, but the half-naked woman's face wore a beatific expression that Belle could swear had not been there before, and a scent like gardenias swirled around her, though no flowers were in sight.

Okay, I thought the dead guy in the crypt was weird, but this is really too much. Now I'm hearing voices? And answering? Am I losing my mind? Maybe spending more time in this place wasn't such a good idea.

Shuddering, she speed-walked to her car and guided it—faster than was probably safe—toward the interstate. The whole drive back to Lawrence, she talked to herself.

That statue did not talk to me. It didn't. *But then, who did?*

Around Junction City, it hit her.

Speakers! That was it. Crazy old Dinsmoor had installed speakers in his statues and set them up to play recorded messages. She wouldn't put it past him. Yes, that was it. It was speakers and recordings and a final practical joke on unsuspecting visitors. It was that simple, and now she could sleep tonight.

But it wasn't, and she couldn't. Only after reading about the fantasy worlds of Tressa "Grandma" Prisbrey's Bottle Village and Howard Finster's Paradise Garden—and whether or not they included audio interactives—was she able to doze off. Though she found herself wide awake halfway through the night, thinking again about the voice in Dinsmoor's domain. Ezra said the creators of these strange environments were visited by otherworldly muses. Did those muses talk to them?

Oh, stop it, Belle. It was speakers in those statues. That's the most logical explanation, and you're a logical person.

She rolled onto her sleeping side but then rolled back to her thinking side. She'd noticed this pattern in her bed habits when she was still working in Chicago. Often she'd wake in the night with some dilemma running through her mind. It might be a problem with flower arrangements or hors d'oeuvres for an event she was organizing, or it might be Jamison's unwelcome advances. It might even be a longstanding heartache like the anguish over her mother's sudden death. Or the breakup, two years later, with Ben, the only man she'd ever allowed herself to love (though he was barely a man at the time—just a college kid like her).

If she lay on her left side, she ruminated endlessly, sometimes coming up with solutions, but more often thrashing in spirals of worry and pain. If she rolled onto her right side, she might continue to cogitate for a bit, but eventually dreamlike mental snapshots would replace her thoughts, and the next thing she knew, she'd be waking in the morning from a full-length dream.

This night, she resisted the urge to roll back to her right and let sleep overtake her. She needed to think.

Those visions and dreams and creations are taking over my life. I've got to stay in control. Stay normal. Stay normal. Stay . . .

And then it was morning, and she was waking from another dream. But this one was unlike the others she'd had lately. Instead of disconnected dramas populated by exotic animals and peculiar personages, this dream took place on a misty riverbank and whispered serenity. Across the water, nearly obscured by the haze, stood Belle's mother. Though they were too far apart to touch, her mother reached out her arms, smiled, and before disappearing completely, spoke one word: "Listen."

Listen? To what? To whom? Belle turned the questions over in her mind as she brewed coffee, poured a cup, and took it onto the side stoop just outside her kitchen door.

Had it been a dream? Or was it a *visitation*—the one she'd been waiting almost half her life for? For the most part, Belle didn't buy into superstitions and New Age nonsense, unlike Miranda, who was always carrying on about crystals and chakras and such. But Belle did believe that once in a while, spirits from the other side might drop by to impart meaningful messages. Her dad, as rational a man as ever lived, had confided to Belle that a few weeks after his father—Belle's Grandpa Jake—died of a heart attack, a strange thing happened. He awoke in the middle of the night to find Grandpa Jake sitting on the end of his bed, a look of utter contentment on his face. "Just wanted you to know, son, that it's not bad where I am," the older man said. "Not bad at all. I miss you all, of course, but I've got no pain, no sorrow. It's a pretty darn good life—or whatever it is." And then he was gone.

"And Belle, it wasn't a dream," her dad told her afterward. "It was as real as sitting here with you. I can't explain it, but I really believe Grandpa came back to tell us he's fine and we needn't grieve for him."

So when Belle's mother died unexpectedly of a brain aneurism just after Belle's nineteenth birthday, Belle was sure it was only a matter of time until she'd wake to find her mother in her room. Every night she rehearsed in her mind the questions she'd ask—all the things she never thought to ask when her mother was alive. Some nights she dreamed of her mother, but the dreams were clearly dreams—convoluted and unreal, with no clear message. This latest one, though dreamlike in some ways, was the most realistic yet. And the message, *Listen*, had to mean something. Didn't it?

Sitting there on the stoop, the neighborhood's morning sounds of clanking garbage cans, barking dogs, and oscillating sprinklers punctuating her thoughts, Belle tried to replay every detail of the dream in her mind.

High above, an oriole trilled a fluty whistle. Belle scanned the treetops until she glimpsed the bird's orange breast.

I'm listening. What are you telling me?

"Good morning!"

Belle's arm jerked uncontrollably, sending what was left of her coffee onto her foot.

"Mom??"

"Belle? Are you okay?" Ezra crouched in front of her and rested two fingers on her arm. "You're pale, and you look a little spacey."

"Ezra! Oh god, it's you." Belle slipped her arm out from under Ezra's hand and clasped her knees, still quivery from the dream and its message.

"Well, that's a greeting I don't often get. A simple 'good morning' would suffice." Ezra grinned, lopsided as ever, and Belle responded with a wan smile as she tried to reenter reality.

"I'm glad you came over, Ezra. There's something I wanted to ask you."

Ezra's eyebrows lifted.

Belle hardly noticed. "Yeah," she continued, looking past him into his uncle's backyard. "I was wondering if you have any chicken wire or hardware cloth over there at Mitchell's place. That book you brought over says to use it as a scaffold for three-dimensional shapes, and that's the direction I feel like I should go next."

Ezra looked toward Mitchell's garage. When he looked back, the grin was gone. "Sure. Mitchell has a little bit of everything over there, and I think I saw a roll of chicken wire behind the garage. I'll bring it over later." He paused. "You're getting pretty wrapped up in that project, aren't you?"

Belle traced a design on the dusty ground around the stoop. "Yeah. It's weird. I feel like I ought to be doing something more—you know—useful with my life, but this silly thing keeps calling to me." She threw up her hands in a helpless gesture.

"Then maybe this *is* the useful thing, Belle. You never know where artistic expression will lead." With that, Ezra stood. For a moment, he looked down at Belle, not saying anything, just looking at her with an expression that could have been thoughtful or sad or tender—it was hard to interpret the odd arrangements of his features.

Belle's eyes met his and then traveled back to her design in the dust.

Ezra turned to walk away.

"Oh, and Ezra?"

He turned back, brightened.

"Thanks."

"Oh." He gave a nod, so slight it barely registered on Belle's consciousness. "Right."

– 9 –
THE ZOOKEEPER

Unpaid bills still littered Belle's kitchen table; towers of dishes still teetered in the sink; dirty clothes still spilled from the laundry basket in her closet. Belle could not be bothered with such things. The project, the creation, the "atrocity" consumed her every thought, waking or dreaming.

Swallowing the last of her coffee and skipping breakfast once again, she wheeled her supplies out to her gray predawn front yard. *Good girl, starting early.*

Not that Belle had ever gotten a late start in her life. Never tardy to school or work, always on time or early for appointments, parties, and meetups with friends. Her more lackadaisical cohorts ribbed her about it. The Princess of Punctuality, they called her. She couldn't help it. Being prompt was as ingrained as being organized. Those tendencies were tightly spiraled into her DNA; she was sure of it. Hadn't her second-grade teacher confirmed that notion when the drawing Belle had worked so hard on wasn't included in the school art show?

Belle thought back to that day, to Mrs. Glick crouching in the aisle beside Belle's desk, the smell of paste and crayons and pencil shavings filling the air around them.

"You know, Belle, we all have different skills," her teacher said. "Some people are just naturally artistic, and some people do other things well. I see you arranging your books and pencils, and I admire your ability to organize things. And your dependability! I bet you'd be just the person to help me organize the art supplies."

As she took in her teacher's words, Belle pictured Andy, another kid in her class. He couldn't play soccer because something was wrong with his heart, so he helped Mr. Silvers, the gym teacher, hand out balls and water bottles. *Andy's a helper because something's wrong with his heart*, Belle told herself. *I guess I'm a helper because something's wrong with my art.*

Yet now, here she was making—it still felt presumptuous to call it *art*, but it was undeniably a creation of some kind. Creating, not just organizing. Sure, she was setting to work early, but that was more to avoid the afternoon heat than to keep to a schedule. Organization? What about those unpaid bills, dirty dishes, unwashed clothes? It was as if the very traits that defined Belle were being uprooted like ancient trees in a windstorm, and dandelions were invading their spaces.

Belle poured gray powder into her bucket, added water, and mixed. Just this much powder, this much water: The process was second nature now, and the mucky smell of concrete slurry like perfume to her nose. She'd have to wait for Ezra to bring the chicken wire before she could go any higher with the figures she was fashioning. She hoped he wouldn't forget. He'd seemed a little . . . strange when he'd left. But then, like many of the people she'd come to know in Lawrence, he *was* a little strange.

No sooner had Belle begun smoothing fresh concrete and pressing in broken china than Reba zoomed up on the tangerine motor scooter she rode around town. Wallace, secure in a backpack, peeped over her shoulder. She vaulted off the scooter, tromped over to Belle's worksite, and stood, hands on hips, giving Belle a look that combined pique and concern.

"Where have you *been*? I've been trying to call you since yesterday:

no answer, no answer. You had me worried—thought you'd made another trip to Lucas and fallen into Dinsmoor's crypt or something." Reba glanced at the section Belle was working on, then bent down to inspect the rest of the structure. "Wow. What's this—a walla-dog? Cool. You've done a lot since I was here last. And from the looks of it, you *have* been back to Lucas."

Belle pulled a rag from her back pocket and wiped her hands. "Yup. Yesterday, in fact. This time, I noticed things I hadn't noticed the first time, like those speakers—they really had me going for a while."

"Speakers?" Reba stood and arched her back. Backlit by the morning sun, her frizz of hair glowed like a halo.

Angels everywhere, Belle thought.

"What speakers? Hey, are you okay? You're looking a little drifty. Maybe you need to eat something?"

"I'm fine." Belle smiled what she intended as an undrifty, *normal* smile. "Just preoccupied with this project. I'm sure you know how that is."

"What speakers are you talking about, Belle?" Reba repeated. "Something else you want to add to the parade?"

"In the statues. Dinsmoor must've installed speakers to scare the bejesus out of visitors. It sure worked on me." Belle let out a laugh but stifled it when Reba frowned.

"Interesting. I've got friends who help maintain the Garden of Eden structures, and they've never said anything about speakers." Reba squinted at Belle. "Though they did say that back in Dinsmoor's day, there was an eye-of-God type thing hanging from one of those concrete branches. Dinsmoor had it wired to light up, and he ran a hose up to it from the basement of the house. He'd yell through the hose at people walking by, acting like he was God talking to them. And there was another tube that went to one of the angels. If people were gawking at the garden from the sidewalk, he'd nag them through the tube to pay the admission fee or move on. But those are long gone. No hoses. No speakers."

"You're sure?"

"Positive. Did you maybe hear a radio from a passing car and think it was coming from a statue? Sounds can be tricky that way."

Belle bobbed her head in an overenthusiastic show of agreement. "Radio! I hadn't thought of that. Yes, that's what it was."

She knew it wasn't. What kind of radio delivered messages like *You will find it . . . or it will find you*? But she also couldn't be sure that it wasn't, and she was in no mood to argue the point.

Wallace nibbled at Reba's ear; Reba reached up to stroke his snout and nudge it away. "Yes, baby, we'll go home soon. Just a few minutes more." Then turning back to Belle: "Well, I'm glad we got that mystery cleared up. And now that I know you haven't gone missing, there's something I need your help with."

Again? Parade costumes were one thing, and stepping up to help with the permit denial wasn't even that big a deal, but now what? Belle really needed time to herself: time to keep piecing together her project; time to start piecing together *herself.*

"It's the zoooooo, Belle."

Oh, no, not the pleading bird-call.

"Lakshmi has to take time off to prepare for her oral exams. For her PhD, you know—evolutionary biology or some such thing. It's all mumbo jumbo to me, but Lakshmi gets it. Anyway, Jax can fill in here and there, but there are gaps in the schedule. I'm totally up to here with the parade." She raised a hand to eyebrow level. "Roscoe's working a double shift at the Pen; DeShawn's juggling his job at the Castle and volunteering as a music teacher for underprivileged kids, and he's the one assembling the inflatables—who knew he used to work for a company that made those wacky, waving air-dancer guys? Olive Pickle is majorly allergic; Mae is—well, you know; and everyone else is too busy with other stuff to pitch in. So that leaves yoooooou, Belle. I know, I know. You're already helping with the parade and working on your art, but it'll only be for a few weeks. Just until Lakshmi's exams are out of the way. Promise." Reba made a cross-my-heart gesture with her index finger and waited—head tilted, eyes imploring—for Belle's response.

Belle stirred the concrete, inhaled its bouquet, and watched it swirl in the bucket. A bright scrap of porcelain, dotted with rosebuds like Polly's calico dress, caught her eye, and she scanned her growing assemblage, searching for just the right place to add it.

When she looked up, Wallace was peering over Reba's shoulder with an expression that so comically mirrored Reba's she had to laugh. A hummingbird buzzed by on its way to Mitchell's feeder. Caring for animals was a good thing, a *useful* thing, and hadn't Belle told Ezra she needed to do something useful with her life? But then, hadn't he said maybe this—her *Belle Jardin—was* the useful thing?

"Well?" Reba said.

"Only a few hours a week?"

"Right."

"And only for a few weeks?"

"Right again."

Wallace still stared at Belle as if awaiting her answer. If the other animals in the roadside zoo were one-tenth as endearing as he was, how could she say no? She'd still have plenty of time for trips to Lucas and working on *Belle Jardin*. Plenty of time.

Temperatures were edging into the mid-eighties when Belle arrived at the zoo for "orientation" that afternoon. She wasn't sure what she'd expected, but the onetime roadside attraction was no longer attractive. Peeling paint, faded signs hung askew, an overall ambiance of neglect.

Lakshmi, dressed all in white and wearing a broad-brimmed

straw hat—this one undecorated—met her at the front gate and looked her over.

"Tank top and jeans. Perfect. It gets warm in here, especially when you're lugging feed sacks around, but you don't want to wear shorts. Some of these creatures have sharp claws. They're all tame, but they can get rambunctious at feeding time. And bright colors seem to agitate some of them, so keep it neutral."

"No problem. Neutral is my color." Belle followed Lakshmi into the compound, a maze of pens, some with branches for animals to perch on, others with rocks to hide behind or small pools to splash in.

"I've been trying to enrich their environments as much as I can. Coogan won't pay for any improvements, of course, so everything's improvised from what I can scavenge." She turned to face Belle, her brown eyes searching. "What kind of experience do you have caring for animals?"

Musky scents mingled with the sharp tang of animal feed and the nose-tickle of straw. Farmy smells, as foreign to Belle as tractor fumes. "Well, I had a cat once." *God, Belle, how pathetic.* "Oh, and I took care of Wallace for a few days." She looked away, lest her expression reveal her negligence in letting the wallaby escape.

"Um-hm. Well, at least you have some idea of the importance of consistency. Being confined as they are, these creatures depend on us for their very lives. Their *lives*, Belle. It's not a matter of keeping them healthy just so old Red Beard can make a few bucks off this wretched tourist trap. It's our responsibility to care for other living beings—an expression of *ahimsa*."

Belle racked her brain. *Ahimsa, ahimsa.* She'd heard Miranda use that Sanskrit word. Something from yoga—one of the eight *yamas* or something like that. *Oh yeah: Doing no harm.* She nodded.

"This little guy's a coati," Lakshmi said, squatting down to eye level with a raccoonish animal snuffling around a log. Its ringed tail looked like a raccoon's, but it had a long snout that curved up at the end. "At one time, Coogan had larger animals—a tiger, a bear, a baboon, an alligator—but they all died, and he wasn't able to replace them, thank goodness. Now it's just smaller species." She stood, dusted off her slender hands, and pointed out other cages. "Squirrel monkey, marmoset, porcupine, bobcat, skunk, turtles. That little fox over there is a recent arrival. Coogan got him from some guy in California. Hasn't even bothered to give him a name."

Belle took in the surroundings. Many pens showed signs of recent repairs—Lakshmi's handiwork no doubt—and the animals looked well-cared-for, again thanks to Lakshmi. Still, the place was dismal. "So people still pay money to come to a place like this?" With theme parks, water parks, zip lines, and real zoos, not to mention all the attractions of the virtual world, Belle couldn't see why anyone would bother.

"Fewer and fewer. Before the expressway came through, this was on the main highway. Travelers would stop to let their kids pee and run around and look at the animals before driving on. Coogan even had a snack bar back then. But now it's mainly local kids who've gotten to know these animals over the years and come back to visit them again and again."

Lakshmi motioned for Belle to follow her into a shed. Once inside, she lowered her voice. "We have to be extra vigilant now. Animal rights groups are shutting down places like this, and I'm all for that, but Coogan's feeling the heat. Between that and his dwindling revenues, he's desperate to sell this place and dispose of the animals any way he can. We've got to make sure he doesn't do anything that will cause them harm."

"Of course." If only everyone were so compassionate, so committed to nonharming. Then there'd be no Coogans, no Jamisons, no wounded beings in their wakes.

Stacks of straw lined one wall of the shed. Buckets, a shovel, a rake, and a pitchfork occupied a corner. Bags and tubs of feed stood in neat rows on shelves, each container labeled with a number. Belle pointed to a label. "What're these for?"

Lakshmi pulled out a laminated sheet and handed it to Belle. "Each animal's needs are listed here. The numbers by the animals' names correspond to the numbers on the feed containers. Just follow the numbers, and you'll be sure to give them the right food."

Belle giggled, clutching the laminated sheet to her chest.

Lakshmi gave her a sharp look. "What?"

"It's not often I meet someone as hyperorganized as I am—or *was*. I'm not laughing at you, Lakshmi, I'm laughing with *us*."

Lakshmi flashed a white even smile. Everything about her seemed to radiate perfection. It was no wonder she was methodical too.

"I'm way too familiar with how a person manages everything they've got going by staying organized," Belle said. "I can only imagine how it is for you, working, studying for your exams, helping with Reba's causes . . ." Belle laid a hand on Lakshmi's arm. "You must really love animals to take on this extra responsibility."

"That . . . and like I said, *ahimsa*. And also *seva*." Lakshmi ran a neatly manicured finger along the edge of a shelf.

Another one of those words. *Seva. Where have I heard that before?* All Belle could think of was Seva Café, a little vegan eatery she and Miranda had gone to a few times. But what did a restaurant have to do with working in a zoo?

"*Seva*?"

"It's Sanskrit," Lakshmi said, gesturing for Belle to follow her back to the gate, and pointing to a water faucet and hose they passed on the way out. "Selfless service for the benefit of all."

Belle looked back over her shoulder at the shed, the pens, the animals snoozing and grooming and grazing. She pictured herself moving down the aisles, delivering appropriate feed from the numbered containers, filling water pans, spreading fresh straw.

Seva.

Propped against the side of her house, the roll of chicken wire was the first thing Belle saw when she pulled into her driveway.

He remembered.

Not even bothering to go inside, Belle headed straight for her backyard shed, gathered the usual supplies—plus the tin snips, new bag of concrete, and trowel she'd picked up on her last trip to the home center—and mixed a fresh batch of sludge.

Then, returning to the shed, she brought out a length of wide plastic pipe, probably left over from the last plumbing repair to her rental.

Just right for the body.

She'd read and reread the instructions in the garden ornament book so often she knew them by heart. Following the memorized directions, she snipped chicken wire and formed it into a circular base for the pipe, then wrapped more wire mesh around the pipe. Toward the top, she attached two plastic platters—yard-sale finds—one to each side of the pipe, and wrapped them in still more chicken wire.

Wings!

She knew her technique wasn't advanced enough to manage outstretched arms, so her winged woman would just have to keep her arms to herself.

Next, she balanced a child's plastic ball atop the pipe to form the base for the figure's head. Then she sheathed the whole figure in concrete, adding embellishments along the way.

As she worked, she circled around and around the piece-in-progress, stopping occasionally in response to advice from the garden ornament book:

> *Sometimes we get so involved with a piece or a project that we forget to step back and view the piece in its entirety.*

Periodically, remember to stop and look, really look, at what you're doing.

That's what she was doing now, wasn't it? Not just with this sculpture, but with her whole life: stepping back to view it in its entirety. Picking up broken pieces and trying to rearrange them into something new and whole.

The longer Belle worked, the more the form resembled the woman in her imagination. Memories mingled with those mental images. In her mind, she traveled to another place, another time when she felt the same connection between imagination and expression.

Belle was seven, just beginning second grade in Mrs. Glick's class, not yet branded as a "helper." She sat at the kitchen table, one hand clutching a crayon, the other anchoring a sheet of slick paper. In her small fingers, the crayon slid across the page like a skater on a rink, moving in time with the tune in her head: "Waltzing Matilda." Everything about drawing enchanted Belle: the crayons' waxy smoothness, their candle-like smell, the array of colors in the box of sixty-four Crayolas that sat before her—a gift from Mommy "for my little artist."

Belle skipped over the plain colors—red, green, yellow—and picked out unusual shades: bittersweet, cornflower, violet, salmon. As she drew, pictures filled her mind. She saw rivers, mountains, and forests unlike anything in her suburban neighborhood of sidewalks, lawns, and tidy flower beds. Opulent castles rose on the horizon. Creatures with scales, fins, horns, and extra eyes galloped across wildflower-carpeted meadows.

The images spilled onto the page so fast her fingers could hardly keep up. The scenes and animals she drew didn't look exactly like the ones in her mind, but they were just as real to her. Mommy said she could see them too. Why hadn't Mrs. Glick seen what they saw?

Belle snapped out of her daydreams when she reached the top of the concrete column. She stepped back and admired the figure her hands had shaped. The body, draped in a long gown, looked body-like; the wings, inlaid with bits of mirror, resembled wings. All that remained was the face. Could she still picture it after all these years? She had photographs, but those were so static they didn't even seem real. She wanted to remember her mother's face as it was in life, to see her standing over Belle in the kitchen, offering encouragement: "Keep drawing, Belle. Practice makes perfect."

She closed her eyes. Dusk had overtaken afternoon, and the air had cooled, if only a few degrees. High above, nighthawks swooped and dived for insects, calling *peent, peent.* Belle sensed she wasn't alone. Someone—a presence—had joined her. Her mother? Could this be the visitation she'd been waiting for? She opened one eye.

"Oh. Ezra. Again."

"I see you've already put that chicken wire to good use." He held out a bottle of Stormchaser. "Thought you might need a break."

Belle bent down to inspect her nearly empty mixing bucket. "Yeah, probably too late to mix another batch. Just let me clean this stuff up, and I'll have a beer with you."

Belle rinsed the bucket and tools, and with one last look at her winged woman, stashed everything in her shed and joined Ezra on the side stoop. With his long limbs bent into sharp angles, he looked like a folded-up ladder.

"Would you be more comfortable inside?" Belle hoped that didn't sound too inviting, but Ezra did look awkward all bunched up like that.

"No, no. This is good. I like to sit out in the evenings and watch the nighthawks and bats and fireflies. And we can admire your handiwork from here. Your angel is shaping up nicely."

Ezra handed Belle a bottle of beer. She took a long swig. "Aahhh. Angel, muse, I'm not sure what she is. I'm waiting for her to tell me."

"As I'm sure she will."

With a loud whiz, a nighthawk nose-dived like a fighter jet, pulling up at the last minute. Belle stared, open-mouthed. "What *is* that? I've never heard a bird make a sound like that."

Ezra scanned the sky. "Amazing, isn't it? No matter how many times I hear it, I'm always astonished. It's wind rushing through the male's primary feathers. Guess that ought to catch the attention of any available lady nighthawks."

"Not exactly subtle, is he?" Belle followed the bird with her eyes as it swooped upward for another dive.

Ezra laughed. "Not exactly." He paused. "Subtle doesn't always get the point across."

Belle took another swallow of beer. From the corner of her eye, she saw Ezra looking at her strangely. "What?"

"Nothing, nothing." He raised his eyes to the sky again. "I was at the library today . . ."

"You just can't stay away from those stacks of books, can you?" Belle gave him a playful poke in the ribs. He mock-flinched and grinned.

"Well, no, and that's what I was about to tell you. There's an opening for assistant director. I'm thinking of applying." His eyes met hers and lingered a moment before traveling back up to the darkening sky. "Uncle Mitchell's getting up in years, and he's going to need me around more. And also . . ."

Fireflies flashed, signaling desire.

"Also, you'd be able to get Stormchaser anytime you want." Belle clinked her bottle against his. "Good luck—if you decide to apply."

"Right. If I do. It's a big decision. But it's not like I'd be leaving that much behind in Nebraska." Ezra shook his head as if clearing the air for another topic of discussion. His black hair cascaded into his eyes, and he swept it back with a careless swipe. "So, Belle, *Isa*belle. I'm not sure I've ever known another Isabelle. Were you named for someone?"

Another dive, another *whizzzz.*

"My great-aunt Isabelle Yakamoto—she met her husband when she was teaching English in Japan. Auntie Izzy, my mom called her."

"So your great-aunt was an Izzy. Does anyone ever call you Izzy?"

"Me? Nope. It's always been Belle or Isabelle." She paused. *Except.* Did she want to go there? She peered into the neck of her bottle. "Except for Ben. He called me Izzy when I was stressed out over some silly thing. 'Izzy's having a tizzy.'" One corner of her mouth turned up.

"Ben? You haven't told me about him." Ezra's voice sounded far away, like he was talking through one of Dinsmoor's speaking tubes.

"My boyfriend in college. We came close to getting married. Funny thing—Ben was Asian, too, like Auntie Izzy's husband. Korean, though, not Japanese. Ben Park. If we'd gotten married and I'd changed my name, I'd be Belle Park. Sounds like a place you'd go to ride a roller coaster." She managed another rueful half smile but felt a pang just below her ribs.

"What happened?"

Belle took another drink. She let out a long breath. "It didn't work out." *Didn't work out because I wouldn't let it work out.* The irony of it. How many weddings had Belle-as-event-planner flawlessly orchestrated for other couples? Yet when it came to her own marriage to the love of her young life, she had wrecked it.

"I'm sorry to hear that," Ezra said, folding his hands on his lap. After a minute or two he shook his head again, and in a lighter tone said, "Well, I think Izzy is a very fitting name for an artist who creates such imaginative works. Izzy . . . Ezzy . . . now all we need is an Ozzy."

Grateful to shift to a less personal subject, Belle let her thoughts drift back over the day. Reba and Wallace; her organizational twin Lakshmi; angels, nighthawks, fireflies. And the zoo, with its miscellaneous menagerie. Salmagundi, for sure. An image of the little fox, timid but bright-eyed, popped into her mind. The *nameless* little fox.

"Ozzy? I think I just met him today."

– 10 –
THE BABIES

For the next week, Belle worked as if in a trance: mixing, snipping, forming, smoothing, smashing, embedding, over and over again, always remembering to step back and take in the whole piece as it grew in new and unexpected ways. When darkness fell, she stayed up late, sketching images she'd run out of time to cast in concrete. Finally, exhausted, she collapsed into bed, knowing her subconscious soon would take over, showing the way to the next day's work. Showing her where she needed to go.

Yes, *needed* to go. For the figures and shapes she was modeling were not mere decorations. Belle was more convinced of that than ever, as increasingly her dreams stirred up every loss, every wound, every upheaval of the past thirty-four years. Everything she needed to repair. All she had to do was fit the fragments of her life back together. And she could do that now, she was sure, by piecing shards of ceramic and glass together into symbolic shapes. Icons.

Fueled by the passion of purpose, she saw no reason to interrupt her work for anything except her shifts at the zoo—carried out on autopilot—and every night's dream-inducing sleep.

And Reba's visits. At least once a day the tangerine scooter zipped into Belle's driveway, and Reba and Wallace clambered off and wandered over to inspect her progress. Reba let Wallace skip around the yard while she rooted through her backpack, extracting parade costume samples for Belle's approval and scrolling through cell phone shots of her other projects: a quilt depicting tornados carrying off cars, outhouses, livestock, and gleeful children; another assemblage made from rusty can lids, feathers, and claws gleaned from roadkill finds. She never failed to bring a sandwich or snack that she coaxed Belle into consuming as they discussed the zinnia bra tops, inflatable headdresses, gold lamé shorts, sunflower masks, and other pieces of apparel the two women had dreamed up.

By the seventh day of her creative blitz, Belle had grown so accustomed to the sound of Reba's scooter, she barely glanced up when she heard it approach. But this day she glanced and did a double take at the sight of not only Reba and Wallace perched on the seat, but also Mae riding sidesaddle on the back, clutching Reba's backpack for dear life.

Reba slid off and extended a hand to steady Mae. Belle jumped up to help. Between the two of them coaxing and bracing, they managed to get her safely onto solid ground. Mae was competent at many things—crosswords, vocal music, even acupuncture, she claimed—but two-wheeled vehicle transportation apparently was not one of them.

She looked around, blinking, taking in the sprawling assemblage on Belle's lawn—the swirls and doohickeys, the walla-dog, the angel. She ran a hand over her wrinkled aqua muumuu. "Goodness, Belle, what a milieu you have here. Reba told me you've been exploring your artistic side, but I never imagined . . ." Mae patted the braids pinned to the top of her head and continued. "I made this perilous journey today because I haven't seen you around lately, and we have a score to settle."

Belle guided Mae to a shadier part of the yard on the perimeter of *Belle Jardin*. "We do?"

"We do. Oh my, would you look at this?" Mae bent over double to peer at a shrub. "Are you aware you have a veritable aphid farm in your yard, Belle?"

Leaning in, Belle could see minuscule green blobs and black specks she hadn't noticed before. She exchanged a look of *what the hell?* with Reba. "A what?"

"Ants tending aphids, like farmers tending cows. The ants protect the aphids from predators. In return, the aphids let the ants milk them for the honeydew the aphids secrete from their—" Mae covered her mouth with both hands and blushed. "—their heinies. Reciprocation, Belle. Even our insect friends understand its importance."

"I guess I wasn't aware of that," Belle said. "Thank you for calling my attention to it."

"No. Thank *you*, Belle. That's why I'm here. You still have not let me repay you for the favor you bestowed upon me the first day we met. I don't like my debts to go unsettled. It's . . . *unsettling*." Mae feigned a shiver. Or perhaps she actually shivered. With Mae, one never knew.

Belle shot Reba another look, this one with a shoulder shrug. "Favor? Debt? What?"

"The crossword puzzle." Reba spoke as if Interpreter of Obscure Remarks were part of her job description. "Remember, you gave Mae the word she needed to finish her crossword puzzle?"

Mae nodded. "Malevolent."

Belle gave her a blank look. "Malevolent?"

"A ten-letter word for sinister starting with M. You supplied it, and that allowed me to finish the crossword, which I *must* do every day before I can get on with my business."

What business might that be, Belle wondered, but she kept the question to herself as Mae went on. "You wouldn't allow me to pay you back at the time; you said you'd put it in escrow. But it's weighing on me, Belle. There must be some favor you need, something I can do to repay your kindness."

Belle took both of Mae's hands in hers, noticing how rough her own had become. Sometimes she got so wrapped up in her work she forgot to put on gloves before fooling with the concrete. Even Mae's liver-spotted hands looked better than hers.

"Mae, you are so kind to care about repaying me. I promise I'll figure out something you can do for me—and soon. In the meantime, please don't worry about it. I'm sure there are days when no aphid predators show up, but the ants collect honeydew anyway. It all evens out in the end. No pun intended."

Mae blushed again and let out a little giggle.

Belle gave Mae's hands a last squeeze before turning toward her workplace. She didn't mean to be rude—especially knowing how touchy Mae could be about the oddest things, like this need for recompense. What was *that* about? But the atrocity beckoned—and finally won out. Belle picked her way through *Belle Jardin*'s pieces-in-progress to a small patch of relatively uncluttered ground and squatted there, hoping her visitors would get the "time to go" message. Instead, Reba crouched beside her, and Wallace hopped over to poke his nose into her armpit.

"We're starting to build floats for the parade," Reba said. "We're repurposing most of them from previous years, but since this is the tenth anniversary of Soulstice, we want one super-spectacular float at the end of the parade. Our dear Mae has consented to ride on the float in the persona of Queen Aquamaureen."

Mae raised a hand and made figure-eight motions like a homecoming queen.

"How nice," Belle said. *Please don't ask me to staple metallic fringe onto two-by-fours. I did that to death in high school.*

"So Belle . . ." Reba began.

Uh-oh. Here it comes.

". . . since you're so good at coming up with novel ideas, especially after your visits to Lucas, I wonder if you could be persuaded to make another trip over there. For inspiration. You wouldn't really be taking time away from your creation here, you know. You'd surely get more ideas for it, toooooo."

There it is. The irresistible, beseeching bird call. Oh, that Reba. She knew Belle was drawn to Lucas like—well, like an ant to honeydew, and now she was turning that attraction to her advantage. But she was right. Another trip to Lucas surely would stoke Belle's imaginative fires, fueling her dreams and providing the vision to repair her life, piece by piece by piece.

At ten o'clock the next morning, Belle found herself once again in the company of Samuel Perry Dinsmoor. She crouched beside his glass-topped coffin as she had by Grandpa Jake's bedside after his first heart attack—the one that slowed him down a tad but didn't kill him.

"So what's with the voices, old man?" She couldn't believe she was talking to a guy who'd been dead almost ninety years, yet she couldn't stop herself. "If you didn't put them here, where are they coming from? Did they talk to you too? Are they what made you so . . . so crazy? Because I think that's happening to me."

Belle half expected Dinsmoor to answer, but her questions were met with silence.

"All right, then." She stood and brushed herself off. "If you're not talking, let's see who is."

As she stepped from the chill of the crypt into the already warm morning, Belle took a moment to lift her face to the sun, then headed for the gift shop to check in with Polly. After exchanging pleasantries—always so exceedingly pleasant on Polly's part—Belle spun the postcard rack, shuffled copies of Dinsmoor's *Cabin Home* pamphlet, ran her fingers along the edges of shelves, and studied the wares displayed there, in case they'd changed since her last trip.

Polly paid her no mind after their initial exchange, puttering around behind the register until Belle blurted, "Do you ever hear strange voices around here, Polly?"

Polly adjusted her glasses and tapped a finger on her round cheek. "Now that you mention it, I have. There was this one time a whole busload of folks showed up here from some church I wasn't familiar with. Seemed like nice, normal folks when they came in and paid their admission—special rate for bus tours, you know." Polly paused, a look of bewilderment clouding her face. "Now, where was I going with that?"

"Voices," Belle prompted.

"Oh yes. Like I said, they seemed all normal-like at first, but after they'd been here a while, I heard strange sounds coming from over by Adam and Eve—kinda babbling nonsense words. I told my niece about it later—that's my niece Teresa who lives with me—she went to college at KU, you know, so she's up on things I'm not up on. She said more than likely they were speaking in tongues. A religious kind of thing."

"Mmmmmm, yes. I've heard of that," Belle said. "What about when no one else is here?"

Once again, Polly looked confused. "Well, how could I hear them speaking in tongues if they weren't here?" She squinched her lips together as if puzzling over a riddle.

"No, I meant, do you ever hear *other* voices when no one else is here? Speaking regular English, maybe just a sentence or two." Belle had the sense she'd said too much, but there was no taking it back. Besides, she really needed to know.

Polly directed her puzzlement at Belle. "Voices? When no one's here? No, hon." She raised an index finger and drew circles in the air around her ear. "Cuckoo! Cuckoo!"

Belle forced a laugh. "Yeah, crazy question. I was just over in the crypt communing with Dinsmoor, and some of his crazy must've rubbed off on me. Forget I asked."

With that and a cheery wave that Polly—all smiles again—returned, Belle made a hasty exit.

Slowly circling the grounds, she took in the now-familiar figures: Adam and Eve, Satan, the winged women, the soldiers, the monsters, the babies. The babies. They caught her attention as never before. Naked and glassy-eyed, one stood atop a pinnacle in a jaunty hand-on-hip pose. Something protruded from its back—a wing? A cherub child of one of the winged women, perhaps? Another baby dangled upside down, as if tumbling through the air.

Babies were supposed to be soft. Cuddly. Irresistible. These concrete children were none of those things. Their expressions and positions perturbed Belle. Or was it her own memories that troubled her?

Seven years before—she didn't have to stop and do the math, the number was etched into her consciousness—Belle had been working at her desk all morning, calling florists and drawing up menus for the event she was tasked with planning: a fiftieth-anniversary party for a prominent local attorney and her husband. She needed a break, but there was no time for her usual pick-me-up: a walk around the block. Maybe a social media time-out would refresh her.

Scrolling through Facebook, she saw a post from her same-age cousin Amy. The picture showed Amy propped up in a hospital bed, a rosy-faced infant, swaddled and newborn-capped, in her arms. "Jason and I are over the moon with the birth of our daughter. Welcome to the world, Emma," the post read.

Wow. Amy, a mother.

Belle and Amy had been childhood playmates, lugging life-sized baby dolls around on their hips. Belle named her doll Ashley; Amy's was Amanda. The girls changed their babies' diapers, poked bottles into their soft plastic mouths, discussed diaper rash and croup, and fantasized about the real-life children they'd have someday.

Amy wanted a big family—five or six kids. Belle thought three would be about right. Being an only child, she wanted her own children to have built-in playmates, but not so many she couldn't give them each plenty of attention, like Belle's parents had lavished on her.

Seeing the Facebook post of Amy with her first baby, those childhood fantasies came flooding back. Belle tried to picture herself in the same pose: exhausted but happy in her hospital bed, beaming for the camera with her infant in her arms. Mother to a daughter. But the image cracked her wide open. How could she love a baby without constantly fearing she might lose her? How could she bring a child into the world, knowing she herself might die—as her mother had—and leave her daughter motherless? Life was just too fragile, too unpredictable, and already Belle was uneasy with unpredictable.

She'd closed Facebook, opened Google, typed "tubal ligation," and found "Pros and Cons of Getting Your Tubes Tied" on WebMD. She read: "It's permanent. This is a big plus if you don't want to have children . . ." and "It works. Only about one in two hundred women get pregnant after a tubal ligation. That's less than 1 percent."

That was all Belle needed to know. She dialed her gynecologist's office and made an appointment for the following week. Life was just too uncertain to take any chances. That was one thing she was sure of, even at age twenty-seven, so she kept the appointment.

Now, transfixed by the concrete babies, she wondered if she'd done the right thing. *What's done is done*, she told herself. *You've moved on.* As if acting out her thoughts, she turned away from the cherubs and continued her tour of Dinsmoor's garden of strangeness, even as the babies' auras traveled with her.

She stopped in front of the statue of the woman astride the hideous eight-legged creature. Pondering its meaning, Belle looked at the woman and beast from every angle. Was the monster attacking the woman, or was the woman attacking the monster? She still couldn't figure it out. Which had the upper hand? And after all these years of struggling against each other, why had one not triumphed over the other?

Another crazy question, Belle. These are statues. They're not real.

Belle had planned on spending the whole morning in Lucas and had even packed a lunch and snacks again in case she decided to spend the whole day. But all of a sudden she had the urge to leave.

She turned to walk away.

"Wait."

That same tuneful female voice she'd heard before. In any other context, it might be comforting. Coming from—wherever it was coming from—it was anything but that.

"What?" Belle didn't mean to sound impatient, but . . . *really*?

"Slay the beast, Belle. You have the power."

That was no radio from a passing car. It was no religious fanatic speaking in tongues. It was a message from the statue—a statue that knew her name, by the way, and possibly other things about her. A message meant for Belle and Belle alone.

That night, Belle dreamed not of monsters, but of babies. Not stony cherubs in disturbing poses, but real toddling, crawling, cooing infants—three of them. They circled around Belle, all just out of reach, giggling as she crooned a lullaby. Then, forming a sort of chorus line, they waved their chubby hands and sang back, "Bye, bye, Mama. We're going to sleep now." And then, just as Belle's mother had on that misty dream-shore, the babies vanished.

After waking from the dream the next morning, Belle went right to work on her creation. With growing confidence in her sculpting skills, rough though they might still appear to others' eyes, she formed sweet little feet, plump little legs and tummies, adorable fingers and arms. Three happy toddlers in a ring around the winged woman, who remained faceless. When Belle came to the figures' torsos, she dashed into the house and returned with a golden charm bracelet, a childhood gift from her mother. Too small to fit her grown-up wrist, it had sat in her jewelry box for years, an abiding symbol of her mother's love.

Five golden hearts dangled from the bracelet's links. One by one, Belle worked three of them off, sealing one deep in the breast of each sturdy child. She pocketed the bracelet with its two remaining charms, one for Belle, the other for her mother. A salty rivulet ran down her cheek. *Sweating already, and it's not even warm yet.*

It wasn't sweat. She knew that. Why couldn't she own up to her grief?

Blinking back tears that now flowed faster, she formed the babies' round faces, their upturned noses, and rosebud mouths. She placed clear blue marbles in their eye sockets and sculpted soft curls atop their heads. As she put the finishing touch on the last one, a sense of well-being settled over her, the likes of which she hadn't felt since her own childhood.

"Bye, bye, babies."

What next? It wasn't yet noon, and she wasn't due at the zoo until mid-afternoon, but Belle felt she'd already fulfilled the day's creative mission.

A scraping sound, like metal on concrete, came from next door. No doubt Mitchell tending the stubborn earth of his flower beds, inexplicably teeming with petunias, marigolds, zinnias, and other flowers Belle didn't recognize. His house—a one-story, white-frame bungalow like most of the others on the street—might be bland as a Saltine cracker, but his garden was anything but. Belle caught his eye and waved, not caring if he interpreted the friendly gesture as an invitation to visit.

Sure enough, Mitchell dropped his hoe and hobbled over. Was he walking that way the last time she saw him?

"That's some thingamajig you're putting together there, Miss Belle," he said. "And I do know it's *Miss*, 'cause Ezra told me."

"Oh, he did, did he?" Belle wasn't about to ask why the two men were discussing her marital status.

"Yessir, this here creation of yours is the talk of the neighborhood." Mitchell pushed his tractor cap back on his head and wiped his brow.

"Is that so? No one's said anything to *me* about it. Although now that you mention it, I have seen the lady across the street—Mrs. Pruitt, is it?—peeping through her blinds when I'm out here working on it."

"Don't pay that busybody no mind," Mitchell said. "She's got nothing better to do than poke her nose where it don't belong. She's the one who was always up in arms about little Rip's barking."

Mitchell shifted his weight and winced.

"Let me get you something to sit on," Belle offered and headed for her shed. She returned with a folding lawn chair, its once-bright aluminum frame dull, its webbed straps frayed.

Mitchell chuckled. "That there chair looks about as beat-up as I been feeling lately. It's the arthur-itis, you know."

"Sorry to hear that. Good thing Ezra got so much time off work to come down and help you." Belle glanced next door. Lawn mowed, weeds pulled, screen door rehung, window frames repainted, porch steps repaired. Ezra had been busy. No sign of him today, though.

Mitchell nodded. "Yep. Too bad he'll be having to go back pretty soon. Unless he takes that library job down here. They told him yesterday it's pretty much his if he wants it. That's where he is right now, talking to the library folks again."

"Well, that's great—for you—isn't it? He'll be around to help out all the time, or at least when he's not working."

"Oh, it'd be great, all right. He could stay here with me, and we'd have us a good ol' time. But I don't know if being my live-in handyman and helper is enough to keep him here. If he had some other reason, you know . . ."

Belle let a beat go by. "Reason? Like . . . ?"

Mitchell pulled his cap down low on his forehead and gave Belle a sly look. "Like a lady friend." He winked.

Flustered, Belle hiccupped and pulled at her hair. "Goodness," she said, tilting her head back to look at the sun, high in the sky. "Look how late it's getting. I hate to cut this short, but I've got errands to run before my shift at the zoo. I imagine Ezra told you about that too."

Mitchell just grinned as he pushed himself out of the chair and limped away.

"See you later, *Miss* Belle."

– 11 –
THE iNFORMANT

Belle was having lunch—sitting at her kitchen table for a change, eating an entire cheese-and-mayo sandwich she'd prepared herself, along with a peach Reba brought on her last visit—when her phone blared out "Soak Up the Sun," the new ringtone she'd just downloaded.

It was Reba.

"Oh, good, I caught you." Reba sounded breathless. "Jax has to leave early today and wants to know if you can get to the zoo while they're still there."

"While who's still there?" Belle hoped "they" didn't mean Jax and Coogan. She wasn't ready to make the zoo owner's acquaintance quite yet. "Who's they?"

"Jax."

"Jax and who else? You said *they*." Was this turning into another of those *what-is-she-talking-about* conversations? The kind that reminded her of the old Abbott and Costello skit that used to crack up Grandpa Jake? He must have watched the "Who's on First" routine a thousand times, laughing just as heartily the thousandth time as the first.

"'They' is Jax. That's their preferred pronoun. You know about those, right?"

"Oh, right, of course." Belle knew all about how personal pronouns were being adapted to reflect a growing understanding of gender fluidity. It was linguistically confusing, but she understood the necessity.

"Tell Jax I'll see them there."

Belle ended the call and finished her lunch, thinking about Jax—their lopsided, chartreuse hairstyle, their androgynous physique and features. Jax fit no particular mold, yet Jax seemed to know exactly who they was. *Or is it "who they were"? What are the rules?*

Once again, Belle had that not-knowing feeling.

Jax was spreading straw in the coati's pen when Belle arrived at the zoo.

"Thanks for coming early," Jax said. "I just wanted to fill you in on some of the animals. The marmoset's been pulling out its hair. You'll need to treat it with that herbal potion of Reba's. Lakshmi's got all the remedies labeled and arranged in alphabetical order—of course—on the top shelf in the shed." Jax laughed. "I've never known anyone so hyperorganized, have you?"

"Um. I did once, yes," Belle mumbled. "So marmoset, potion. Got it."

"And that little fox doesn't seem to be adjusting too well—off his feed. You might have to sit with him—at a distance—while he eats. You'd think that'd make things worse, but he's apparently accustomed to having company at mealtime. Hope you don't mind."

"Not at all. I'm kind of partial to that little guy," Belle said. "It's all right to have favorites, isn't it? As long as all the animals get proper attention?"

Jax pulled a strawberry from a plastic bag and held it up to the coati. "Sure. This coati's my favorite. It's raccoonish, but it's not a raccoon. It looks kinda doglike, but it's not a dog. It's not like any other animal. It just is what it is, its authentic self, and there's nothing wrong with that. Nothing wrong at all." Jax's expression turned wistful.

"Are we still talking about animals?"

"Animals and everything else. Every*one* else. Imagine how this world would be if we all felt free to be our authentic selves." Jax's phone chimed a reminder. "Oh, hey, I've got to get going. Remember: marmoset, potion; fox, meal-tending."

"Right. And coati, authentic self."

Jax gave a thumbs-up and sprinted toward the gate, then turned back. "Oh, I almost forgot—Coogan might be back this afternoon, but he hardly ever comes out here, so no worries."

No worries? I'm not so sure about that. What if he's another Jamison?

Belle tried to dismiss the thought as she set to work, first feeding and watering the animals that needed no special attention. When all those were taken care of, she opened a can of cat food, carried it to the fox's pen, unlatched the gate to let herself in, and settled onto the ground a few feet away from where the fox lay curled up like a cat.

"Hey, fella. Hey, Ozzy. Look what I've got for you." She spooned a blob of cat food into a bowl and waved it around. "Yum!"

Rousing, the fox uncurled himself, stretched, and tilted his head from side to side, following the bowl. His expression reminded Belle of Wallace, which made her laugh. Who knew animals could have so much personality? More than some people, it seemed. She pushed the bowl toward him. He eyed her warily but gobbled down a mouthful.

"Attaboy, Ozzy. There's more where that came from." The fox ate until the bowl was clean. Belle loaded it up again. Ozzy emptied it again, and with a look of contentment, returned to his napping spot.

Belle sat for a while, watching Ozzy doze and considering what Jax had said about being true to one's nature, one's authentic self. What was Belle's authentic self? Who was she before she was labeled, lost, and damaged? Was that person still somewhere inside her, captive like these animals in their pens? Could she set her true self free the way the animals in that strange quilt of Reba's had been sprung from their cages? Is that what *Belle Jardin* was all about—releasing Belle's authentic self?

The marmoset's twitters reminded Belle she still had work to do. She left Ozzy's pen and went into the shed, leaving the door open for more light to read the remedies' labels. Aloe vera, CBD, flaxseed oil—Belle ran a finger along the shelf. Ah, here it was, a dark bottle labeled simply "Potion." As she reached for it, a sound distracted her.

"Yeah, yeah. I know you're over capacity, but can't you at least take a couple?" The gruff voice came through an open window in a one-story, concrete-block building attached to the shed. On a previous visit, Belle had peeked through that window and seen a rickety office chair, a computer tower and monitor that looked past their prime, and a desk overflowing with papers. Coogan's office, no doubt.

Belle sidled to the shed door and took a furtive look in the window. The chair swayed beneath the bulk of a massive masculine figure. She recognized the long red hair and beard. Turned sideways, Coogan probably couldn't see her, but just in case, Belle crouched below the windowsill and continued to eavesdrop.

"I'm getting sick of this whole thing, and it's costing me an arm and a leg," Coogan growled. "If I can't find another zoo to take these last animals, I might just shoot 'em all. I woulda done it sooner, but now I got this gang of looney-tunes working here—this foreign-looking girl, Indian or something; another green-haired weirdo that's half girl, half boy; and this new girl that seems almost normal, but you never know. They'd probably turn me in to some bullshit animal-rights group."

The decrepit chair creaked. "Uh-huh. Uh-huh. Yeah. Well, think it over, will ya?"

A scuffling sound signaled the call's end. Belle scrambled into the shed to retrieve the potion and made her way to the marmoset's pen. She hurried through the final task and out the gate to her car. Driving just far enough to be out of sight from the zoo, she pulled onto the shoulder and called Reba, who answered on the first ring.

"Mayday!" Belle panted. She filled Reba in on the conversation she'd just heard. "We've got to stop him."

"Okay, okay." Reba's voice was annoyingly calm. "First of all, Coogan can be a jerk, but he's also given to hyperbole. He's probably not going to kill any animals as long as he thinks he might make a few bucks off them. That's why he's so desperate to sell the ones he's got left, or trade them for something he thinks he can sell for more money. That's his MO. Lakshmi's been documenting and analyzing all his sales and trades over the past year—ever the scientist, you know—and she's noticed patterns."

A grasshopper landed on Belle's windshield and fixed its bulbous eyes on her. How strange it looked close up. How alien. Yet it was only an ordinary insect. Nothing to fear. "I don't know," she said. "He sounded pretty disgusted with the whole zoo thing."

"Well, you're right about that," Reba said. "He's definitely getting more desper—"

The line went silent. *Damn! Not a dropped connection. Not now.*

"Reba! You still there?"

"Oh, sorry—I just went brain-surfing for a minute. What if we could—okay, this is probably totally crazy, but hear me out. What if we could buy the zoo and all the animals? We could find them homes in proper wild animal shelters—or even convert the zoo into our own shelter."

"Buy the zoo? Us? I don't have that kind of money, do you?" Belle mentally scanned her dwindling bank account—an account she hadn't bothered to balance in quite a while, come to think of it. A wobbly sensation rose up as she realized she had no idea how much money she had left. Definitely not enough to buy a zoo.

"Me? Are you kidding? I'm an artist, remember?" Reba said. "But we could *raise* the money."

With a growing sense of confinement, Belle rolled down the driver's side window for some air. "How?"

"Well, that's the part I have to figure out. *We* have to figure out."

Not even waiting for Reba's cooing plea, Belle sighed and lifted her hands, palms up in surrender. "What do you want me to do?"

"Just keep doing what you're doing: putting in time at the zoo, keeping your ear to the ground—or in this case, the window. I'll call a meeting of the Soulstice gang and get their input. Matter of fact, we're all getting together at Roscoe's to work on floats tonight, so I'll bring it up then. Which reminds me: What'd you come up with for Mae's float?"

Mae's float. Shit! Between babies, beasts, and messages from disembodied voices, Belle had completely forgotten to seek parade float inspiration on her last trip to Lucas.

"What? I didn't hear that. You're breaking up," Belle fibbed. "I'll have to get back to you."

Thoughts spiraled as Belle drove home: Mae's float, Coogan's call, monsters, madmen. To calm herself, she accessed her Happy Tunes playlist. Its assortment of hits from her high school years—Beyoncé, Pink, Sheryl Crow—and old Beatles favorites of her parents always did the trick.

The first track, "Here Comes the Sun," flooded her mind with brighter images.

I've got it! Queen Aquamaureen, your float awaits.

By the time Belle got home, she lacked the strength to haul out her tools, yet she was too keyed up to rest. She took out her colored pencils and drawing pad and sketched her ideas for Mae's float. All the while, she kept thinking about the zoo and the last cryptic message from the Garden of Eden voice: *Slay the beast.*

What beast was she supposed to slay? Surely not an actual animal. Unlike Coogan, she was all about saving animals, not destroying them. Wait—Coogan? Was he the beast she was supposed to slay? Not literally, of course. Belle was no killer. But maybe the voice was urging her to neutralize Coogan in some other way.

Miranda would know. Belle grabbed her phone and just as quickly, laid it back down. The last time they'd talked, Miranda had seemed—distant. Come to think of it, she'd been more and more distracted ever since her engagement a few weeks earlier to Nick, the guy she'd met at an ashram in West Chicago (of all places). Miranda, the one person Belle could always count on. She'd been Belle's *person* and Belle had been hers, just like Meredith Grey was Cristina Yang's person on *Grey's Anatomy.* Miranda and Belle had teared up and clutched each other when they watched that episode together as twenty-somethings. Meredith totally got it when Cristina called her "my person" just like Miranda totally got everything Belle said—or felt, even when Belle couldn't put words to her feelings. She'd been there for Belle through every disappointment, every loss. She'd been the only person Belle confided in about Jamison and the one who persuaded Belle to sever that destructive connection.

But now, this connection—this healthy, sustaining connection with Miranda—was fraying. Now Nick was Miranda's *person* and she was his, and that was as it should be. Still, Belle couldn't help feeling abandoned again. No longer could she count on Miranda to figure things out.

You're on your own now, Isabelle Marsden. On. Your. Own.

Or was she? All at once, she was struck by an impulse. Tucking the drawing of Mae's float into her purse, she scooped up her keys. As she backed out of her driveway, she caught a glimpse of Ezra standing in Mitchell's yard, rake in one hand, bottle of Stormchaser in the other. He held up the beer with a question in his eyes.

"Wish I could," Belle called through her open window, "but I'm off to a meeting. Another time?"

Ezra made a pouty face. "Okay. I just bought another six-pack. I'll try not to drink it all before then."

With a hasty wave, Belle drove on. At the junction for Highway 59, she turned right, away from the center of town, and headed into the surrounding countryside. She'd never been to Roscoe's farm, but Reba had pointed out the driveway once.

"That's where we're building the floats," she'd said. "In Roscoe's pole barn."

Belle had peered down the long drive but saw only a dusty lane lined with sycamore trees. "What's a pole barn?"

"Oh, you really *are* a city girl, aren't you? It's like an oversized garage. Roscoe's is the only one around with portraits of famous poets and authors painted on the sides, courtesy of *moi*."

Now, scanning breaks between cornfields, Belle searched for driveways and pole barns. Plenty of both, but not the ones she was looking for. At last, she saw the mailbox she remembered: black and white striped like an old-time prison uniform, with the word "Box" printed in red letters on the side. A bit of Roscoe's dry humor, labeling a mailbox as a box, Belle had assumed when she and Reba passed it that other day. But no, Reba had informed her, "That's his name: Roscoe Box."

Gravel crunched as Belle turned into the drive and followed it to a clearing where cars and trucks were parked willy-nilly, as if their drivers had pulled up and scrambled out to escape some looming disaster. Just beyond the parking area stood a steel-sided structure decorated with faces. "Ginsberg. Ferlinghetti. Burroughs. Kerouac." Belle read the captions beneath the portraits, vaguely recognizing the names.

Chickens fluttered and pecked patches of bare ground. Two dogs (*box*ers—what else?) roused and trotted over to sniff Belle when she opened her car door. She patted the dogs' heads and made her way to the barn, half expectant, half apprehensive about what she'd find inside.

The interior resembled a barn less than an over-bright gymnasium—the kind where you'd see people camped out after a tornado. But this was no glum refuge; it was a hive of busyness as the ragtag bunch Belle had come to know as the Soulstice gang hammered, sawed, and decorated half a dozen floats-in-progress, chattering among themselves all the while. Wallace bounced around the room, collecting ear scratches and chin rubs from the workers. When he spotted Belle, he hippity-hopped over to nuzzle her behind the knees.

DeShawn, sporting an inflated headdress shaped like sunflower petals, greeted Belle. "Here for the meeting? It's about to start."

Belle reached into her purse for the sketch of Mae's float. "Would you mind? It's for Aquamaureen, and it'll need some of your handiwork." She looked around the room. "Hey, where *is* Mae?"

Studying the sketch, DeShawn replied absently, "It's after five." Then looking up: "Sorry, I was just awestruck by your idea. We can definitely do this—it'll be spectacular. So like I was saying, Mae's not a night person. She has dinner at five on the dot, and she's tucked into bed with a book by seven. Except on choir nights, when she sacrifices her routine for the sake of 'vocal exaltation,' as she calls it."

Just then, Reba climbed onto a watermelon-shaped float and, using it as a stage, addressed the crowd. "Folks, I know you're all on board with our efforts to protect the animals at the horrific establishment called a roadside zoo. Well, it seems we need to step up those efforts—Coogan's getting hinkier by the day. Call me crazy, but I think the only solution is to buy the place. How, you might ask? That's what we need to figure out, so the floor is open for fundraising suggestions. Think . . . what's Kansas famous for?"

Olive Pickle fluttered a hand. "Sunflowers! We could sell sunflower seeds."

"True enough, Olive," Reba said. "We'd have to sell a helluva lot of sunflower seeds, though, to buy anything more than dinner at the Eldridge House."

Titters rippled through the room.

"Leavenworth!" Roscoe shouted. "How about a reading of penitentiary poetry? I've been collecting work from guys in the prison's writing class for an anthology. Some pretty powerful stuff. And you know, the theme of confinement is relevant to the zoo." He paused, took a swig from a bottle of Bud, and rubbed the top of his buzz-cut head as if it were a lucky charm. "On second thought, scratch that. It's hard enough to get anybody to listen to poetry when it's free. If we're asking for donations—even for a good cause—forget it."

"Wagon trains," DeShawn volunteered, his sunflower headdress bobbing emphatically. "The Oregon Trail passed through Lawrence—right over Mount Oread, as a matter of fact. You can see the historical marker up there. And the Santa Fe Trail ran just south of town. We could organize covered wagon rides."

"Thank you, Mr. History," Lakshmi said. "But aren't there already companies that do that? And where would we get the wagons?"

Reba raked her fingers through the tangle of curls that spiraled like morning glory vines from her Rastacap. "Nice tries, Olive, Roscoe, DeShawn. Appreciate the ideas. Let's keep going, people. We're brainstorming here. No idea is too far out." Then scanning the crowd: "Anybody taking all this down?"

Lakshmi whipped out her phone and tapped its screen. "I'm on it."

"Dorothy and Toto," Jax called out. "A *Wizard of Oz* costume ball."

"I like it!" Reba said. Lakshmi's fingers danced.

"Yeah, but didn't the art museum do something like that a couple years ago?" Zebulon said.

Reba squinted and tapped her cheek. "You're right. I remember you dressed up like Dorothy. How could I forget that juxtaposition of gingham and pigtails with tattoos and piercings? Okay, what other Kansas claims to fame can we come up with? There's wheat, of course, but that wouldn't go over too well with the gluten-free crowd. Let's get creative here. Belle?"

Belle hiccupped. "What?"

"You're our brilliant idea generator. What've you got?"

"I've . . . well . . ." Belle shook her head and looked at the floor. DeShawn patted her shoulder.

"Think, Belle." Reba prompted. "What have you been spending time on lately? *Where* have you been spending time?" Around the room, faces turned toward Belle. She tried not to notice.

"The zoo? But isn't that . . ."

"Where else, Belle? Come on."

Belle shrank back. She felt like she was getting smaller, literally. *Is this what it's like being grilled in an oral exam like the one Lakshmi's cramming for? Mercy!* Forcing herself to focus, she searched her brain. "You don't mean Lucas, do you?"

Murmurs went through the crowd.

"Bingo!" Reba crowed. "And what is Lucas famous for?"

"The Garden of Eden, of course." Belle didn't see where this was going. "And grassroots art," she added as an afterthought.

Nodding encouragement, Reba made "come on" motions with her hands.

DeShawn stage-whispered a prompt: "Exhibit."

At once, Belle saw the whole thing: a grand exhibit of visionary art gleaned from Kansas and neighboring states. Blown-up photographs of pieces too big or distant to move displayed along with smaller pieces. Emery Blagdon's "Healing Machine" assemblages, Herman Divers's pull-tab car, Betty Milliken's chewing-gum portraits, Ed Galloway's carvings and totem pole park, T. J. Jenkins's Bear Head Road. A gala opening reception with pricey tickets, sure to attract arts supporters from near and far.

With works scattered around in various museums and installation sites, it was a ridiculously ambitious idea. It could be done—she knew that from experience with equally challenging events—but it would take tremendous planning and organization, and who was up to that? Not Lakshmi, with her exams coming up. And Belle? She just wasn't that organized anymore. Still, she might be capable of putting together a task list and timetable for the others to follow.

"Yooo-hoooooo." Reba's voice brought Belle back from her mental meanderings. "What are you seeing, Belle?"

"It's a crazy-ass idea," Belle began, "but we're all about crazy, right?"

Whoops and whistles erupted from the crowd. Someone started a chant, and everyone joined in: "*Cra-zee! Cra-zee! Cra-zee!*"

Reba held up a hand like a traffic cop. "Let Belle finish."

And that was how Isabelle Marsden, on her own (more or less), came to propose the most ridiculously ambitious, crazy-ass exhibit of outsider art ever undertaken in the state of Kansas.

– 12 –
THE PARADE

Three days later, parade day dawned cloudless and sunbeamy—everything summer solstice should be. An hour earlier, a mix of excitement and jitters had jolted Belle awake. Now thoroughly caffeinated, she was a human whirlwind, fussing with her hair, applying extra-strength eyeliner and mascara, and slipping into her costume.

Checking her reflection in the full-length mirror on her closet door, she clapped a hand over her mouth, not sure whether to laugh or cry at the sight of herself in gold lamé shorts. *I look like the guy in that awful Austin Powers movie. What'd they call him? Oh yeah, Goldmember.*

She'd been aiming for something more like Beyoncé's character Foxxy Cleopatra. Maybe the zinnia bra top would help. She left it in the fridge until just before time to leave, then slipped out of her T-shirt and into the skimpy top, praying it wouldn't wilt or slip as the morning warmed. Did she dare take another peek in the mirror? She couldn't resist.

Still not Foxxy, but maybe a tad less Goldmember. And it was—she had to admit—daring and unique, very un-Isabelle. Not that long ago she would've been mortified to appear this way in public. Now she was . . . giddy?

Definitely coloring outside the lines. Oh, Miranda, you should see this. Belle grabbed her inflatable headdress and without another thought, skipped out the door.

Floats and marchers already were assembling when Belle reached South Park. The atmosphere sizzled: Musicians tootled instruments, acrobats warmed up with sun salutations, jugglers practiced routines, and paraders mingled, comparing costumes. And what costumes! Every imaginable symbol of the season was represented: sunflowers, of course, as well as other summer blossoms and various forms of greenery. Frogs, turtles, brightly colored birds, bugs, and all manner of dreamed-up creatures. Hot dogs, ears of corn, strawberry shortcakes.

The floats, equally imaginative, echoed many of the same themes, plus wading pools, miniature golf courses, and baseball diamonds.

Belle made her way to the last float in the lineup: Queen Aquamaureen's Soulstice Spectacular. DeShawn and the others had done a masterful job of translating Belle's "Here Comes the Sun" motif into three-dimensional reality. Giant inflatable flowers lined a yellow brick pathway that led to a massive golden throne topped with a beaming sun the size of a backyard blow-up pool.

DeShawn bustled around making last-minute adjustments and testing the loudspeaker that would play a continuous loop of the Beatles tune.

"It's glorious," Belle told him. "Way beyond what I envisioned. Where's our queen?"

DeShawn tilted his head toward the gazebo, where Mae sat cradling a bouquet of sunflowers like a newborn baby. Dressed in a sleeveless aqua gown and sporting a coronet studded with jewels the color of sea ice, she looked positively regal.

"Um, I'm sure you've thought of this, but how's she going to get onto the float?" Belle recalled the ordeal of helping Mae off Reba's scooter.

"Never fear," DeShawn said. "Roscoe's here."

Just then the Penitentiary Poet drove up on a tractor with a pillow-lined bucket on the front end.

"No one but Roscoe could ever talk her into this," DeShawn continued, "but we've practiced, and she's okay with it. Jax and I will load her into the bucket, and I'll ride up with her to make sure she doesn't fall out. Jax will climb up and meet me at the top, and we'll unload her and get her onto the throne."

"That ought to be a sight."

"For sure." A voice behind Belle came from a sandalwood-scented cloud. She turned to see Lakshmi fiddling with her phone. "I'll be taking video." In her gold shorts and zinnia top, Lakshmi's perfect face and figure made her resemble Foxxy Cleopatra far more than Goldmember. A pang of envy pierced Belle. *Smart, organized, and beautiful too. Not fair!*

Belle adjusted the inflated sunflower on her head (already askew), hiked up her zinnia top (already drooping), and threaded through the crowd until she spotted Reba buzzing around, collecting slips of paper from parade participants.

"What're those?" Belle asked when she caught up with Reba.

"Pledges." Reba kept moving, gathering more papers and tucking them into a pocket on the Snugli where Wallace, apparently not a morning wallaby, dozed.

"Pledges? Like for money?"

"No, you ding-a-ling. Remember? You promised the Parks and Rec guy?" Reba pulled a slip and a pen from another pocket and handed them to Belle. "Here—sign."

Belle read the printed form:

> I, ________________, promise for the duration of the Soulstice parade to refrain from immodest conduct, profanity, or any other behavior that might reflect negatively on the Soulstice celebration.

Signed: ______________________ Date: ______________

Print name: ____________________

Using Reba's back for support, she filled in the blanks and handed the slip back. "Hope it helps."

"I just hope we don't run out of pledge forms," Reba said as she scanned the overflowing park. "There must be twice as many people as last year."

An amplified voice rang out from the gazebo. "Can everyone hear me?" A round of cheers confirmed everyone could. Speaking through a bullhorn, Zebulon—dressed as Sunbonnet Sue in pinafore and sunbonnet—continued. "We're counting down to step-off time, so we need everyone to line up. Our parade marshals are circulating to get everyone in the right order. It's a spectacular day for a solstice celebration, so let's all radiate positivity and have a good time!"

Reba waved a slip of paper in the air.

"Oh yeah," Zebulon added, "and don't forget to honor your pledge."

There was a momentary melee as paraders scrambled into position. Reba grabbed Belle's hand and pulled her to the front of the line, where the rest of the Soulstice gang, all decked out and humming with nervous energy, prepared to lead the procession. "I need your help with this," Reba said, leaning down to pick up a long fuchsia banner with SOULSTICE FOUNDATION in gold letters. "I'll hold one end, and I need you to hold the other."

Belle glanced out at the street, where throngs of spectators jostled for good viewing spots to set up lawn chairs, and thought she spotted Arthur MacAdams, the Parks and Rec director, herding his family to claim theirs.

"You mean, like, at the head of the parade?"

"Yes, at the head of the parade. You got a problem with that?" *My, but Reba was snappish this morning.*

"Well, it's so . . . conspicuous."

"Right. Like otherwise you'd just blend into the crowd in that outfit and makeup."

A sudden urge overtook Belle: to dash home, scrub her face, and change into her standard jeans and tank top. There was no time for that. The marching band struck up "You Are My Sunshine," and DeShawn, now at the head of the parade, waved a sunflower-topped drum major's baton and led the procession out of the park and onto Massachusetts Avenue.

As the parade proceeded up the town's main street, the band segued into "Walking on Sunshine," "Soak Up the Sun," "Sunshine of Your Love," "Don't Let the Sun Go Down on Me," even "Black Hole Sun," which wasn't nearly as ominous without the lyrics.

The music, the spectators' cheers, and the high spirits of the other marchers exhilarated Belle. Before she knew it, she'd forgotten her self-consciousness. Reba, too, relaxed and flashed a grin at Belle as Wallace, now awake and wide-eyed, looked on. Roscoe, marching between them, held up two thumbs. "We've done it again!"

"I'm walking on sunshine!" Belle sang as the parade neared the endpoint at Watson Park, though by then the band was playing a different tune.

"Isabelle!" a voice called out. "Ms. Marsden!" Belle turned to see MacAdams, his family in tow, waving and smiling as if he and Belle were old friends. "Good job!"

Belle waved back just as energetically with her free hand. A moment later, the strap of her zinnia top snapped. She looked down and—*horrors!*—her bare breast bobbed in time with the music.

"Shit!"

Colors swirled around Belle's head. A wave of seasickness churned in her stomach.

Oh noooo—don't let me puke, too!

Before she could make a move, Roscoe slipped behind her. With one hand, he pulled up her top. He clapped the other hand over her mouth and stage-whispered into her ear, "No profanity! The pledge!"

Belle nodded and ventured another peek at the crowd, specifically the spot where she'd seen the Parks and Rec director. *Whew!* MacAdams, his family, and the rest of the spectators appeared to be focused on the Bermuda shorts–clad push-lawnmower brigade behind the Soulstice Foundation marchers.

Roscoe slid the hand from Belle's mouth but remained behind her, discreetly holding up her top until they reached the end of the route. As marchers streamed into Watson Park, he whipped off his camouflage T-shirt and helped her into it, shielding her from view as best he could. "Looks good with those gold shorts," he teased.

"Omigod, that was a close one." Belle doubled over and wrapped her arms around her still-lurching stomach. "You saved my skin."

"Your skin. Yes. Some guys would have a smart-ass, sexist comeback for that remark, but feminist that I am, I'll refrain." Belle sensed he wasn't kidding about the feminist part. Despite his macho looks and swagger, Roscoe's attitudes seemed surprisingly enlightened.

"I owe you big for this one," Belle said.

"Not so big, really. I jumped in to save the parade's honor as much as yours. But you can do me one favor."

"Anything."

"I gave Reba and Mae a ride to South Park in my truck this morning before I went back home for the tractor. Once we get Queen Aquamaureen unloaded from the float, I need to skedaddle back to the farm to get things ready for the after-party. If you could take Reba and Mae home, it'd be a big help. You know where Reba lives, and Mae's house is on the way."

"Of course." Belle spotted Reba and started toward her, calling over her shoulder, "I'll return your T-shirt at the party tonight. Looking forward to it!"

Smells of grilling meat swirled with the sweet scent of ganja.

Dance music—more sunshine songs—blared from loudspeakers as revelers gyrated, spun, skipped, twisted, pranced, gavotted, whooped, and hollered. The fun and games would be going on all afternoon and into the night.

Belle and Reba sauntered through the craft and artisan food booths, in no hurry to return to South Park to retrieve Belle's car. Something big and wonderful was happening here, and Belle was part of it. She wanted to hold onto that feeling as long as she could.

Even strolling back to South Park through streets still teeming with jubilant people, the two women took their time, exchanging smiles and high-fives with merrymakers all along the way. Belle's spirits danced. "Do you think Mae will be peeved at having to wait for us to pick her up?" she asked Reba.

"Are you kidding? She's in her glory being Queen Aquamaureen for a day." Reba shifted the Snugli and fed Wallace a grape she'd stashed in a side pocket. "People will be taking selfies with her, and she'll eat up the attention."

Sure enough, when Belle, Reba, and Wallace circled back to pick up Mae at the float, four college boys in Jayhawk T-shirts and backward ball caps were clustered around her, snapping pictures with their phones for a parade montage they were creating.

"I have a virus," Mae called out. "But Jax says it's a good one."

Jax, leaning against a tree that shaded the folding chair where Mae held court, laughed. "Not vir*us*, vir*al*. I said you'd be so popular you might go viral."

Mae's face squinched. "Isn't that the same thing?"

"Jax means people everywhere might see your picture and admire your queenliness," Reba said as she and Belle popped out of the car they'd finally picked up and driven back from South Park.

Mae adjusted her crown. "Will I be on that book-face thing?"

"Facebook? I imagine you already are," Reba said. "And Twitter and Instagram too."

Wide-eyed, Mae cupped a hand over her mouth. "If I'd known I was going to be famous, I would've gotten one of those dry blow jobs."

The college boys, still loitering around, snickered. Jax waggled a finger. "Mae! I'm shocked!"

"What?" Mae's eyes went wider, and her head jerked from Jax to the college boys to Belle to Reba, all of them suppressing titters.

"She means a blow-dry job—at the salon," Reba said. "I don't think they blow-dry braids, Mae. And you look perfect without a dry blow job." She guided Mae toward Belle's little Chevy.

Mae stopped short and squinted at the car. "What's this?"

"I'm giving you a ride home," Belle said. "Roscoe needed to get back to the farm to set up for the party."

A cross expression creased Mae's face. "Oh, no. This won't do."

Belle had little patience for mulishness, but she tried to summon a shred. "I know it's a small car, Mae, but we don't have far to go. This has got to be more accommodating than Reba's scooter."

Mae drew herself up. "It's not that. It's just—I can't accept a ride from you, Belle. I'm already indebted, and you've come up with no way for me to repay you."

Belle rolled her eyes at Reba, who shrugged in a *what-can-you-do?* way. She slipped an arm around Mae, and in a voice she hoped came off more comforting than exasperated said, "We'll just add it to your escrow account for now. There's no expiration date, you know."

Still frowning, Mae grumbled, "I might reach *my* expiration date before you let me reciprocate."

Belle gently guided Mae into the car seat. "Then we'll just have to roll it over into our next lives. But I promise I'll find a favor you can do for me as soon as I can."

With that settled, Mae buckled in, and Reba and Wallace tucked into the back seat, Belle drove away, Mae offering directions to her house. Mae-style directions.

"Here! Right!" she blurted as Belle was halfway into an intersection. "Wait, no! It's the next one."

At the next corner, Belle signaled and began to turn.

"No, the one after this." Mae looked around in her stop-motion way.

"You do know where you live, right?"

Mae shot her a sharp look. "Of course I know where I live. It's just—different from this perspective. I'm not feeble-minded, you know. I have degrees in modern languages."

"Geography might've been a better choice," Belle muttered under her breath. She turned at the next corner, and Mae pointed to a cottage barely bigger than Belle's backyard shed. "Here we are."

Geraniums bloomed in window boxes. Marigolds, black-eyed Susans, and coneflowers flanked the aqua front door. Belle wasn't sure what she'd expected, but the house surprised her with its tidiness. "It's charming," she said. "And your flowers are amazing."

Mae's scowl softened. "I tend the garden. The fellows do the rest."

"The fellows—you mean . . . ?"

From the back seat, Reba piped up: "Her boyfriends."

Mae flushed and pressed her lips together. "Stop it! They're my *helpers*. Roscoe and DeShawn maintain everything for me. Without them, this place would be a hovel."

As Belle and Reba drove away after unloading Mae and seeing her into the house, Reba waved a hand in the general direction of the little cottage. "The place *was* a hovel before Roscoe and DeShawn stepped in. I gather the inside still may be. The guys are tight-lipped about what they see when they help her with chores, but every once in a while, Roscoe lets something slip. It seems our Mae is something of a hoarder. And it's not only stacks of *New York Times*. Rumor is, she's sitting on a stash of dough—over a mil. 'Course that's just a rumor."

“People always want to make up extraordinary stories about ordinary folks,” Belle said.

“Mae isn’t exactly ordinary, though, is she?”

Belle turned onto Mass Ave., headed for Reba’s house, with its eyeball doorknob, grotesque masks, roadkill assemblages, and faux food. “Granted,” she said. “But when it comes right down to it, who is?”

– 13 –
THE ULTIMATUM

Driving home after dropping Reba off, Belle couldn't get that song out of her head. "I'm walking on sunshine," she sang. "And don't it feel good!" She *did* feel good. Windows rolled down, she breathed in a potpourri of warm asphalt, lawn-sprinkled grass, house paint, and her own sunscreen, feeling the glory of summer in a way she hadn't since childhood.

Had it really been just over a month since she'd arrived in this leafy, loony town? In that short time, she'd not only come to know the whole eccentric Soulstice crew, she'd been embraced by them. Hell, she'd just marched in a parade, side by side with all those colorful folks, dressed as crazily as the rest of them. Good thing she'd taken selfies. No way would Miranda believe this without photographic evidence.

She smiled to herself, thinking about the outfit she planned to wear to the after-party: the sequined gold top Reba had picked out at the resale shop, the Goldmember shorts again, and topping it off, the feathered wig.

Her mind drifted like desultory clouds over sunflower fields. The parade, the zoo, the Soulstice gang, her strange artistry—all fitting together in a pastiche as satisfying as her front-yard creation. *Salmagundi.*

As she turned onto her street and drove past Johnny's, an image of Wallace nosing around the tavern's back door flashed into her mind. And then the memory of Ezra helping her corral the runaway wallaby and fix the screen. Ezra. Always there at the right moment, with his tools and books and chicken wire. His gentle usefulness. *What has he decided about the library job?* she wondered.

Her wandering thoughts screeched to a whiplash stop when she pulled up to her house. Yellow caution tape encircled her yard art. A notice tacked to a window frame glared at her. With her heart crashing against her chest wall, Belle scrambled out of her car and rushed to read the note.

DEMOLITION NOTICE
JUNE 21, 2018
TO: ISABELLE MARSDEN, RESIDENT
FROM: CITY OF LAWRENCE ZONING DEPARTMENT
SUBJECT: UNAPPROVED STRUCTURE IN FRONT YARD

You are hereby informed that the structure located on the front lawn of this residence is in violation of residential zoning regulations and is scheduled for demolition in twenty-one days.

You may appeal this decision in writing or by appointment with Code Enforcement staff.

Belle crumpled to the ground beside her beloved *Belle Jardin.* Zoning regulations? Who knew there were such things? In the fancy historic districts maybe, or in the McMansion developments on the outskirts of town. But here on the *other* side of the river? Where overgrown lawns rubbed crabgrassy shoulders with tidier, yet still modest yards? Did some zoning zealot cruise neighborhoods looking for violators to satisfy his ticketing quota, like an overzealous cop lurking behind a billboard at a speed trap? Or did one of her neighbors simply not like the looks of it—that snoopy Mrs. Pruitt, perhaps? Belle squinted at the woman's house across the street and thought she saw a slit in the closed blinds. Or did she just imagine it? In a matter of minutes, her reality had gone topsy-turvy, and she was no longer sure of anything.

Twenty-one days. Not even a whole month. She'd appeal, of course. She was still thinking clearly enough to know that. She'd successfully reversed the parade permit denial, hadn't she? Surely she could save her creation. Meanwhile, she'd just have to redouble her efforts to finish the work—if such a thing could ever be considered finished—to repair as best she could the remaining broken bits of her life.

Reflexively, Belle reached into her purse for her phone and speed-dialed Miranda's number, momentarily forgetting that her go-to gal pal was wrapped up with Nick now. Even as the phone rang, Belle asked herself why she didn't just call Reba. Habit, she guessed. Plus Miranda's good sense and skill at coming up with solutions.

The call went to voicemail.

"Oh. I was hoping I'd get you—you know, in person. Well, I'm in a major mess down here. Apparently, I've colored too far outside the lines for some people's taste, and I'm in trouble with the city. Call me. Miss you."

What to do now? She could skip the after-party and get right to work on her creation, but somehow she lacked the heart for it. She could go back to Watson Park and join in the festivities to take her mind off her predicament, but she had no enthusiasm for music and dancing, either.

At least get yourself up off the ground, Isabelle Marsden.

What she felt more like doing was crawling to the side door and curling into a ball on the kitchen floor, but she willed herself to get up and walk—no, march!—head high, in her gold shorts and Roscoe's camo T-shirt, right into the house, where she poured bourbon into a glass and sat down to drink and think.

For about a minute. Then she sprang from her chair and paced—kitchen to living room, living room to kitchen—waiting for a callback from Miranda that she only half expected, debating whether to call Reba, but deciding not to, knowing Reba was busy helping Roscoe with the after-party. As she paced, images trickled and then cascaded into her mind. The physical movement and mental ramblings finally steadied her enough to sit down with paper and pencils and sketch out more designs for her so-called—and now officially recognized—atrocity.

Belle sketched people and places, totems and talismans from her past. Time passed, but she scarcely noticed until the slant of sun through the catalpa tree in her side yard reminded her it was time for the party at Roscoe's. She was hardly in the mood for it; still, she needed to talk to someone about the impending demolition, and Miranda hadn't come through for her. Reba and her gang might not be as insightful as Miranda or as intimately acquainted with all things Belle, but one thing they always were was *available*. And right now, available sounded good enough.

The party was well underway when Belle slipped into Roscoe's barn. A country band, complete with fiddle and pedal steel guitar, was playing "Take Me Back to Tulsa," and at least half the party guests twirled and pretzeled on the makeshift dance floor. DeShawn, still wearing an inflated sunflower atop his microbraids, circulated through the crowd, bearing a tray of something that looked only semi-edible.

"Catfish sushi," he shouted to Belle over the party din. "Better than it looks. Trust me."

Trust me. Such a throwaway expression, but one Belle couldn't take lightly. She reached for a piece and summoned the nerve to take the smallest possible bite. Surprisingly tasty—though by now, such a contradiction shouldn't have been a surprise. "Drinks are over there."

DeShawn pointed to a corner where Jax tended a bar stocked with booze, beer, soft drinks, and punch that exactly matched Jax's chartreuse hair.

Belle scanned the crowd for Reba and spotted her doing a push-pull dance step with Olive Pickle as Wallace bounced in place beside them. When the music died down, Belle threaded through the crowd, exchanging hasty greetings with the revelers. Breathless, she grabbed Reba's arm.

Reba gave her a sideways look. "Belle! We've been looking for yoooooou. Where's your outfit?"

Only then did Belle realize that in her distress over the demolition notice and her bourbon-fueled flurry of creative scrawling, she'd completely forgotten about her party ensemble and unconsciously changed from her parade clothes into an old tank top and cutoffs. She hadn't even bothered to comb her straggly hair, much less conceal it under the feathered wig.

"Something's happened," she panted.

"Well, obviously." The band launched into "San Antonio Rose," and Zebulon pulled Reba back onto the dance floor. Reba held up her pointer finger and gave Belle an apologetic smile. "Hold that thought. I'll be back in a minute. Watch Wallace for me, will you?"

So much for *available.*

Sensing someone behind her, Belle spun around. To her relief, it was only Roscoe.

"You've got to stop doing that," she said. Ever since Jamison, she couldn't stand anyone sneaking up from behind. It was a wonder she hadn't punched Roscoe when he'd slipped behind her to fix her wardrobe malfunction in the parade. If he hadn't been so smooth, and she hadn't been so fixated on her bare boob and nausea, she just might've.

"I see you're more modestly attired than when I saw you last," Roscoe said. "A bit drab, perhaps, but definitely decorous."

"Spoken like a poet." Belle couldn't help cracking a smile. "Listen,

Roscoe, something's come up." Unlike Reba, Roscoe didn't budge until Belle had spilled out the whole story. By that time, Reba was back from the dance floor, flushed and perspiring, but attentive, and Belle repeated the details.

"So I'll appeal, of course," she finished. "I just hope my landlady doesn't get wind of this. She's already threatened to evict me if my 'atrocity' doesn't shape up into something more—I don't know—*acceptable*?"

"Yeah, like art is supposed to be *acceptable*," Reba snorted. "That woman probably has a painting over her sofa that she bought to match the upholstery."

"Who's your landlady—Mrs. Dumbass?" Roscoe asked. "She owns half the rentals on that side of the river."

"Mrs. Dumas," Belle said. "It's *du-MAHS*."

"No, in her case I'm pretty sure it's Dumbass. But anyway, you go and put in your appeal, and if that doesn't work—" Roscoe and Reba exchanged knowing looks, "—we might know someone who knows someone who yada, yada, yada."

Belle had no idea what that meant. Before she could ask for clarification, Roscoe and Reba were spinning and ducking under each other's arms, and Belle was left with Wallace. He looked up at her with an expectant expression.

"What? You want some of my sushi? I have a feeling that's not on your diet plan, pal." Belle crouched down to scratch Wallace under his chin. He tilted his head back, and she mimicked him. That's when she saw a familiar pair of legs—very long legs.

"Ezra! You're *here*. I mean *you're* here. Are you a friend of Roscoe's?"

"I'm a friend of *yours*, Izzy." He extended a hand to help her up from the floor. "I got home late from the celebration in the park and saw that god-awful caution tape and demo notice. You weren't home, so I came looking for you."

"But how'd you know I'd be here?"

"You forget I'm an information specialist." His smile teeter-tottered on his face. "No, actually your friend Reba tipped me off. One day when you were at the zoo, she came looking for you. I walked over to tell her where you were, and we got to talking and well, you know how it is with Reba—one thing leads to another. She told me about the parade and invited me to the after-party. I hadn't planned on coming, but when I saw you were in trouble I had to find you."

How did he *do* that? Always showing up at the right time. Was he stalking her? *Don't be ridiculous, Belle. He's only trying to help.*

"I assume you'll appeal. I'll be happy to go with you, as long as it's before I go back to Nebraska."

"You're going back?" The disappointment in Belle's voice took her by surprise. "But I thought you had the library job here cinched."

"I do. It's mine if I want it. But I need to get back to Nebraska for the wrap-up of the children's summer reading program. We have a drawing for a bicycle, and there's a big party where the kids and staff dress like characters from their favorite books. So there's that. And I just want to get some space to think things over."

"While dressed as a book character."

"Exactly."

"Which one?" With wildly costumed solstice celebrants whirling around them, dressing up struck Belle as de rigueur. Not at all odd, no matter how odd Ezra might be in other ways.

"I was the Cat in the Hat last year and Waldo the year before that," Ezra said, his eyes shining. "This year I'm thinking Max from *Where the Wild Things Are.*" He made a snarly monster face and held his hands up like claws. "But I promise I won't wear that costume if I go with you to appeal the demolition notice."

"That's a relief. Listen, Ezra—Ezzy—you are so kind to offer, and I really do appreciate all your help. But I think I can handle this on my own. I think I *need* to handle this on my own, like you *need* to go back to Nebraska for a while. I hope you understand."

Ezra's expression turned grave, with a pinch of puckishness, just as the music slowed and the crowd quieted down. "How could I not? The king of the wild things knows as well as anyone that sometimes you have to forge your own path."

– 14 –
THE INITIATION

It was mid-morning when Belle awoke from a dream more convoluted than ever. This dream had no clear plotline, just a mishmash of unrelated vignettes: Belle marching naked to "Walking on Sunshine"; Mr. MacAdams in a zinnia bra, twirling in dizzying circles; Ozzy the fox playing pedal steel guitar; Ezra dressed in a child-sized Max costume; Reba peeking out of a Snugli strapped to Wallace's chest; Mae with a fluffy, blow-dried hairdo. All bright, smiley images—even the marching-naked one—until the end, when a monster shaped like an enormous thundercloud with fangs and lightning-bolt eyes threatened them all.

Slay the beast, Belle. The cryptic Garden of Eden message came back to her. *You have the power.* But powerful was not what she felt just now. Overwhelmed, confused, fuzzy—those were better descriptors.

She picked up her phone and replayed the breathless message Miranda had left the night before.

"Belle, I'm *so* sorry I missed your call! Nick and I were at a *kirtan*. God, what's going on? I can't believe *you* are in trouble with the city. Do you need me to come down there? Because I absolutely will. Call me as soon as you get this."

Belle laid the phone back on her nightstand. She needed to think, to sort things out. And to sort things out, she needed to work. A plan took shape in her mind: First, she'd call the zoning department to set up an appointment. It was Friday, so they'd probably schedule something for next week. That'd be good—she'd have all weekend and possibly longer to outline her defense. Once the appointment was set, she could spend the rest of the day adding to and fortifying *Belle Jardin*. If the city was going to destroy her concrete creation, she'd make damn sure they had to work at it.

Good plan, Belle. See? You do have power. Maybe not a lot, but enough to figure things out, one step at a time.

She picked up the phone again, called the zoning department, and in a businesslike tone identified herself and asked to schedule an appointment with the director for the following week.

"I'm sorry Ms. Marsden, but Mr. Schwann will be on vacation for the next two weeks. Today's his last day in the office until July 9."

July 9? She couldn't wait that long—the demolition was scheduled for July 12. That would be cutting it too close.

"But I . . ."

"Wait a minute—" The secretary's voice was kind. Did she know who Belle was and why she was calling? Was she secretly an ally? Belle wanted to think so. "He actually has an opening in his schedule this morning. Could you be here in, say, half an hour?"

Half an hour! No way. But it took Belle only a fraction of a second to realize she had no other choice.

"Certainly," she heard herself say. "Thank you."

Belle rummaged through her closet for something more formal to wear. Where were her pencil skirts and tailored blouses? Her trim slacks and jackets? Oh, that's right, packed away in boxes. She'd seen no need to unpack clothes she had no intention of wearing, much less ironing and organizing. And the casual skirt and top she'd worn to the Parks and Rec meeting lay heaped in the laundry basket with all the other clothes she hadn't gotten around to washing.

Gold shorts and camo tee? *Oh, good heavens, Belle, no! Jeans and tank top it is.*

She grabbed the closest ones she could find, rumpled and sweat-stained as they were. Sliding into a pair of well-worn Dr. Scholl's sandals, she reached for her purse and keys on her dresser and caught a glimpse of herself in the mirror. Yikes. The hair.

The feathered wig sat on a featureless plastic foam head next to her purse. Without another thought, Belle snatched the wig and stuffed her own hair beneath it.

She raced to city hall, too scattered to think in complete sentences, much less formulate a defense. *Something will come to me. I'm good at thinking on the spot.* Belle smiled at the memory of Mr. MacAdams crossing out "Denied" and writing "Granted" on the parade permit.

Breathless after bounding up the stairs to the third-floor zoning department office, Belle paused before pushing open the solid-wood door. The secretary—twentyish with long hair, well-defined eyebrows, and a pulled-together presence—looked up with a smile that shrank only slightly when she caught sight of Belle. She smelled like a cinnamon roll. No, that was the candle burning on her desk. Belle didn't care for nonedibles that smelled like food—green apple soap, sugar cookie bath salts, and such turned her stomach with their synthetic mimicry—but she didn't hold it against the young woman.

"Sorry to make you rush in like this," the secretary said, "but I know you need to see Mr. Schwann before he takes off for Colorado. You can go on in—he's expecting you." The young woman's smile widened, and she gave Belle two thumbs up.

Head high, feathers flopping against her cheeks, Belle strode in, projecting—she hoped—confidence and above all, *normalcy.*

The man behind the desk stood, unsmiling, and extended a hand. "Steve Schwann." He was lean, in a joylessly athletic way. The type who worked out daily just to check off a box.

She shook his hand. "It's a pleasure to meet you, Mr.—" It took every ounce of concentration not to say *Schwanz*. Roscoe was rubbing off on her. "Mr. Schwann." Belle exhaled loudly and sank into the chair the director gestured toward.

"So," Mr. Schwann said, still expressionless.

Why did people begin sentences with "So"? Such a meaningless word in that context, which was no context at all. So *what*? Sometimes Belle mentally substituted some inappropriate word—poop, for example. She did that now and choked back a giggle.

Get a grip! she admonished herself. The old Belle, the professional Belle, never would've lapsed into such silliness. Was stepping out of line part and parcel of coloring outside the lines?

Mr. Schwann gave her a strange look and continued. "I understand you're here to discuss the demolition order." He glanced at his watch—one of those gargantuan quartz analog jobs. Costly. "I'm not sure there's anything to discuss. Neighbors have complained about the eyesore, which doesn't fit any definition of allowable structures. It might even be considered a safety hazard. I understand there's broken glass, sharp things." He shook his head. "Not the kind of thing Lawrence residents want in their neighborhoods."

Belle began to wish she'd had more time—hell, any time at all—to prepare. Then she reminded herself: *I'm good at this. I can think on my feet. Or seat.* A giggle bubbled up again, and with the feathers tickling her cheeks, she couldn't hold it back this time. She collapsed forward, head to knees, shoulders shaking, and tried to collect herself.

"Ms. Marsden? Are you all right?" Mr. Schwann's tone was not sympathetic. "Can we get on with this?"

Belle straightened with a jerk that felt so Mae-like she almost broke out giggling again, but she forced a serious expression. With no scripted speech, she rattled off whatever snippets popped into her head. It was as if her muse was now feeding her words instead of images.

"Well, you know, Mr. Schwann . . ." *Whew, said it right again.*

". . . *Belle Jardin* is not supposed to be *acceptable.* Oh no, not at all acceptable. It's art, you know, but I'm not planning to hang it over Mrs. Dumbass's sofa. It's more of a Lucas-y kind of thing, but without the dead guy under glass or the disembodied voices. Or Polly Perm. No, probably no gift shop at all. Just pure art for art's sake." She hiccupped three times in a row.

Mr. Schwann aligned the corners of a stack of papers and looked at his watch again.

"At least give me more than twenty-one days," Belle continued. "I have to put all the pieces back together. I *have* to. Like the king of the wild things *has* to go back to Nebraska. And see, there are *so* many pieces I have to repair, and that's the only way—*the only way*—we can both be whole. Not you and me, I mean. You already look pretty whole, actually. But it's the only way for *Belle Jardin* and me to be whole again." Belle flashed a triumphant smile.

She waited for Mr. Schwann to smile back and nod in agreement.

Mr. Schwann did not smile back. He did not nod. Mr. Schwann scowled. "With all due respect, Ms. Marsden . . ." Was that a mocking tone? "It's my understanding that you're the one breaking things *into* pieces. At all hours of the day and night. Now, noise complaints are not under our jurisdiction, but all things considered, I see no reason for us to allow this rubbish—and that's precisely what it is—to persist any longer. In fact, if we had the resources, I'd have scheduled the demo for next week."

Stunned, Belle sat motionless, staring at Schwann. Had Dinsmoor suffered such indignity? The director pushed a button on his desk. "Allison, in here, please."

Allison. Ally. Surely that friendly young woman, her *ally*, would come to her aid.

The secretary burst through the door, filling the room with a scent like day-old donuts. How much bigger she looked now than when seated behind her desk! Big in a kickass, Queen Latifah way.

"Escort her out, please," Mr. Schwann said. "I think she's—" He pantomimed drinking from a bottle.

The secretary grabbed Belle's arm, yanked her out of her chair, and marched her out the door.

"Ow!" Belle shrieked. Then, over her shoulder: "I'm not drunk. I am an artist, Mr. *Schwanz*."

The tangerine scooter was parked in Belle's driveway when she got home. Reba and Wallace stood in her front yard.

"We just stopped by to see if you needed anything, but you weren't here. Where'd you go?"

"Oh, Reba! I totally, totally blew it." Belle dissolved into tears.

Reba threw her arms around her, and Wallace squeezed between them. "Blew what?"

Between sniffs and hiccups, Belle described her visit to the zoning department.

When she'd finished, Reba handed her a tissue. "Congratulations!"

Through Belle's tears, Reba was a blur of turquoise, coral, and curl. Was Belle's hearing bleary, too? Did Reba really just say . . . "Congratulations? *Belle Jardin* is about to be desecrated, I'm talking goofy, and you're congratulating me?" Belle crumpled to the ground and held her head in her hands.

Reba squatted in front of her. "Yes, I am." With a solemn expression, Reba took Belle's hands in hers, raised the right one, and placed the left on an imaginary Bible. "Isabelle Marsden, you have just been initiated into official artist-dom. By suffering in service of your art, you have joined the ranks of artists throughout time. Rejection, misunderstanding, mockery—all of that goes with the territory. But so does the joy of creation, the *necessity* of creation, the healing power of creation. So we carry on, Belle. We persevere."

It was all too much for Belle to absorb—the shock of the demolition notice, the humiliation of the morning's meeting, the sense she'd somehow lost control and instead of pulling her life back together, she was shattering it even more with her blunders.

"Piece by piece, Belle," Reba said. "That's the only way to proceed." She signaled Wallace with a hand gesture. He stuck his nose into an open pocket in her backpack, came out with a small drawstring bag in his mouth, and hopped over to deliver it to Reba.

"Look what we have for you!" Reba said. "Hold out your hands."

Belle hesitated, then cupped her open palms.

"Everyone's been saving stuff for you. Salmagundi, you might call it." Reba poured out an astonishing assortment of trinkets. It was like watching circus clowns tumble out of a miniature car—mind-boggling that so much could fit into such a small container. "Roscoe found the old marbles under his front porch—don't ask me what he was doing under there; Lakshmi went through her jewelry box and culled all the unmatched earrings; Mae busted up her favorite plates—lord knows what she's eating off of now. Zebulon threw in those antique buttons. He's in a men's sewing club, you know, The Seamsters' Union. And finally—*ta-da!*—Olive Pickle wanted you to have this." Reba reached into her own pocket and pulled out an eyeball. Glass, but disconcertingly realistic. "It was her late husband's."

Belle stared at the eyeball. The eyeball stared back.

"Now, if all this doesn't get you inspired, nothing will." Reba stood and whistled for Wallace, who stopped licking the fingers of one of Belle's babies and bounded to her side. "We've got a busy day, and so have you. Now, get to work, and I'll be back soon to see what you've done."

She bundled Wallace into the backpack and fired up the scooter, calling out as she rode away, "Artists don't let artists drive discouraged!"

The eyeball, nestled in the grass where Reba had laid it, winked at Belle in a conspiratorial way. A trick of light, no doubt. Already high in the sky, the sun danced off bits of mirror and glass embedded in concrete. Now as long and wide as a king-size mattress, with some additions reaching a good three feet high, *Belle Jardin* was truly a sight to behold. Belle laid the other donated treasures next to her sculpture and pocketed the eyeball. She'd find a special place for it in her creation eventually, but for now, she wanted it as a talisman.

Comforted by Reba's kindness and exhausted from her meeting with Schwann, Belle dozed off on a strip of grass beside her creation. On a day so snoozily warm, with lullaby breezes, sleep should've been narcotic. Yet Belle's was fitful, disrupted by dreams of masked men violently attacking *Belle Jardin*. Chunks of concrete, shards of glass and china, marbles and baubles flew everywhere. The walla-dog's head went one way, a baby's hand another.

She awoke with a mission: protect *Belle Jardin*.

But how? Barbed wire? Booby traps? Explosives? In Belle's frame of mind, nothing seemed too extreme.

The question was, where could she get—or how could she make—what she needed? Google should know. She fetched her laptop from the house and settled onto the side stoop to search, oblivious to the late-afternoon sounds: kids splashing and shrieking in backyard pools and springing on trampolines, grown-ups rolling out barbecue grills and popping open beers.

Just as she entered search terms, a distant siren—the only sound that penetrated her consciousness—stopped her short.

Could I get in trouble for this? Can't the authorities find your browsing history somehow?

A moment's pause.

Oh, come on, Belle, what authorities? You're getting paranoid.

She typed "how to make explosives" in the search box and clicked on the first result returned. Before she could read it, Mitchell's back door opened and Ezra appeared, headed toward the garage.

Mitchell's garage—of course! The source of so many needful things.

"Hey, Ezzy," Belle called out, "got any barbed wire over there?"

Ezra trotted over, puzzled concern pleating his face. "What do you need that for? Keeping out cattle rustlers?"

"Something like that." Belle tipped her head toward *Belle Jardin*, with its damning necklace of yellow tape. "Gotta protect my investment. What about ammonium nitrate? Got any of that?"

"Ammonium nitrate? Hold on there, Izzy." Ezra stooped to see her laptop screen and recoiled. "I get where you're coming from, but let's not do anything rash. Someone could get hurt. Let's think this thing through."

Exactly what Belle didn't want to do. She was desperate to *act*, not contemplate and deliberate. She knew from the Jamison experience that she tended to spend too much time deliberating and waffling when she should take swift and decisive action. Yet deep down, she knew Ezra was right.

- 15 -
THE DEFENDER

The Garden of Eden was an altogether different place in the dark of night. So Belle discovered the following evening. Throughout the day she'd been interrupted by visitors and phone calls—Reba and Wallace with another load of trinkets, Ezra checking back to make sure Belle wasn't concocting hazardous cocktails, Miranda wanting details on the zoning department meeting, Mrs. Dumas reminding her the rent was due and needling her again about *Belle Jardin*, Jax asking if she'd pick up a bale of straw on the way to her next zoo shift—all preventing Belle from making the early morning run to Lucas she'd had in mind.

Postpone it until the next day? That would make sense. Sense was not what Belle was making. Not anymore. It was mid-afternoon when she hopped into the Spark and sped west, arriving at the Garden of Eden just before the gates closed for the night. She pulled into an out-of-the-way parking space on a side street, grabbed her backpack, and slipped into a shrubby corner of the grounds.

Once she was sure Polly had locked up and driven away, Belle staked out her campsite: a sheltered spot just big enough for her sleeping bag. No need for cookstove or campfire; she'd brought granola bars, caramel corn, an apple, and water for sustenance. She stayed hidden until dark, then crept around walkways so familiar in daylight, so eerie at night. The sculptures that hovered overhead—the same ones she'd become accustomed to on her daylight visits—now made her skin prickle. Never mind Dinsmoor in his mausoleum. It was locked tight, thank goodness, but even if Belle had been able to pay him a visit, she'd have been scared out of her wits to venture in there after dark.

She'd hoped clarity would come here at her source of inspiration, beneath the waxing moon. Instead, only shivers and apparitions. She slipped into her sleeping bag and closed her eyes, but startled at every strange sound: wind creaking branches like bones, owls calling *woooo-woooo* like phantoms. Even the quiet was spooky. In Lawrence, night sounds drifted through her open bedroom windows: train whistles and rumbles, barking dogs, neighbors' TVs, rambunctious revelers leaving Johnny's tavern. Here, long stretches of absolute silence for Belle's mind to fill with fearsome fantasies and endless loops of worrisome thoughts.

Should she throw all her energy into girding and defending *Belle Jardin*? Or should she just admit defeat and destroy it herself before the city could lay hands on it? She could pack up, go back to Chicago, and pretend this whole strange experience never happened. Or could she? Chicago was her past, and some of that past—especially the recent past with Jamison—was troubling to recall. Why return to a setting filled with reminders? Besides, what was there for her? She had no job, no home to return to. Miranda, though still her bestie in principle, would be more and more consumed with coupledom. Here, at least she had Reba, Roscoe, Mae, and the rest of the gang for company and creative encouragement. And Ezra. *Oh, Ezra.* The very thought of him set off new cycles of perseveration. Was he just being helpful with his constant attention—helpful did seem to be his default setting—or was he trying to start something more? And if he was, well, then what? Belle had been unattached since her breakup with Ben—dear, solid, grounded Ben—more than a decade earlier, and she had to admit she'd had lonely moments. But loneliness was no reason for taking up with someone; there had to be feelings. Did she have feelings for Ezra (dear, solid, grounded Ezra)—besides gratitude, that is? That was a question she hadn't allowed herself to consider. And just as she began to turn it over in her mind, crawly things started creeping over every exposed inch of skin, distracting her from weightier matters.

If she slept at all the rest of the night, it was only for brief snatches, fragmented by pangs of fear she'd oversleep and be discovered. Before dawn, she rolled up her sleeping bag, stuffed all signs of her presence into her backpack, and hurried away, feeling more disoriented than ever.

I thought I'd find answers here—what to do next, how to save Belle Jardin. *All I got was a sore back and bug bites. I should've known it's a hopeless cause. I'm no artist—not even an eccentric one like Dinsmoor. I'm just a lost soul making a mess of my front yard.*

As Belle drove home, the rising sun lit up limestone fence posts. Fence posts that had stood firm for a hundred years or more, since early settlers heaved them into place. With that sight, a flash of clarity: *The best way to protect* Belle Jardin *is to keep building it. To make it indestructible.*

At home, when Belle set to work later that morning, it wasn't a fortress she constructed. It was feet. Solid, grounded feet, standing firm.

As she shaped the ankles, insteps, and finally toes, she realized they were not just anyone's feet. They were Ben's. And as she sculpted, she found herself reciting a snippet of a Pablo Neruda poem Miranda had memorized—and practiced endlessly on Belle:

But I love your feet
only because they walked

upon the earth and upon
the wind and upon the waters,
until they found me.

So many things she'd loved about Ben—his gentle spirit, his energy, the way he encouraged her in her own pursuits, their shared passion for venti nonfat Caramel Macchiatos, the music of Coldplay, and orderliness. But she absolutely adored his feet. Not in a fetishy way, just in the sense of finding them adorable. Smallish for a man, perfectly proportioned, with nails that always looked like he'd just had a pedicure, though he swore he never had. And capable! Yes, capability was a quality you could ascribe to feet. Hiking, skating, dancing—especially dancing!—Ben's feet never faltered, never stumbled, always seemed so sure of themselves. Like Ben. Always so sure.

Belle had been sure, too. Until she wasn't.

It was at a wedding (oh, the irony again!) that her certainty began to unravel. Now, as she smoothed the concrete likenesses of Ben's feet, thoughts of that evening fourteen years ago unspooled in her mind.

The wedding chapel—small, with sloped walls that gave it a cloistered feeling. A single arrangement of calla lilies flanked by candelabras decorating the altar. Belle and Ben seated in the front row, waiting for the other guests to arrive. Ben squeezing her hand and giving her a sad, knowing smile.

And then the ceremony. Her dad in his best suit, Shelley in a cream-colored lace dress, her hair in an updo with a spray of tiny rosebuds. The minister—a country-club friend of Belle's dad's—saying the usual words. It all passed in a blur. And then they were kissing. *Dad and Shelley. Husband and wife. Mr. and Mrs. Marsden.*

Belle held it together until she and Ben were in his car, heading toward the restaurant where there'd be a small dinner in lieu of a reception. All of a sudden she was sobbing, tears spotting her gray silk dress. Ben turned into a supermarket parking lot and found a space near the back with no other cars around. He shifted the car into park and wrapped his arms around her.

"I know. I know. A lot of changes." He stroked her hair.

She pulled away and leaned against the passenger door. "I just feel so . . . so *alone* in the world now."

"*Alone*?" Ben looked stricken. "But babe, you're not alone. You've got me. For better or worse." He laughed weakly.

She knew he was trying to lighten things up, but his reference to wedding vows sent a tremor deep into her core. What if they weren't always together? What if he left or died? (*Till death do us part.*) Or what if they stayed together but drifted apart?

After that night, they did stay together one more year. Outwardly, they were a couple sailing in the same direction, toward careers and a shared life. Inwardly, Belle was no longer on board.

Everything came to a head one morning as Belle sat at the kitchen table in the apartment they shared. The time had come for Ben to choose a graduate program and Belle to apply for internships—a key requirement in her tourism, hospitality, and event management major. Ben was considering universities in Seattle, New York, Boston, and Los Angeles, schools he'd chosen specifically because Belle could intern in the same cities. For weeks, the table had been littered with brochures and printouts on the attractions of each place: Seattle's ferries and Pike Place Market, New York's neighborhoods and ethnic restaurants, Boston's harbor and historic sites, LA's sun and Hollywood dazzle.

All appealing. So why had Belle felt paralyzed, unable to read a single sentence, leaving all the promotional materials untouched?

A key clicked in the front door lock. Ben breezed in, back from an early-morning meeting with an engineering prof who was writing him a letter of recommendation. He stopped short at the sight of Belle cradling her coffee mug, staring at the pile of literature.

"Time's running out, hon," he said gently, sliding into the empty chair across from her. "We need to make a decision about this." His voice, usually soothing as warm milk, had a peevish edge.

Belle shifted her gaze to her coffee cup, watched steam rise from dark liquid. She couldn't look Ben in the eye.

"I don't know. I really don't know."

"*What* don't you know?" His tone tightened; the pitch rose. "Can we at least rule out one or two? It'd save me a lot on application fees."

"Well . . . *I* haven't ruled out Chicago, you know."

Ben threw up his hands. "But that's where you've spent your whole life—except for coming here to college. This is your chance to get out in the world, experience something new, something bigger. And besides, Belle—look at me, Belle—you know Chicago isn't on *my* list."

Ben waited for Belle to respond, but she couldn't find words that fit her feelings. The silence between them expanded like a seeping stain.

Ben pushed away from the table, paced to the living room and back. Belle sat, still staring at her cup. Finally, Ben broke the silence. "Are you telling me you don't want to go where I go? You don't want us to stay together? Jesus, Belle! This is what we've been moving toward all this time, and now all of a sudden you're backing out?"

Belle lifted her eyes at last and searched Ben's. His pupils were dark pools. The rest of his face was constricted: brow furrowed, cheeks drawn in, mouth a tight line. She searched for words and still couldn't find the ones she needed, the ones that would tell him, *I care about you, but I can't let myself care* that *much.*

Ben turned away, paced some more. "Then why don't we just call it quits right now?" He dragged a hand across his jaw. "I've given my all to you, but it seems like I'm getting back less and less. I'm not sure what you want anymore, Belle, and I don't know if *you* do. But I know this isn't what I want."

His footsteps fell heavy on the wooden floor. The door slammed behind him.

Silence filled the apartment. In a strange way, it felt comforting.

See? Belle told herself. *I knew I might lose him, and I did. Good thing I didn't let myself get any closer than I did.*

She poured herself another cup of coffee, brought out the recycling bin from under the sink, and swept into it all the papers from the table.

If only it had been as easy to sweep Ben from her mind, to wring every trace of him from her memory. Yet here she was, thirteen years later, memorializing her long-gone lover's feet. *Pathetic, Belle.*

It wasn't like she was still hung up on him, unable to move on. There'd been a time—after Ben but before Jamison—when she believed she might allow herself to love again and felt eager to try if she met the right guy. If she could somehow convince herself he wouldn't leave or die, or that if he did, she'd be all right. Look at her dad. How desolate he'd been when her mother died. How quickly he'd recovered enough to take up with Shelley and build a new life around her.

How quickly Ben recovered, too. He moved to Seattle for grad school, and by the time he earned his degree he'd married a marine biologist and started having kids with her. Forgotten all about Belle, no doubt.

Meanwhile, Belle concentrated on her career—landing an internship at a Chicago hotel, running her closet- and event-organizing business for a few years after that. Then hired full-time at the prestigious Magnus hotel chain and impressing her boss—the good one, before Jamison—with her ideas and efficiency. She dated, sometimes half-heartedly, sometimes hopefully. No one struck the chords Ben had struck.

Then the thing with Jamison happened—an episode so tawdry Belle stuffed it into a dark recess of her mind and snipped off every tendril of memory that intruded. After that entanglement, she felt so sullied, so unworthy of any good man's love, she stopped believing in love at all.

As she put the finishing touches on Ben's feet, she had the sense she was sealing away a part of herself—the squishy, vulnerable part that had put her in the path of pain. But then it struck her that perhaps that part had been sealed off long ago, sealed as securely as Dinsmoor in his tomb, and that by casting Ben—or at least his feet—in stone—or at least concrete—she might open a window, just a crack, and allow her shut-in spirit to breathe.

Yet before she could draw a single easy breath, her chest seized up at the thought of yet another loss. Everything she'd just sculpted, everything she'd created in the past month, which was pretty much all she'd created in her whole life, could be gone in a matter of hours if the city carried out the demolition.

Who am I kidding? No matter how strong I build this thing, they'll find a way to destroy it. Schwanz will make sure of that.

As if to underscore that thought, a city truck crawled by, the workers inside gawking and pointing at Belle and *Belle Jardin*. Laughing. *Laughing!*

How dare they disrespect her art! Whatever other indignities Belle might endure, she would not stand for that. She'd go on building—as an act of defiance, if nothing else.

Never had Belle felt so zeroed in, so *present* as she did now. Hands, hammer, concrete, trowel all working as one, guided by imagination and the alchemistic specter of her muse. She sculpted and sketched, sketched and sculpted. From time to time, she stroked the glass eyeball in her pocket and seemed to get an extra charge of inspiration.

Her next addition to *Belle Jardin* was a likeness of her second-grade teacher, Mrs. Glick: pencil-thin and all angles, with her wash-and-wear bob and small gold hoop earrings—the same ones every day. In real life Mrs. Glick didn't wear glasses, but Belle fitted her with an oversized pair like Polly's that made her look googly-eyed. Maybe with those she could finally see the artistry in Belle's drawings.

As if to confirm that, Belle held her sketchpad in front of the statue's face. Its stony features registered no reaction, but Belle had all the affirmation she needed. She was an artist for certain, expressing her visions as she saw them.

She doodled on the pad, trolling for ideas. What else in her life needed mending?

Miranda. Distant now—not just in miles, but in ways that counted more—yet for so many years, the only person Belle fully trusted. She could trace the roots of that trust to a single event, twenty years earlier.

One afternoon, at the start of ninth grade, Belle was killing time at the mall while Miranda visited the orthodontist. She wandered in and out of shops, not really looking for anything. Spinning racks of earrings, fingering blouses she had no intention of buying. Then, there it was: a T-shirt the color of her birthstone—sapphire—with a design of her zodiac sign: Libra. She had to have it. She flipped over the tag and read the price. Ridiculous. Maybe it would go on sale eventually. But what if someone else bought it before it got marked down? It was the only one of its kind on the rack.

She carried the shirt to the full-length mirror and held it up to her chest. *Oh yes.*

That's when she noticed the T-shirt had no plastic security tag. She glanced over one shoulder, then the other. One clerk was leading a customer to the dressing room; another was folding jeans on a table at the rear of the store. No one else was in sight. Belle stuffed the T-shirt under her own and scurried out into the concourse.

Walking to the bus stop, she congratulated herself on her boldness. *Belle, the victorious warrior princess, returns from battle with her spoils.* Sitting on the bus, she smoothed the rumpled T-shirt on her lap and admired the design again. It was made for her. She *deserved* it. Miranda would agree, she was sure.

A pesky thought intruded: *What if my parents find out I've shoplifted it?* She tried to dismiss the thought, to reason and rationalize it away, but it itched like a rash in her brain. And like an irksome rash, it spread.

What if there's a surveillance video? What if the police show up at my house?

By the time she reached her stop and started walking toward Miranda's house, Belle was a ragged bundle of anxiety, regret, and indecision. Miranda met her at the door, braces glinting in a smile that deflated when she saw Belle's pained expression.

"What happened to you? I thought you were going to the mall." Her eyes traveled to the bulge under Belle's T-shirt. "Omigod. You didn't."

"Can we just go to your room? Please."

Cloistered in Miranda's bedroom, Belle spilled out the story as their idol Freddie Prinze Jr. stared down from a poster above the bed, with eyes that on other days enticed but now condemned.

Miranda thought for a moment, then gave a brisk nod.

"Okay, I've got it. I'll hide your T-shirt here until we're sure the coast is clear. Then the next time we go shopping, we'll slip it into your bag before you go home, so it looks like you actually bought it."

The plan was brilliant, the friends agreed. Handling the shirt like a sacred vestment, Miranda folded it and buried it beneath seldom-worn sweaters in the very bottom of her bottom dresser drawer.

But over the next few weeks, a veil of guilt trailed Belle through her days and tangled her sleepless nights. It wasn't only that she'd committed a crime. She'd also put her best friend in jeopardy by allowing her to hide the stolen property. Made her an *accessory*—wasn't that what they called accomplices? An accessory—as if she were no more than a scarf or an earring.

As much as she loved that T-shirt, Belle loved Miranda more, and now she knew she'd never wear the purloined piece of clothing. But what to do? She couldn't let Miranda keep it, yet if she took it home and hid it in her own room, she'd have to live with a constant reminder of her misdeed. She could throw it away, but what a waste of something another shopper might legitimately enjoy. She could donate it, but she'd still be burdened with the shame of cheating the store. She could return it and apologize, but she might still get in trouble.

She outlined the options and possible outcomes to Miranda, who once again came up with a brilliant plan. Miranda would sneak the T-shirt back into the store and leave it in a dressing room. Which is exactly what she did on their next trip to the mall, as Belle waited, nibbling a dry scone at the Starbucks down the hall. The deed was done, Belle's conscience cleared, and Miranda never mentioned it again.

Just as, years later, she never told anyone what Belle had confided about Jamison. Miranda was a vault where Belle could lock her deepest secrets and know they were safe.

Now, surveying *Belle Jardin*, Belle found an empty spot just the right size for her next addition. She mixed more concrete, smashed some of Mae's china, shaped chicken wire scaffolds, and set to work on an image of her lifelong friend. She sculpted Miranda's messy bun, her oversized ears, her sympathetic eyes, and her hands covering her mouth like the speak-no-evil monkey. When Belle finished, she sat on her haunches, face to face with concrete Miranda, satisfied with her depiction.

Her contentment didn't last long. Minutes later, the city truck rolled by again, and Belle was left with no one to console her but the silent likeness of her longtime friend.

– 16 –
THE FOX LIBERATION FRONT

Ozzy raised his head and sniffed the air when Belle slipped into his pen with an open can of cat food. Was that a flicker of familiarity in his eyes, or was it only the smell of food that perked him up?

Belle didn't delude herself. Adorable as she found the little fox, she knew he was still a creature of the wild, leery of strangers and unfamiliar settings—and rightly so. She understood leery. Oh yes, she did.

Stationing herself in the corner opposite Ozzy, as far from him as the cage's confines allowed, she sat quietly as minutes ticked by, letting him grow accustomed to her presence. Then slowly, she spooned food into his dish and pushed it toward him. He pattered over, emptied the dish, and sat with head cocked, awaiting another serving. Belle scooped the rest of the can's contents into the bowl. He gobbled down every bite and licked the bowl clean, looking up once or twice with an expression Belle read as gratitude.

She wanted to reach out and stroke Ozzy's lustrous cinnamon fur, but she held back. Somehow she knew any attempt at physical contact might shatter the timid bond growing between them. She needed more time. Time to build trust with Ozzy and the other animals, time to gather information about Coogan's plans and pass it along to Lakshmi, Reba, and the others, and of course, time to build more of *Belle Jardin*. But as the tick-tick-tick in the back of her mind kept reminding her, time was exactly what she lacked.

She picked up the empty bowl, let herself out of the pen, and returned to the shed for the food and remedies she needed to complete her rounds. As she loaded a wheelbarrow with supplies, Coogan's gruff voice drifted through the open window and shed door.

"Yeah, I got that fox you said you wanted. It's a beauty—fur like you wouldn't believe."

Belle dropped the wheelbarrow handles and slipped beneath the windowsill.

"Well, sure it's young, but that just means it hasn't been around to get beat up. Let's talk some numbers here."

Leaden footsteps punctuated Coogan's words as he paced around his office. Belle pulled out the pocket-sized pad and pencil she'd started carrying to sketch ideas on the go. Instead of drawing, she scribbled down everything Coogan said.

"Listen, I don't give a shit what you do with it, as long as I get my money. You can skin it and make a fur toilet seat cover for all I care."

Belle's hand flew to her mouth to muffle a gasp. *Ozzy? A toilet seat cover? Not on my watch.*

More footsteps and a long pause, as Coogan seemed to be listening to the person on the other end of the line. Belle strained to hear what he'd say next. Would he seal the deal over the phone, or would he soften and hedge?

When Coogan spoke again, his voice came not from indoors but from right behind Belle.

"What the hell's going on here?" he bellowed.

Belle swiveled to find him looming over her, his chest heaving, his face florid as his hair and beard. She scrambled to her feet and stammered, "I dropped my um, my um, mmmmmy list. Yes, my list of um—you know, things. For the animals."

Coogan snatched the pad from her hand and held it close to his face. "Spying on me? You little sneak. I knew you were a mole. I *knew* it!" With his monstrous hands, he ripped the whole notepad into pieces, reducing Belle's notes and sketches to fluttering scraps.

"What else have you got there? You better not be recording on your phone." He lunged forward, reaching for her hands. She jumped aside, and he crashed into the cinder block wall. Cursing, he pushed away and reached a hand toward Belle again, but she was already skittering down the path toward the gate.

"That's right—get out!" Coogan yelled after her. "And stay out! If I ever see you snooping around here again, I'll have you arrested for trespassing."

When Belle came home in tears after fleeing the zoo, Ezra was watering Mitchell's flowers. He dropped the hose and hurried over to see what was wrong. As Belle recounted the morning's events, Ezra said appropriately soothing things, then shifted into action mode.

"All we have to do is figure out how much that fox is worth and offer Coogan more than the buyer he's got on the hook. Simple."

Simple? Except for the matter of where the money to make that offer would come from. Ezra didn't mention that detail, and Belle didn't ask. She knew she didn't have it, and no one she knew seemed to have extra cash. With the possible exception of Mae's rumored stash, but that was probably a rumor.

Belle fetched her laptop from inside, and she and Ezra huddled side by side on the stoop, engrossed in a Google search. Other times, such close proximity might make Belle uneasy, but now, united as they were in a mission, it seemed perfectly okay.

Ezra peered at the screen, furrows of concentration throwing his features even more out of alignment. "Says here red foxes can go for hundreds of dollars. Now, does that mean two hundred or nine hundred? Big difference, you know."

Wasn't that just like him to be a stickler for details? Moving closer, Belle read and reread the paragraph as if clarification might magically appear.

"You're sure you didn't hear him mention any numbers?" Ezra prodded.

"Oh god, Ezra, I don't know. I might've? I was so upset, and everything happened so fast. If only I still had that notepad instead of—" Belle fished around in her pocket and pulled out a handful of paper scraps she'd scooped off the ground when Coogan slammed into the wall.

She dropped the torn bits into Ezra's outstretched hand, and they both stared at the scrawls. Doodles swirled around snippets of cursive.

"Shorthand?" Ezra asked.

"I wish. I guess I was unconsciously drawing whenever Coogan wasn't talking. Some notetaker I am." She sprang off the step and paced back and forth on the driveway, holding her head with one hand and fingering the glass eyeball in her pocket with the other.

"Well now, wait." Ezra scrutinized the scraps as if divining oracle bones. "We must be patient. And sly. We are, after all, the Fox Liberation Front." He gave Belle a sideways look, one eyebrow arched.

With a weak smile, she rejoined him on the stoop. Once again, Belle found herself trying to piece together fragments to find answers.

Using his thumb and forefinger like tweezers, Ezra plucked one scrap from his palm and held it up. "Is this a figure eight?"

Belle leaned in and squinted. "Well . . . it could be. Or an infinity symbol. I draw those sometimes when I'm doodling."

Ezra turned the bit of paper this way and that. "Looks to me like an eight. So just for the sake of argument, let's say the buyer is offering eight hundred dollars. We'll offer nine. That's near the top of the price range, so even if we're guessing wrong, we'll probably have the high bid."

Belle pondered his logic, then nodded. "I gotta say, Ezra, you are a wonder. Is there anything you can't figure out?"

Ezra got that faraway look again, and his voice softened. "One or two things, yeah." Then his tone shifted back to businesslike. "Leave the negotiations to me. Coogan doesn't know me and won't have a clue I'm working with you. I should be able to clinch the sale before I go back to Nebraska. I've postponed my return a bit to help Uncle Mitchell with a couple more repairs. While I'm at it, we can build a pen for Ozzy in his backyard—that way you won't get in trouble with your landlady about another quote-unquote dog. Mitchell will be thrilled to have another critter for company, even if it's only temporary, and I'm sure you'll help him out with the care and feeding, right?"

"Of course." Now that she'd been unceremoniously relieved of her zoo duties, Belle certainly would have time to tend to one little fox, even as she devoted herself to *Belle Jardin* in its rapidly dwindling days.

"Now all we have to figure out is where to get $900."

Belle dropped her gaze to her hands and sat silently for a long moment. Then she lifted her eyes to Ezra's. "Leave that to me."

– 17 –
THE CELEBRATION

The shop wasn't what Belle had envisioned. The only other time she'd been to a pawn shop was with Grandpa Jake on a bargain-hunting expedition at a dusty, junky storefront where a sad stream of folks shambled in and out seeking cash for meager treasures. The modern brick building before her now was nothing like that. With its sturdy columns and shiny windows, it looked more like a branch library. She checked the bright yellow sign to make sure she was in the right place:

SUNFLOWER PAWN & JEWELRY

$$ MONEY TO LOAN $$

Though the shop looked inviting—not the least bit forbidding—Belle couldn't bring herself to open the car door. She sat, hands in lap, fixated on the ruby ring on her right hand.

A scene flashed across her mind's movie screen: her father placing the ring next to her mother's in the velvet box. Her chest felt trapped between boulders. She struggled for a deep breath, then opened the car door, slid out, and trudged slump-shouldered across the parking lot, one word playing over and over in her mind: *sellout.*

"Hello, there! How's it going today?" The young man behind the counter flashed a smile that perfectly matched his chipper voice, both at odds with Belle's frame of mind. "Are you browsing, or are you here to barter?"

Belle slipped the ring off her finger and handed it to Perky Boy. He held it up to the light and gave an approving nod.

"Sell or pawn?"

Belle stared through the glass-topped counter to the shelf below, where diamond solitaires, strings of pearls, hefty gold chains, turquoise-encrusted belt buckles, and vintage lockets were arrayed. For a moment, her thoughts drifted to Dinsmoor in his glass-topped coffin. A different kind of death was on display here. A death of dreams, of promises.

Or was the display a testament to life, to new beginnings bankrolled by this business? She pictured Ozzy's shining eyes and glossy coat.

I'm saving a life here, not ending anything—except Coogan's greedy scheme.

This was *ahimsa*: doing no harm. This was *seva*: an act of selfless service. She had to believe Grandpa Jake would approve. Hadn't he always told her to be kind to animals and help the helpless? She could almost hear his voice urging her on.

Go ahead, girl. Do whatcha gotta do.

"Sell or pawn?" the young man repeated.

"What's the difference?" Belle had watched that TV show a few times—the one with the three generations of Las Vegas pawnbrokers—but all she'd absorbed was that people never seemed to be offered as much as they thought their valuables were worth.

"If you pawn it, it's like a loan. I give you money and hold onto the ring until you pay me back and reclaim it. If you don't pay me back within ninety days, the ring is mine to keep and sell. If you sell me the ring outright, you give up ownership on the spot."

"Oh." She sort of knew that was how it worked, but hearing the process described in such clinical terms made her throat clench. This was a family heirloom they were discussing, not a hunk of scrap metal. How could she?

She picked up the ring from the countertop where the pawnbroker had laid it and gave it a longing look. The ruby glowed like a Christmas bulb, illuminating memories: long-ago holidays with her mom and dad, Grandpa Jake, cousin Amy, and other relatives gathered around a splendid tree. Heaps of wrapped packages hinting at untold delights inside. How she'd taken all that bounty for granted—not just the material goods, but the close connections, the lavish love.

"Pawn it, I guess," she said, her voice squeezing out in a croak. Ninety days. That would be around the end of September; she'd figure something out by then. She'd only be a temporary sellout.

"Based on the estimated value of this ring, I can offer you $500." The young man flashed another polished smile that seemed to say, *Isn't that fantastic??*

It wasn't fantastic.

"That's all?" Belle peered at the price tags on the jewelry in the case beneath the counter. "But what about—?"

The clerk followed her eyes. His tone suddenly crisp, he explained, "If you were to sell it, I might be able to offer more. But we still have to make something on it, you understand." He nodded to another customer who'd just come in and was eyeing a wall of guitars. "Be right with you. We're finishing up here."

He looked back at Belle with a *what'll-it-be?* expression. Then, gently: "Look, I can tell this ring means something to you. I'm sorry I can't offer you more, but if you need money, this is probably the easiest way to get it. It'll be safe here, trust me."

Trust me. Those two troublesome words again.

The pawnbroker extended a hand. Belle hesitated, then laid the ring back on the counter and shook on the deal. After counting out

$500 in fifties and twenties, the young man handed Belle the cash and a claim ticket.

"Don't lose that. You'll need it to reclaim the ring."

"I'll guard it with my life," Belle said. *I've lost enough already.*

All the way home, Belle drummed her fingers on the steering wheel, eager to show Ezra the cash and get on with their plan but still conflicted about how she'd come by it. She had barely pulled into her driveway when Ezra bounded out of Mitchell's house wearing cargo shorts, a short-sleeved safari shirt, and an Aussie slouch hat. Shaking her head and laughing, Belle crawled out of her car and met him on the lawn.

"You never cease to amaze me. Where on earth did you get that outfit?"

"Too much?" Ezra made a worried face that melted into mirth. "Just trying to look the part. I hit the resale shop while you were out—couldn't believe they had all this stuff, and in my size."

"What—or who—exactly, are you supposed to be? The Crocodile Hunter?"

"Hmmm, subconscious inspiration perhaps. But no . . ." He swept the hat off with a flourish and bowed. "I am Max Mitchell, simulated owner of the entirely fictitious Nebraska wildlife park, Where the Wild Things Are."

"Brilliant!" Belle pantomimed zealous applause.

Ezra clamped the hat back on his head and tilted it in a jaunty way that enhanced his facial asymmetry. "The Fox Liberation Front—code name FLUFF—is nothing if not clever. And what about you, Agent Izzy? Any luck acquiring funds?"

The lightness Ezra's antics had aroused in Belle turned heavy, and her smile flattened into a grimace. "Yes and no." From her purse, she extracted the stack of bills, careful not to pull the claim check out with it. "I got money. Just not enough."

Ezra took the cash from her outstretched hand, fanned the bills like a hand of cards, and looked them over. "So, how much—about five hundred?"

"You got it. Not exactly nine."

"That is true. But don't look so glum. We have $500 more than we had two days ago. And when it comes to making do with limited funds, I'm your man. I'm forever applying for library grants and coming up short. I'll figure something out. Trust me."

Belle wished people would stop saying that. But the funny thing was, when it came from Ezra, she sort of—*sort of*—did . . . you know, that thing he just said.

Two hours later, Ezra returned from his trip to Coogan's zoo. As he pulled into Mitchell's driveway, Belle looked away, half trusting he had Ozzy with him, half afraid to confirm he didn't. Then hope won out, and she snuck a glance.

Disentangling himself from the Jeep's front seat, Ezra emerged—empty handed—and Belle's hope sank like dregs in the bottom of her bucket. His face impassive, Ezra strode toward her, then veered to open the Jeep's cargo compartment and slid out a large carton with circular holes cut in its sides.

"Here you go, Miz Iz," he called out in a poor imitation of an Aussie accent. "A fox in a box."

Belle's mouth fell open. This guy! She'd never known anyone quite like him. Even Ben, with all his skills and competence, couldn't—or wouldn't—have pulled this off.

"Omigod," Belle said. "You did it. *How* did you do it?"

"Must've been the outfit. So convincing." Ezra set the box on the ground and opened the top flaps. Huddled in a corner, the fox looked up and seeing Belle, seemed to relax ever so slightly.

"Okay, I lied," Ezra said. "It wasn't the outfit. Turns out the so-called interested buyer disappeared and stopped returning Coogan's calls. I showed up at the right moment with cash in hand. Consequently, I was able to liberate Ozzy for a mere four hundred bucks, which leaves us a C-note for fox chow."

Belle crouched down to look Ozzy in the eye. "You're safe now, little one. Uncle Ezzy's going to build you a new home, and Auntie Izzy will visit you every day."

"Don't forget Uncle Mitchell," came a scratchy voice behind Ezra. Angling in for a better view, Mitchell bent to look at the fox. "Looks like you got yourself another funny-looking dog, Miss Belle. Let's get him over to my place before somebody—" he nodded in the direction of Mrs. Pruitt's house, "—calls your landlady."

Ezra and Mitchell scurried to set up a portable dog pen in Mitchell's backyard; Belle carried over the carton and released Ozzy into his temporary quarters. The fox explored the space, sniffing every inch, then settled into a corner and laid his head on his paws.

As Ezra gathered wooden posts, wire fencing, and tools to build a sturdier pen, Belle stood by, ready to pitch in. Then it dawned on her: They had nothing to feed their new tenant. She headed home to collect her keys and purse, but just as she opened the screen door, an unfamiliar car pulled into her driveway—one of those boxy models that look like a cross between an ice cream truck and a sneaker. DeShawn sat at the wheel, with Reba, Wallace, Mae, Jax, and Roscoe crammed inside. They all piled out, Reba and Mae bearing balloons, Jax carrying a cake with chartreuse frosting, and Roscoe lugging a large cardboard box imprinted with the name of a cat food brand.

"Word travels fast, and we thought this event called for a celebration," DeShawn said, brandishing a champagne bottle. "A pop-up homecoming party for the newly liberated creature, if you will. And a celebration of Belle's marvelous creation, *Belle Jardin*, no matter what Steve *Schwanz* thinks of it!"

Stupefied, Belle stared at the ebullient bunch. Then, coming to her senses, she opened her arms wide. "Welcome! I'll get plates and glasses." She started inside again but saw Wallace leaping toward Ozzy's pen and rushed to intercept him. "Reba, help me. Ozzy just got settled in—I don't think . . ."

"Relax," Reba said, tying a balloon to the chubby finger of one of Belle's concrete babies. "They know each other. Coogan got them from the same guy—a Hollywood animal wrangler named André Legrand. He's been selling off his animals 'cause there's not much demand for live critters in movies nowadays. Everything's computer-generated, you know? Plus, animal rights. Pressure on filmmakers to stop using live animals."

"Huh," Belle said. "That's good, though, right?"

"Sort of. But the sad thing is, sometimes the animals end up worse off. Legrand took better care of them than Coogan does, that's for sure."

Belle watched Reba tie another balloon on another baby's hand. Her eyes traveled over *Belle Jardin*: the babies, the walladog, Ben's bare feet, Mrs. Glick's googly glasses, the winged woman. She lingered at that figure, remembering Dinsmoor's winged women and their cryptic messages.

"If I can't go back to the zoo, I don't know how I'll ever slay the beast," Belle mused, unaware she was thinking aloud.

DeShawn, Roscoe, and Reba exchanged worried looks; Mae's hand shot to her mouth; Jax laid down the cake knife they'd brought, mid-slice.

Reba finished tying the balloon and rested a hand on Belle's shoulder. "What did you just say?"

"The message. From Dinsmoor's statues," Belle said, sounding dreamy. "The last thing they said to me was, 'Slay the beast, Belle. You have the power.' I think they meant Coogan. I mean, not actually *kill* him, but render him powerless, you know? He's kind of a monster."

Another round of concerned looks passed among the comrades, their festive mood dampened. Reba spoke slowly, as if calming a panicky child or talking a jumper down from a skyscraper ledge. "Okay now, Belle. Number one, we talked about those voices, remember? They're not coming from the statues. You're probably hearing someone's radio, and it's not actually talking to you. Maybe it sounds like it's saying your name, but it's probably saying something else that your ear interprets as your name."

DeShawn and Roscoe nodded, urging her on. Mae's eyebrows tilted into a quizzical furrow, but she said nothing.

"And number two, Coogan might seem like a villain, and sure, he's a bit of a hot reactor. But he's not a monster. You have to realize, the zoo was never his idea." Reba moved closer and reached for Belle's hand. "It was Audrey's."

"Audrey?"

"His wife."

"He's married?" Belle couldn't imagine that brute ever caring about anyone but himself.

"Was. She died about five years ago. Audrey was such a kind soul—an animal lover of the first degree. She collected all the animals and nurtured them like her own children—see, she and Coogan never had any kids. So Audrey took care of the animals, and Coogan ran the business end of the zoo, and it all worked fine until Audrey died. It was totally unexpected—some freak thing with that big artery that comes out of the heart—the whatchamacallit." She paused and looked up, as if the vessel's name hung from a catalpa tree branch.

"Aorta," Mae prompted. "Five-letter word: A-O-R-T-A."

"Right. So anyway," Reba continued, "Coogan pretty much fell apart—Audrey and the zoo had been his world. He kept the place open as a sort of memorial to Audrey, but he had no clue how to care for the animals. Then when the highway was rerouted, things got even harder. That's when he started dealing in exotic animals to make ends meet, but that meant he neglected the animals in the zoo even more. So yeah, he screwed up royally, and he acts like an ass, but you gotta understand—sometimes people act heartless when they're really heartbroken." Reba gave Belle a meaningful look.

Belle returned the look, letting Reba's words sink in.

Reba squeezed her hand. "Fight your own monster, Belle. I know you have one. I've seen it in your eyes since the moment we met."

All this time Belle thought she'd been keeping her secrets to herself, her wounds tightly bound. But Reba had intuited her deepest pain. Intuited, or deciphered the messages in Belle's body language, expressions, and demeanor. Leave it to an artist to pick up on those nonverbal cues. Who else had? Belle searched the faces around her: Reba, Mae, Jax, DeShawn, Roscoe, and now Ezra, who'd left his pen-building task to join the group, with Wallace bouncing behind him. All looked at her with a warmth and tenderness a more trusting soul might have interpreted as love.

DeShawn shook his microbraids and smiled. "On a lighter note . . ." Soft laughter rippled through the group, and everyone's shoulders slipped down. "Just make sure you don't do what the warrior queen Amanircnas of the ancient kingdom of Kush did when she slew her beast. That could land you in the pokey."

"Explanation, please," Jax said, returning to cake-cutting. "You and your obscure historical facts."

DeShawn cleared his throat. "Well, after Amanirenas slew the Emperor Augustus, she buried his head beneath the steps of a temple dedicated to victory."

"Ewwww," Belle said. Something awfully Dinsmoorish about that.

"Not his actual head," DeShawn continued. "A bronze likeness. Still, head-burying of any kind is probably frowned upon these days, and you've already gotten in enough trouble with the city. Yes, we've heard all about your little chat with *Schwanz*.

Belle flushed. "Thanks for reminding me of that mortifying encounter."

"Mortifying. Ten-letter word for humiliating," Mae interjected.

"Let's drink to mortification!" DeShawn said. "And to liberation. And to Belle's utterly unacceptable 'atrocity.'" He popped the champagne cork, and fizz erupted from the bottle's neck and flowed down the sides. "Three cheers for the Fox Liberation Front! Three more for *Belle Jardin*!"

"*Now*, I'll get those plates and glasses," Belle said and headed into the house, with Ezra—always the helper—close behind.

"I can carry the plates," he offered. Of course he could. And contrary to the impulse she would've had mere weeks earlier, she wouldn't resist.

"What are we going to do without you, Ezzy?" Once again, Belle was surprised to hear herself speaking her thoughts and still more surprised to be having them. "I mean, you've been so helpful to Mitchell—and me." Entering the kitchen, she opened a cabinet and stacked mismatched plates on Ezra's outstretched hands.

"You'll manage fine, Izzy," he said. "You don't need anyone's help."

"Hmmm," Belle said. She stopped what she was doing, shot him a quick look, hiccupped, then returned to her task. "I thought I had more of these, but I must've smashed them. Guess we'll have to share."

"Sharing is caring," Ezra said, backing out the screen door and winking the eye that was already smaller than the other. "I'll get forks from Mitchell's." As Ezra set about his tasks, Belle lingered in the kitchen a few minutes more, wondering just how she—Isabelle Marsden, so dedicated to detachment—ended up with a yard full of zanies whose company she actually welcomed.

Once forks, plates, and glasses were assembled, the crew consumed every crumb of cake and swigged gallons of champagne, with

DeShawn returning to the car to retrieve bottle after bottle from a cooler. Belle found herself giggling and weaving as she traipsed back and forth between her yard and Ozzy's pen with Wallace in her wake, delivering cat food, water, and reassuring words to the fox.

About an hour into the festivities, she noticed Mae sitting alone on the stoop, a tattered piece of newspaper pressed against her knee. Belle wobbled over. "Mind if I join you? All that sugar and champagne got me woooozy, and I think I'd better—whoops!" She toppled onto the stoop. Mae scooched over to make room.

The arch-shaped trellis between Mitchell's yard and hers swirled like a carnival ride. The catalpa tree pulsated. "Whoa!" Belle pressed a hand to her forehead and looked down to steady herself. Catching sight of the scrap on Mae's lap, she leaned in for a closer look. Mae covered the paper with both hands.

"It's another crossword, isn't it? How's it going?"

Mae spread her fingers, revealing bits and pieces of the puzzle—some squares filled with peacock blue letters, others blank. "Not so well, I'm afraid," she said. "I got pretty far this morning, but now I'm stuck on fourteen across—a ten-letter word for hodgepodge. Starts with S, blank blank, M . . ."

"Salmagundi?" Belle blurted without hesitation, then hiccupped twice.

Mae counted on her fingers. "Ten letters, all right. You've done it again. How can I . . ."

"Please," Belle said, "not that recip . . . recip . . . recip-ro-cation thing again. But if you really want to do something for me—" she tilted sideways and struggled to right herself, "—see if Reba and Roscoe can help me into the house. I gotta lie down."

– 18 –
BALANCE

Her head still pounding, Belle opened one eye and squeezed it shut again at the sight of sunlight streaming through slits in her bedroom blinds.

She groaned. Could it really be time to get up? Did she have to?

No parade to prepare for, no meetings with city officials, no zoo duty. She curled into a ball.

Wait! Zoo duty! She sat bolt upright. *Ozzy! Omigod, I've missed his morning feeding. My first day as caretaker and I've already blown it.*

She clambered out of bed and stumbled into the kitchen, where she found cans of cat food stacked in a pyramid on the counter. She opened a can and ran barefoot next door without bothering to change out of her nightclothes. Ezra, already at work on the new pen, held up his hand.

"Already done, Miz Iz," he said. "When you conked out last night, we figured you might not be up so bright and early this morning. So we unpacked the case of cat food, and I brought some over here for emergency backup."

"Of course you did. I should've known Ezra the Good Samaritan would have it covered." She smiled to make sure he knew she wasn't being snide. "Ezra, I'm sorry."

"For what? Showing up late for feeding time? Not a problem."

Belle hung her head. "Not just that. For drinking too much and checking out last night. That party wasn't just a celebration of Ozzy's release and *Belle Jardin*'s creation, you know. It should've been a celebration of all you've done in the short time you've been here. A toast to Ezzy."

Ezra laid down his staple gun. "Toast. Sound good? Bet you haven't eaten yet, and toast is probably the only thing you can manage right now. And guess what—you're in luck! Toast is one of the few foods I know how to make. Give me a minute and I'll serve you breakfast al fresco."

The screen door closed with a whoosh from the pneumatic closer Ezra had installed. Belle sank onto Mitchell's back step and regarded the half-finished pen. How could Ezra be so consistently good-natured, so generous with his time, talents, and gentle humor? Had he experienced no trauma, no betrayals, no disappointments? Or had he simply found ways to steam steadily through them? She had no idea, and that realization, coupled with her failure to pay tribute to him the night before, weighed on her.

Ezra returned carrying a tray laden with coffee mugs, a teetering stack of buttered toast, a jar of strawberry jam, a bear-shaped squeeze bottle of honey, and two tin plates. He set the tray on the porch and pulled two cloth napkins from his back pocket.

With a flip of his wrist, he fluttered one napkin like a flag, laid it on Belle's lap, and handed her a mug of coffee. She took a sip.

"I needed this."

"I know."

"I know you know." She set down the mug and reached for a slice of toast. Squeezing honey onto the crannied surface, she let its sweetness sink in before taking a bite. "How do you keep your balance, Ezra?"

Ezra, slathering jam on his toast, laughed. "Balance? You're joking, right? Haven't you noticed what a klutz I am? Just this morning I tripped over a four-by-four and went sprawling. I was hoping you weren't looking out the window to witness that graceful display. And carrying that tray out just now? I nearly dumped the whole thing on your head. So balance? You're asking the wrong guy."

"Not that kind of balance," Belle said. "I mean like when bad stuff happens. Bad stuff happens to everyone at some point, right?" That question was way less personal than the ones she really wanted to ask, but it was all she was capable of at the moment.

Ezra chewed a mouthful of toast, his face skewing every which way. He swallowed but didn't answer right away. "It's all about grounding," he finally said. "And that's different for everyone. Me, I meditate every morning—ideally before Mitchell turns on that blasted TV. Other people, like your artistic friends, they probably get grounded through their creative work. You, too, right?"

"Ideally," Belle said. "I guess I'm still trying to find out."

"All the more reason to get you up to speed again this morning," Ezra said. "More coffee?"

More coffee, a shower, and Belle was back in creator mode. Before mixing another batch of concrete, she stood back and looked over *Belle Jardin*. She held the glass eyeball skyward to let sunlight shine through, awestruck at the whole scene. The assemblage had expanded beyond its previous bathtub- and mattress-sized boundaries and now sprawled across half her front yard. Hardly the size of Dinsmoor's square-block domain, but Belle's garden easily occupied the area of two minivans parked side by side and covered the path that once led from driveway to front door, making the side door the only way in and out of the house. She'd never meant for her creation to take over so much space—physically, mentally, or emotionally. Yet she couldn't resist the urge to keep picking at her wounds, opening her heart—if only to herself—and smoothing the jagged edges of her life into something whole. Something *acceptable*—if only to herself.

– 19 –
THE INTERCESSION

For the next two days, the sky scowled and streamed torrents. Downpours gave way to drizzles, which yielded to still more deluges. Belle sat on her futon, alternately sketching and fretting. She would've lost track of time altogether if her phone hadn't kept reminding her the demolition deadline was only a few days away.

So much more work remained to be done—or so it seemed to her. How could she ever heal if she couldn't finish piecing everything together? The urgency to keep working and the frustration of being at a standstill verged on physical pain.

She called Miranda for solace. Despite the changes in their relationship brought about by Belle's move and Miranda's engagement, Miranda still knew Belle better than anyone and always had level-headed advice.

"There are other ways to heal, you know," Miranda told her.

"Yes, but . . ." Clearly, Miranda didn't understand. She hadn't seen *Belle Jardin*, couldn't know its curative power, its enchantment. "OK, thanks. I'll give that some thought," Belle said and hung up.

She paced, fretted some more, stared out at the sodden yard, puddles collecting around the winged women and babies, like a reflecting pool surrounding sculptures. A reflecting pool! She could see it now, doubling every image she'd created. But no chance of that.

The whole thing would be demolished before she'd have time to craft anything so grandiose.

More anguished hours passed. Belle couldn't stop sketching the figures and flourishes she'd be sculpting—very likely her last additions to *Belle Jardin* before its demise—if only the weather would cooperate.

For two solid days, the weather refused. Nothing but rain, rain, rain, and gloom, gloom, gloom, brightened only by friends' gestures of kindness. Reba and Wallace hitched a ride in Roscoe's truck to deliver a crossword puzzle book from Mae; Ezra braved the storm to bring books, pizza, and beer and assure her Ozzy was safely sheltered and well-fed; Miranda checked in more than usual, just to lighten Belle's dreary mood with idle chitchat.

Finally, Monday morning, a single shaft of sunlight pierced the gray. Belle would've taken it as a good omen if she hadn't been so aware of the looming deadline. Schwann would be back from vacation today. Demolition was set for Thursday.

Was adding to *Belle Jardin* pointless now? Maybe. But doing nothing felt even more futile. Belle did the only thing she knew how to do: put on her work clothes, walk around the yard to survey the weather's impact (minimal, *thank goodness*!), gather her supplies, and get to work.

Just as before, she soon was so engrossed she wasn't aware of time passing—or anything else. Her absorption was so absolute, she hardly noticed the city truck when it pulled up in front of her house. Not until a door slammed and a worker called her name did she look up with a start.

What now? They can't be starting the demolition already. Not for another three days.

Belle jumped to her feet and stood, arms outstretched, in front of *Belle Jardin*.

"*No!*" she shouted. "Not yet!"

Just then another truck pulled up behind the first one. Inside the cab, Roscoe, Reba, and Mae grinned like chimpanzees.

What the hell is wrong with you people? Can't you see I'm in the midst of a crisis here?

Her friends piled out of the truck just as the city worker walked toward Belle, palms out in a "calm down" gesture.

"Hold on, now, Ms. Marsden," he said. "We're not here to tear anything down." He handed her a sheet of paper and began rolling up the yellow tape that still encircled *Belle Jardin.*

Reba, Mae, and Roscoe crowded in to read over her shoulder. Wallace jumped up and down to see what they all found so interesting.

To: Isabelle Marsden
From: Steven Schwann, Director, City of Lawrence Zoning Department

This is to notify you that, yielding to pleas from members of the city's artistic community, demolition of the structure at your residence has been postponed until after Labor Day, Monday, September 3. If by that time you have demonstrated to the community at large the artistic merit of your "project," demolition will be called off altogether. If you have not, demolition will proceed.

"Members of the artistic community?" Belle searched the faces around her.

Reba and Roscoe pointed at Mae. Mae hung her head, a sheepish smile playing at the corners of her mouth.

"Mae has known Steve Schwann since he was a kid," Reba said. "They've sung in the choir together forever. When I heard about your trouble at the zoning department, I told Mae. Consequently, she and

DeShawn—he's in the choir, too, you know—were waiting in Steve Schwann's office the minute he got back from vacation. Somehow they convinced him to give you more time."

Slack-jawed, Belle took Mae's hands in hers. "How can I ever thank you?"

Mae snapped her head up and shook it so hard bobby pins went flying.

"No, no! This is *me* thanking *you*, Belle. For the crosswords and the ride home from the park." With her index fingers held horizontal and parallel, she formed an equal sign. "Now we're even."

Belle watched Roscoe's truck pull away, Reba and Mae waving like keyed-up kids, Wallace pressing his nose against the passenger-side window. She waved back, then settled herself onto the stoop and let the latest developments sink in. She still faced a deadline of sorts, but now it was more than two months away. The drive to heal wounds and reassemble her life remained, but with anxiety lifted—at least temporarily—that urge was coupled with a new kind of creativity: freedom to explore, to be (did she dare?) playful.

Fresh sparks of spirit zinged Belle into action. She collected every bit of blue and blue-green she could find—chips of cerulean and celadon china, turquoise baubles, swirly aqua marbles—and piled them beside *Belle Jardin*. Caught up in the moment, she dashed into the kitchen, threw open the glass-fronted cupboard, and reached for the blue china cup—the one that belonged to the yard-sale woman's mother. The one she liked to imagine her own mother had given her.

No! Not that. With a whisper of a gasp, she drew her hand back. Though the connection to her mother was only imaginary, that cup was too sacred to sacrifice.

Returning to her worksite, Belle began to sculpt: a broad,

beaming face, crowned with pinned-up braids tucked beneath a tiara. All decorated with every last bit of blue miscellany.

When she finished and stepped back to look over her creation, there was no doubt about it. The crowned head reigning over *Belle Jardin* was none other than Queen Aquamaureen.

– 20 –
THE MESSAGES

That Joni Mitchell song kept running through Belle's mind as she drove to Lucas the next day—the one about getting back to the garden. Yes, she knew it was about Woodstock, but certain words and phrases jumped out in a way that made her think Joni intended its message just for her. The part about trying to get her soul free. And that line about being caught in the devil's bargain. Belle pictured the demon looming over Adam and Eve in Dinsmoor's garden. Its face morphed into Jamison's.

By the time she reached Lucas, Belle knew where she would direct her attention on this visit. She bypassed the crypt, skipped the usual check-in with Polly, and headed straight into the garden. It wasn't the winged women that called to her today. It wasn't the babies. It was the figures that comprised most of the park's population: the men.

Her impression from previous visits was that they were a violent bunch. Yet now she saw at least a few involved in peaceful pursuits. That fellow holding a hoe, for instance, and the one beside him keeping watch over a ram. How pastoral.

Oh, but then Belle remembered reading about those two figures in Dinsmoor's *Pictorial History of the Cabin Home* booklet. They represented Cain and Abel, and as anyone who hadn't slept through Sunday school would know, that story is as brutal as they come.

All around the garden, other figures glared and squinted from the branches of concrete trees. Here a soldier sighting down a rifle, there a guy brandishing a knife and another swinging a sword. A Native American in feathered headdress shooting an arrow from a bow. Even a few women were engaged in savagery, like the one poised to stab the rifleman.

It was all terribly unsettling. Belle had come here seeking solace and guidance, but now she felt as if she'd been jabbed in the chest with one of those weapons. She circled the grounds in one direction, then pivoted and circled the opposite way. That's when another set of figures caught her eye. She'd seen them before but paid them little mind; now the statues pointing into the distance intrigued her. A naked woman, a bare-chested man wearing short pants and a floppy hat, a sarong-clad man with African-looking features—all seemed to see something important enough to encourage others to look. What could it be? Their expressions—neither fearful nor eager—offered no clues. If only they would speak.

Belle was sure they would if she waited long enough. She found a shady spot beneath a cedar tree and sat on the ground, listening. The patch of shade protected her from the blaze beating down from a cloudless sky, but it did nothing to fend off the humidity. Coupled with the crush of discomfort the barbarous statuary had aroused in her, the heavy air left her gasping for breath.

The longer she sat, the easier breathing became. *Grounding, Belle.* Ezra's words echoed. *Your artistic friends get grounded through their creative work.* He was onto something there. Belle pulled out her sketch pad and pencil, stared into the blank blue beyond the cedar's branches—and found herself unable to draw a single line. Reaching again into her tote bag—public-radio swag from her former life—she brought out a Thermos and a snack bag. She popped a handful of raisins into her mouth and chewed. The dried fruit clung to her teeth and glommed in a sticky lump at the back of her tongue. A gulp of cold tea from the Thermos sent the glob on its way and ignited . . . a tiny spark of inspiration. Picking up the pencil, Belle doodled abstract shapes and intricate patterns that took off in all directions across the page. A whisper overhead interrupted her scrawlings. She inclined her head to listen. The message at last?

No. It was only starlings rustling the cedar branches.

All right, so nobody's talking. But I know you're still trying to tell me something.

A memory floated in: a troupe of mimes Belle once saw performing at Navy Pier. She marveled at how they told whole stories without speaking a word, communicating through facial expressions, gestures, and dance-like movements.

Could her mute companions be miming a message to her? Belle pulled herself up from the ground and followed the walkway to stand beneath each pointing statue in turn. The naked woman pointed one way, the hatted man the opposite, the African man still a different direction.

Belle got the message: It was up to her to find her own way.

No music ran through Belle's mind on the drive back to Lawrence. No Joni Mitchell, no sunshiny songs, no Happy Tunes playlist. Not even a jazzy Brubeck riff from that Chicago station she used to listen to. There simply wasn't room in her overstuffed brain for any more than she'd just absorbed in Dinsmoor's garden. All those aggressive stances and expressions on the shooters and stabbers. And the three placid pointers, each with its own notion of which way to go.

She was so fixated on the imagery and the road right in front of her, she failed to notice the darkening sky and huddling clouds. When the wind jerked her car sideways, she looked around, startled, as if she'd been airlifted into a different world.

The dark clouds now bore down like sinister locomotives. Trees whipped back and forth with no more resistance than paper cutouts. Belle scanned the horizon and checked her rearview mirrors for funnel clouds. What was it she was supposed to do if she spotted one? Ezra had drilled her on tornado safety, but now it was all a blur.

Pull over? Try to outrun it?

Get off the road. She was pretty sure that's what Ezra had said. Then what? Stay in the car or lie in a ditch?

Oh god, oh god, oh god, why can't I remember?

She gripped the wheel and reminded herself she hadn't actually seen a tornado, only ominous clouds. *Steady, Belle. Just keep driving.*

Just keep driving. The way her mother had when they'd run into a storm on the way home from a shopping trip in the city. Belle was ten and terrified. Her mother: the picture of stability, her only outward sign of distress a barely perceptible tightening of her grasp on the wheel. Eyes on the road, hands at ten and two, Dana Marsden hummed along with the radio. Was she really that calm or only acting brave for Belle's benefit?

Just as it had that day on the road with her mother, rain curtained from the clouds, and the highway disappeared. Torrents swept sideways, changed direction and swept the other way. Thunder crashed; lightning splintered clouds, lighting them up with an otherworldly glow. Fleeting nebulae in a perilous galaxy.

Belle clenched the wheel and drove on. She pictured Dorothy Gale whirling in her farmhouse higher and higher, over the rainbow, into the Land of Oz. The house landing on the Wicked Witch of the East. Bam! Dead!

If only it were that simple to do away with every monster. Belle imagined her car, the little Chevy Spark, lifting off the road, twirling and somersaulting through the air, first propelled by a cyclone, then flying on its own power, high above the clouds. And then barreling down like a space capsule, smashing through a high-rise window, and landing smack on top of Jamison as he swiveled in his Herman

Miller Aeron chair to see what all the racket was about. Bam! Dead! Gone for good. Not even a pair of ruby slippers—or oxblood loafers—left behind.

But that was only how things happened in made-up stories. In real life, demons lived on and on. Even when you escaped, they trailed you, hovered like storm clouds over even the sunniest day.

As Belle drove on through the tempest, all the messages she had received in her dreams and on her visits to Lucas swirled around her and coalesced, fragments piecing themselves together like shards of china in *Belle Jardin.*

You will find it. Or it will find you.

Listen.

Slay the beast, Belle. You have the power.

Even Miranda's urging to *color outside the lines* and Ezra's comment that *maybe this* is *the useful thing* fit into the mosaic of messages, and their meaning became clear.

The monster she had to conquer was Jamison, of course. She'd known it all along, even as she tried to push away every thought of him. And by *listen*ing to and studying Dinsmoor's mad magnum opus, she'd been led to create her own, *Belle Jardin. She had found it. Or it had found her.* She had stepped *outside the lines* of her orderly life to enter the delirium of artistic expression. And that was the *useful thing* that would help her fix her remaining broken pieces. But first she had to get home.

Hours later—though it seemed like days—Belle sank into fathomless sleep in her stone cottage, drained from the turbulent drive. A tornado could have ripped off the roof and scooped her into the sky and she wouldn't have awakened. For most of the night, her dreams were murky, plotless conglomerations. Near dawn, a storyline emerged. Once again, she found herself standing high above the ground, looking out on treetops, her feet rooted to her perch, her sturdy body stuck in one place. A female figure in Dinsmoor's creation.

She scanned the branches of the concrete garden. All around her, other statues stood firm in their appointed spots. Except for one. A male figure in a three-piece suit reached down and lifted his feet, one at a time, as if pulling them out of muck. Arms extended, he tightrope-walked across the intertwined branches, edging closer and closer to Belle's roost. She recognized the angle of his jaw. This was no jaywalking lookalike; it was Jamison, her monster, and he was coming straight for her.

Pressing her lips together, she strained every muscle, trying to free herself. Her stony brain sent signals to her feet. *Pick up, pick up.* They felt like concrete. They *were* concrete. She was cemented in place with no escape. She knew that feeling.

Jamison reached her branch and sidled toward her. He pressed himself against her, and though her body was rock-solid, her skin puckered in revulsion.

She reached behind her back, groping for the knife the woman on the next branch held. It was just beyond her grasp.

Jamison wrapped her in a crush more straitjacket than embrace.

With a mighty heave and a guttural jungle sound, Belle shoved him off the branch. Did he land with a terrific crash? Did he liquefy into a puddle like the Wicked Witch of the West? Belle couldn't say for sure. She woke herself with her cry.

Awake but still cobwebbed in strands of remembered dream, she rolled onto her side, the air bed soughing beneath her. A trickle ran from the corner of her eye into her ear. Another. And then she was sobbing, wailing, pounding the bouncy mattress. Emotions she had sealed away spilled out and flowed into a wave of relief. As her tears crusted into salty tracks and the cobwebs spooled back into her dream world, Belle realized the dream was only the first step. She had more work to do to banish Jamison from her waking life.

- 21 -
THE EFFIGY

Ezra was nowhere to be seen when Belle made her morning feeding visit to Ozzy.

"Where's your pal today, Oz?" The fox offered only an uninformative blink. "Oh well, it's just as well he's not around. No time for chitchat today." She spooned cat food into Ozzy's bowl and set it in front of him. He sniffed the food and set to devouring it.

"Voracious little creature, aren't you?"

Ozzy cut his eyes toward Belle but kept eating.

Belle picked up the empty cat food can and slipped out of the pen—the spacious new one Ezra had whipped together in no time. "Like I said, I can't dawdle here this morning—I'm starting a big project—but I'll be back later, okay?"

The fox lifted his head and blinked again, which Belle took to mean, "Whatever."

She strode across the patch of lawn between the pen and Mitchell's garage. Leaving the side door open to admit a shaft of light, she poked around all the recesses, assembling more than her usual supplies. Broken flowerpots, rusty hand tools, and dusty coils of rope thunked into the wheelbarrow.

Instead of wheeling everything to her front yard, she dumped it all in a heap on her back lawn. Returning to her neighbor's garage, passing his petunias, his marigolds, his zinnias on the way, she shoved aside paint cans and plumbing supplies, clearing a path to the mannequin that stood like a castoff Chippendale in a far corner. She wrestled it into a kind of dry-land cross-chest carry, calling on skills dimly remembered from Girl Scouts. The irony—using a life-saving technique to ultimately slay a monster—was not lost on her.

As she mixed her first batch of concrete, memories intruded—memories she usually blotted out but now needed to fuel her fury.

The first flashback was the most innocuous, or so it seemed at the time. Marcus Jamison, her new boss, had invited her to a get-acquainted lunch—just the two of them at Joe's Seafood, Prime Steak & Stone Crab, a Chicago legend. After tuxedoed waiters delivered menus and filled water glasses, Jamison glanced at the list of selections and said, "We'll both have the stone crab." Belle was thinking more along the lines of the chopped salad or ahi tuna burger, but she didn't want to get off to a bad start by objecting to her boss's choice.

"Sure. Fine," she said.

"And leave room for the key lime pie."

Was that a wink? Or just a smile that squinched one eye shut? Most definitely a wink. But okay, older men did that sometimes. Uncle Gary, for one, and Grandpa Jake. Just a friendly, conspiratorial twinkle. Okay.

Belle smiled and unconsciously clutched the top buttons of her blouse. She tried to think of something to say, something light, yet professional. Conversations never had been awkward with her former boss. From the time Belle was hired at Magnus, Lucy Bailey had taken her under her wing, praised her initiative and ideas, and encouraged her to stretch her abilities. Lucy was a mentor, yes, but Belle—having lost her mother not long before—also saw Lucy as a surrogate parent.

"So, Isabelle, tell me about yourself," Jamison said.

Belle sat up straight and summoned her TED talk voice. "Event planning is more than a job to me, Mr. Jamison. I really feel like it's a calling. I'm a detail-oriented person, and I love the variety of opportunities working for a hotel chain provides."

Jamison laughed. "This isn't a job interview, Isabelle. I've read your stellar performance reviews. What about your life outside of work? Family? Boyfriend?"

A flush spread up Belle's neck and crept onto her face. She studied the knot-shaped roll on her bread plate and weighed her words.

"No boyfriend at the moment. No siblings. Just me." She looked up, and Jamison's sympathetic expression prompted her to spill out more than she meant to—the whole litany of her losses. She told him how bereft her mother's death had left her. How her father's remarriage and move to Phoenix and her breakup with Ben had made her feel even more alone.

"I can see how you'd feel that way," Jamison said when she'd finished. He leaned across the bread basket and inclined his head in a way that conveyed concern. "You have every right to. I'm just glad you've found a home—perhaps a sort of family—here at Magnus. It seems to be a perfect fit for you."

Belle's tension drained away. *He gets me. Just like Lucy did.*

A waiter arrived bearing heaping platters of crab claws, and the complications of cracking claws, squeezing lemon wedges, dipping the succulent flesh into mustard sauce, and eating in a relatively civilized manner took precedence over intimate conversation.

It was after that lunch that Jamison, like his predecessor, seemed to take a special interest in Belle, asking her opinion on decisions and dropping hints about promoting her to assistant events manager, exactly the move she felt ready to make. So when he asked her to put in extra hours helping him organize a gala for the Chicago Botanic Garden, she couldn't refuse.

The thought of what came next stuck somewhere in her subconscious and refused to move.

No. Not going there. Not yet.

Belle shut out those disturbing thoughts and returned to the task at hand. She finished stirring the bucket of concrete and laid the mannequin face-up on the ground in the shade of an overgrown lilac bush. Then she sifted through her collection of colorful broken crockery and pushed it all aside.

Nope. No color on this one. No decorations. This one is for the unembellished truth.

She slapped a trowel full of concrete on the mannequin and smoothed it over the figure's skin, starting at the shoulders and working her way down. She covered the arms, then the hands, sealing away their touch.

Never again.

She encased the torso, and as she worked, she allowed slivers of memory to intrude through slits in her consciousness. In her mind, she returned to Magnus, to that first night.

The hour was late—it had been dark outside for hours—and she was tired. But she wouldn't let Jamison see that. Not when the promotion seemed within reach. When he asked her to work late on the gala project, she canceled plans with Miranda for cocktails at that chichi restaurant atop the Hancock building and stayed at her desk pulling together the information Jamison had requested.

She checked and double-checked every detail, printed out pages, assembled them into a presentation folder, and walked the packet down the hall to Jamison's office. Normally she would've emailed him the documents, but he'd said he wanted to go over the plans with her point by point, so the hard copy seemed in order.

Jamison sat at his desk, fiddling with the keyboard and mouse. The printer fired up.

"Oh, Belle, could you grab that for me?"

She crossed the room and stood at the printer, waiting for it to stop spitting out pages. All of a sudden she felt something behind her. In a split second she realized it wasn't some*thing*, it was Jamison.

Thinking he'd come to retrieve the printout himself, she tried to move out of the way, but he grabbed her shoulders and pressed himself against her. The cedary scent of his cologne overpowered her.

His mouth close to her ear, he whispered, "You could go places in this company, you know. New York, San Francisco, London. Wherever you want." Then his hands were moving all over her, around her breasts and hips, under her skirt. She squirmed, but he didn't let up.

"I could make that happen for you." He was breathing harder. "If you make things happen for me." He laughed, but it wasn't a laugh of amusement. "You know what I'm talking about."

Oh god, not this. Is this how it always is when you're a woman and your mentor is a man?

She wriggled out of his grasp, tugged her skirt down, maneuvered herself away from the loveseat he was guiding her toward.

"Mr. Jamison, I don't think . . ."

Her boss's voice took on an edge like sharpened steel. "Suit yourself, Ms. Marsden. You struck me as the kind of young woman who wanted to move forward, but obviously that was a misconception. You may go now. I'll let you know if I have any questions on the event plan."

Ugliness seeped through Belle as she slunk back to her cubicle. *Did I make that happen? Did I send the wrong signals?* No, she assured herself, she hadn't done anything wrong. And saying no to Jamison had been the right thing to do, no matter what it cost her. She'd just try to forget the incident, and maybe Jamison would too.

But that night was only the prelude to what was to come. Time and time again, Jamison made excuses for her to stay after hours to help with a project. Over and over, he trapped her in uncomfortable situations. She always managed to extricate herself, though each time with less conviction. Not that Jamison's advances outraged and offended her any less. They just no longer shocked her. Fending him off became almost routine, just another part of her job, like filing. And like those tedious chores, it wore her down.

Jamison passed her over for the promotion, and every other advancement he dangled in front of her seemed to evaporate just when he assured Belle she was next in line.

Belle was no fool. It didn't take her long to realize Jamison wasn't the least bit interested in her as a person or even as a member of the Magnus team. He only wanted to use her for his own gratification, perhaps made more perversely pleasurable by her resistance. Miranda knew it too, when Belle finally admitted why she canceled so many girlfriend dates to work late. She pleaded with Belle to quit her job and report the ongoing harassment. "Call your old boss Lucy and ask her what to do," she urged. "Call a lawyer. I'll help you find one."

Belle knew Miranda was right, yet the longer it went on, the more she felt paralyzed. The more she wondered if giving in was the only way she would ever advance in the company. As much as she hated the situation she was ensnared in, as much as she loathed Jamison—and herself for weakening—she still loved her work. It was no exaggeration when she'd told Jamison event planning was her calling. The idea of moving up in the hotel chain, overseeing events in some other exciting city, thrilled her as nothing else ever had. If she stood even the slightest chance, she didn't want to sabotage it.

Still, she had her principles, so she continued resisting with what strength remained. Until one night when Jamison kept her even later than usual. When the groping and mauling began, Belle wriggled away and made for the door. But this time it was locked. Before she knew what was happening, Jamison wrenched her grip from the doorknob and, summoning strength beyond anything he'd ever shown, forced her onto the loveseat, ripped her clothes, and . . . *raped her.*

And then treated the whole thing like a joke. "So, you finally got what you wanted, didn't you, after playing hard to get for so long," he said, laughing.

Belle went home that night and never returned to work. She turned her back on everything she'd worked so hard for—just walked away from it all.

No police report, no lawyer call, nothing to force her to relive any of the experience.

Now, the memory flared as she slapped another trowel of concrete onto the mannequin, perhaps more forcefully than necessary.

"Wow, are you sculpting or slaughtering that thing?"

Belle turned to see a pair of long legs she recognized as Ezra's.

"A little of both, I guess," she said.

Ezra crouched beside the figure, taking in the coarse concrete sheath around the upper body.

"I've never seen you attack your work so aggressively," he mused aloud. "And this shroud here—it strikes me as a kind of symbolic entombment." He thought for a moment. "Would this have anything to do with that Me Too incident you mentioned?"

Belle had hoped Ezra wouldn't remember the slip-up she'd made over pizza and beer at her kitchen table. She'd never meant to reveal anything so personal, and even though she hadn't gone into detail, she felt she'd said too much that night. She wasn't about to divulge any more now, especially after just reliving in her mind what happened when she let down her guard and confided in Jamison.

"It might," she finally said.

"Enough said." Ezra leaned back and stretched out one leg, then the other. "I didn't come over here to dredge up ugly memories. Whatever it is you're doing, I'm sure you're doing it for a reason, even if it looks—if I may say so—mighty strange. I'm not sure it's going to help your cause with the zoning department. And not to alarm you, but you should know snarky comments about your artistry have been cropping up on Nextdoor Lawrence—I check it every so often for Uncle Mitchell."

Belle laid down the trowel and shot an appreciative smile Ezra's way. "Thank you, sir. I will take that under advisement." If anyone else had intruded on the work she was so intent upon—and then dropped another stress bomb—she would've felt resentful. Yet resentment was the last thing she felt when Ezra was around, and his presence never felt like an intrusion. "So what's up? I fed Ozzy this morning, so I know you didn't come over here to scold me for dereliction of fox-mama duty."

"Nope. You done good. Our little friend is sleeping off his breakfast right now, contented as a Carnation cow. I'm actually here to say goodbye—for now, at least. I'm heading up to Nebraska right after lunch."

As if on cue, Mitchell's screen door banged, and the older man shuffled out with a pair of suitcases that he stowed in the cargo compartment of Ezra's Jeep.

A pang of something Belle couldn't—or wouldn't—name hit her right in the solar plexus, like the time she had the wind knocked out of her in a volleyball game.

"Today? But it's only Thursday. I thought you weren't leaving until the weekend."

"I've pretty much wrapped up my work at Mitchell's for now, and things have come up back home, so . . ."

So Nebraska was still "home" to him. The thought triggered a twinge of melancholy in Belle. Where was *her* home? The house she grew up in belonged to another family now; her father's house, the adobe-style condo she visited at holidays, was his and Shelley's home, not Belle's; her Chicago apartment had been little more than a crash pad. She guessed this was it—this stone cottage with its long-lived-in smells and strange yard art—this was where her heart was, so that must make it her home.

"Okay, then. I guess I'll see you—sometime."

"Right." Ezra raised onto one knee and pushed against the ground to stand. He looked down at Belle. "I'll keep you posted on my plans."

"Make sure."

"Yep." He gave an over-the-shoulder wave much like Mitchell's and crossed the lawn to his uncle's back door.

Belle watched him walk away, then turned her attention back to the mannequin and stirred the concrete slurry with renewed vigor.

Whump! She slammed another load of sludge onto the figure and spread it down from the torso. As she neared the pelvis, she let out a rueful laugh. Not being anatomically correct, the dummy had no genitalia, only a smooth expanse between its legs. *If only* . . . Still, Belle felt the need to seal off that part of the body, symbolically neutering Jamison and every sexual predator like him. She covered the whole area with concrete, leaving it rough instead of smoothing it out. Leaving it untouched.

The broken flowerpots caught her eye. She'd planned to leave the figure unadorned, but the pots' jagged edges gave her an idea. She picked up a hammer and smashed the terracotta into smaller shards that she placed in a circle around the whole pubic area like razor wire around a restricted zone. With a twig she found on the ground, she scrawled "Danger."

More concrete, more coverage. Belle worked her way down the rest of the body, then took on the head. She covered lips—insistent lips. She covered eyes—leering eyes. With each glop of concrete, a trickle of relief coursed through her. Only a trickle at a time, but altogether the trickles swelled into a tide.

The front of the mannequin would need to dry for a few hours before Belle could flip it over and finish encasing the whole body. She cleaned her tools, tidied her worksite, and suddenly ravenous, went inside to fix herself a snack. As she puttered around the kitchen, unearthing a loaf of artisan bread and a wedge of cheese Jax had dropped off, she kept glancing out the window, watching Ezra and Mitchell finish loading up the Jeep. When the driver's side door slammed and Ezra drove away, Belle flopped onto a kitchen chair and stared at her plate of food, no longer particularly hungry. She forced down a few mouthfuls, then picked up her phone and speed-dialed Miranda.

Answer. Answer. No voicemail, please!

Miranda picked up on the third ring.

"Hey, how's it going down there? Any more parades? Indecent exposure arrests?"

"Very funny. No, and there's been so much going on, I'd practically forgotten about that incident. Thank you so much for reminding me."

Miranda laughed, and the familiar sound of her friend's laughter was like salve. Belle couldn't help but laugh with her.

"God, this feels good," she said. "But I'm calling about something serious."

Miranda's tone darkened. "Oh, no. What's happened now? Are you in trouble again? I can take off work tomorrow and be there in a flash."

"No, no, nothing like that. It's about Jamison. I've found a way to deal with him." She picked up a hunk of bread from her plate and shredded it into crumbs.

"Finally! I mean, I know you needed to do this on your own timetable, but those are the words I've been waiting to hear. So you're finally going to call that lawyer Nick recommended?"

Belle traced the edge of her plate with her finger.

"Well, no, not that. Yet. It's more of a ritualistic solution." She chose the word "ritualistic" deliberately, certain Miranda could relate, given her penchant for pujas and such.

"Okaaay," Miranda said. "I get that. Not something I would've expected from you, but . . ." She trailed off. Then struck by a sudden thought, she yelped, "Omigod, Belle, you're not involved in some kind of cult down there, are you? You're scaring me."

Belle held the phone away from her ear until Miranda finished.

Drawing on her old skills, she spoke in the voice she always used to calm bridezillas and other anxious clients. "No, no, nothing like that. It's just—sometimes you have to do things that defy expectations, you know? Things that defy logic. I know there are more logical, *acceptable* ways of dealing with Jamison, but for now, it's the emotions I need to deal with, and this thing I'm doing is my way of dealing with them."

It took a bit more explaining, but once Miranda understood that Belle's ritual was artistic, not cabalistic, she congratulated her friend on finding a creative way to process her feelings. *Color outside the lines.*

Belle ended the call and pushed away from the table. Miranda approved of what she was doing, so why the lingering sense of disquiet?

It's not enough.

Perhaps the effigy was all she was capable of doing right now. But the day would come when she would have to speak up, not so much for herself—*Belle Jardin* would do that—but for other women who might fall prey. That lawyer's number? She'd keep it handy.

– 22 –
THE INTERMENT

With her mission endorsed by the friend whose opinion still mattered most, Belle returned to work on the mannequin, sealing up the backside and leaving it to dry. She thrust a fist into the air. *Belle, the warrior princess, victorious again.*

The gesture and thought reminded her of something. It came to her in a flash: DeShawn's account of the warrior queen Amanirenas burying a likeness of her enemy's head. Now she knew what her next step would be.

But first, she had a promise to keep. Remembering she'd told Ozzy she'd be back, she dashed next door for a visit. The fox's eyes glowed golden in the late-afternoon sun. His fur, she noticed now, was not a uniform reddish color; it shaded from spice-cake brown to auburn, with darker rings around his eyes.

"You're a handsome fellow, you know," she said. "But just remember, looks aren't everything. Take our friend Ezzy . . ."

"Not even gone one day and already you're pining for him."

Belle hadn't seen Mitchell standing inside the screen door, but the gravelly voice was a giveaway. Her face warmed—not from the sun. "Who's pining? I was just commenting."

Mitchell opened the screen and stepped onto the porch. "It's okay, Miss Belle. I miss him already too." He winced with each step toward Ozzy's pen. "I just hope he's not taking up with Ursula again."

That pang again. That hollow sensation that felt both familiar and unnamable.

"Who's Ursula?"

"That woman. You know. Ezra musta told you about her."

Belle thought hard. In all their conversations—even the one where she told Ezra about her breakup with Ben—she couldn't remember him ever alluding to his own romantic past. He might have hinted at heartbreak, but she was quite sure he'd never spoken the name Ursula.

She shook her head.

"Oh, they was quite an item. It was gettin' so serious I thought for sure I'd be having grand-nieces and -nephews before long. Then she up and left him for some college professor. She'd gone back to school, see, and got all uppity. Now, outta the blue, she calls him up and says she wants to see him and talk things over. Guess she figured he'd always be there waiting for her if she decided to come back, and now she's heard through the grapevine he might be moving down here. I don't trust her not to break his heart again, and he ought not, either. But you know how love is. Dontcha?"

"Yeah, I know."

Did she? Did she know anything about love? In her mind, love was a desirable thing. In her heart, love equaled loss.

Belle stuck two fingers through the pen's wire. Ozzy didn't scurry away or even flinch; he sat staring into her eyes. Still, she couldn't bring herself to touch his snout. Not yet.

"Ezra's a good man," Mitchell said. "He could do a lot better than Ursula."

Belle pretended not to see the sideways look he gave her.

"I don't know about Ursula, but you're right about Ezra," she said. "He *is* a good man."

By the time Belle got back to work, dusk was shading to dark. She checked the figure and satisfied, fetched a flashlight from the kitchen and made her way to Mitchell's garage, where she poked around until she found a plastic tarp and a shovel.

With great effort, she maneuvered the mannequin—now considerably heavier—onto the tarp and dragged it into her front yard. She returned with the shovel and sank it into the ground beside *Belle Jardin*. Or tried to. The earth was unyielding. Of course. She thought now of Mitchell and his flower-tending, forever scratching around in the hardpacked soil to loosen it enough for life to take root.

A trip to her own shed yielded the garden hose she'd been using for concrete-mixing. She attached it to the faucet and stretched it to her digging site. She soaked the ground and dug as far down as she could, then soaked the next layer and dug some more.

No wonder Amanirenas buried only the head!

Belle worked doggedly into the night, soaking and digging, soaking and digging, all to the music of crickets and katydids. Finally the hole was big enough. She heaved the effigy into the grave and without a parting word or gesture, heaped shovelful after shovelful of saturated soil into the yawning cavity. The night was barely cooler than midday, and between the exertion and her haphazard handling of the hose, Belle was soaked head to toe. Intent on her task, she hardly noticed that or anything else.

When the hole was finally filled, Belle's strength was sapped. She left shovel, tarp, and hose in the front yard, stumbled into the house, wiped off the worst of the mud, and fell into bed, satisfied her essential work was done.

The dream came quickly, a rerun of the last one. Again, she stood high above the ground, looking out on treetops, firmly cemented to her perch. Again, the Jamison figure approached her on the concrete branches. Again, she recoiled and reached for a weapon as he pressed against her. Again, she summoned more strength than she'd ever known and shoved him away. But this time, she didn't wake herself with a cry; she remained in her dream state, watching Jamison falling, falling, falling, as if from a thousand feet in the air.

And then a strange sensation in her shoulder blades: an ache that gave way to a stretching and bursting feeling. She reached over one shoulder and touched a protuberance. A wing! And on the other side, another. She channeled her strength into her new appendages and willed them to flutter, and as they did, she lifted off from her roost and rose into the air. Soaring, gliding, swooping like a nighthawk, she laughed with glee. She circled the Garden of Eden, then flew across fields and farmsteads punctuated with ponds and grain elevators. At last, she came to rest atop a spire on her own *Belle Jardin*. With that, the dream faded into wherever dreams go, and she slipped into the sheltering cave of untroubled sleep.

Until a tremendous pounding intruded. Still half asleep, Belle's mind constructed a dream scenario to explain the racket. Drumbeats from a pole-barn party at Roscoe's. Reba, Zebulon, and Olive Pickle dancing with wild abandon, hands in the air, feet stomping and kicking.

The pounding continued, now accompanied by shouting, until Belle roused. Her heartbeat echoed the hammering when she realized it was coming from her side door. She threw on a bathrobe and hurried into the kitchen. Through the windows, lights flashed. Her first thought was that Mitchell had had a heart attack, and EMS workers needed her help.

But why would they?

That's when she noticed the men at her door didn't look like EMS workers. They looked like—police?

- 23 -
THE SUSPECT

Belle shifted her weight on the padded bunk. Surprisingly comfortable, though not a place she wanted to linger. Until now, the only jail cells she'd seen were in movies: grimy cages filled with drunks, derelicts, and other questionable characters. This one could almost pass for a minimalist hotel room, with its polished concrete floor, gray and white walls, stainless steel shelves and lavatory, and narrow slit of a window. Still, definitely not a place she wanted to linger.

I'm in jail. Thinking those words was the only way she could wrap her head around the reality that she, Isabelle Marsden, orderly, organized, law-abiding Isabelle Marsden, had ended up here. *I'm in jail. On suspicion of murder.*

When the police had shown up in the middle of the night, it had been too dark to dig down and show them the effigy, but she'd tried to tell them they were making a big mistake. She hadn't really killed anyone; it was only a symbolic slaying and burial. Yet the more she tried to explain, the more flustered she got, and the more twisted her thoughts and words came out. It was like Steve Schwann's office all over again, except with far higher stakes. That glass eyeball they'd found in her pocket when they brought her to the station hadn't helped matters. The looks the officers had given her—and each other—suggested they not only didn't believe her, they thought they were dealing with a mental case.

Now, here she sat, relieved of her possessions—including the eyeball—and her dignity. At least they had let her get dressed before hustling her into the patrol car, shoving her head down like in an episode of *Cops*. The clothes she'd salvaged from her bedroom floor were the grubby jeans and T-shirt she'd worn the night before, so she looked every bit the part of a criminal. She could only imagine what her mug shot looked like.

She'd been allowed a phone call. Her first impulse was to call Miranda, but then she realized Reba was in a better position to help.

"No worries," Reba had said. "We've got this." Whatever that meant. Maybe Belle should've called Miranda after all.

Miranda. Oh, that was funny. She'd just been read her rights—Mirandized—and here she was thinking about Miranda coming to her rescue. She laughed out loud. The guard on watch shot her another one of those nutcase looks.

Belle choked back the laugh and smoothed her T-shirt, trying to affect an air of normalcy. The guard looked away.

How long would she have to stay here? How long had she already been here, for that matter? She'd lost track of time, but it had to be near morning. What needed to happen before she could go home? She'd overheard the officers say something about "exhumation." Who knew what damage they might do to *Belle Jardin* with shovels—or worse, a backhoe. How dare they! How had they known about the burial anyway? Some suspicious someone must have alerted them. But who, at that time of night?

The clank of a metal door diverted Belle's attention. She couldn't see it from her cell, but she heard approaching voices and a distinctive rasp she immediately recognized as Roscoe's.

"What're you guys doing hassling Izzy-Belle, anyway?" he was saying. "Why don't you jamokes go after some real criminals? Go bust some pot-smoking hippies or something." He laughed.

"Yeah, yeah," the cop escorting Roscoe said in a good-natured tone nothing like he'd used with Belle. "I see you haven't changed since you worked here. Still the cocky sonuvabitch you've always been. Guess I shouldn't be surprised this one's a friend of yours. You gotta admit she's doing some weird shit over there. We're still investigating, but we can release her to you if you promise she won't skip town."

Roscoe laughed again. "Skip town? She wouldn't get far in that little hooptie of hers. But don't worry, she's not a flight risk. And if weird shit gets you hauled in, then book me. She's just got some stuff going on, trying to work it out. Right Izzy?"

Belle nodded mutely, mindful that anything she said might be used against her.

The officer unlocked the door of her cell and escorted her to a desk where she signed papers and was handed an envelope containing the few belongings she'd had on her, minus the eyeball, which was being kept as evidence.

Before the cops could change their minds, Roscoe hustled her out the door and into his truck. As he turned onto Massachusetts Avenue and headed toward North Lawrence, he shook his head and chuckled. "I never would've thought it of you, but you attract trouble like a farmer attracts sweat bees, you know that?"

Belle stared out the window at townspeople going about their morning routines: sipping coffee at outdoor tables, scrolling through their phones on benches, jogging in running shorts, striding to work in summery business-casual attire. Perhaps they all had their troubles, too, but it didn't show.

She looked at Roscoe, who also appeared unruffled. "That thing you said about stuff going on. What'd you mean by that?"

Roscoe gave her a quick glance, then fixed his eyes back on the road. "Darlin', we've all got stuff going on, don't we? The way I see it, the point of life is to work that stuff out—find a way to deal with it. Why do you think I write poetry? Same reason Reba makes weird things out of dead animals, and Mae—bless her little Aquamaureen heart—sings in the choir and works those brain-busting crossword puzzles. We've all got stuff going on, and we've all found ways to deal with it. Yours is that highly imaginative expression of angst and beatification in your front yard. But hey, aggravating Mrs. Dumbass and The Schwanz is one thing, but seriously, the cops? I doubt you really buried a body in your front yard, but what the hell, Izzy-Belle?"

Belle pictured the scene she'd left the night before—shovel, tarp, fresh mound of earth. It did look suspicious, she had to admit.

"I swear, Roscoe, it was nothing like that. Well, actually it was *something* like that."

Crime scene tape encircled *Belle Jardin*. Real crime scene tape, not just caution tape from the zoning department.

Belle groaned at the sight when Roscoe drove up to her house, where Reba and Wallace waited in the driveway.

Across the street, Mrs. Pruitt stood with hose in hand, sprinkling a planter of scraggly petunias but missing most of the flowers as she turned to watch Roscoe's truck turn into Belle's driveway.

Her! I should've known. Hadn't Belle glimpsed a sliver of light through Mrs. Pruitt's blinds as she heaved the mannequin into the hole the night before? She'd thought nothing of it at the time, but now she was sure it was her nosy neighbor who'd called the cops on her.

When Belle slid out of the truck, Mrs. Pruitt's mouth fell open and her face turned even paler than its usual pasty shade. She dropped the hose, and without bothering to turn the water off, scurried into her house and slammed the door.

Reba and Wallace wrapped Belle in the tightest of hugs. "Congratulations on another rite of passage. Been there, done that myself a few times," Reba said.

Belle wriggled free. "Thanks, but I'm really in trouble, aren't I?"

"Well, there's trouble, and there's *trouble*," Roscoe said. "You want to fill us in on the details?"

"I can do better than that," Belle said. "Wait here." She went to her backyard shed and returned with a garden spade from the stash of tools and supplies she kept there. She'd buried the effigy at a slant—not intentionally, only because she hadn't made the hole quite long enough at first and had to excavate an addition to accommodate the head. The hour had been so late, and she'd been so exhausted, she hadn't dug that part as deeply as the rest. Consequently, only a few inches of soil covered the head and shoulders. She scraped away a patch—still damp from last night's soaking—to reveal the concrete-covered face. "See? It's a body, but not a human one. It's *symbolic*. You get symbolic, I know. Your poetry is all about symbolism, Roscoe, and so's some of your art, Reba."

Roscoe tilted his head and leaned in for a closer look in a way that suggested he'd watched too many episodes of *Law & Order*. "Sure, I get symbolism. What I don't get is why you buried it. I mean, you've filled half your front yard with very visible symbols. What're you hiding this one for?"

Reba peered at the figure's head. "It's about your monster, isn't it?"

Belle hesitated, then realized there was no need to hold her tongue. She no longer cared if her secrets were out in the open. If it really was true, as Roscoe said, that everyone was "dealing with stuff," then why should she be ashamed of the stuff she was dealing with? She started to speak, but all at once felt too fatigued to go into it. She pulled out her phone and scrolled through her contacts to

Ezra's name. "Here. Take down this number and call Ezra. He saw me working on the mannequin, and he knows what it's about. He can tell you more."

Roscoe punched the numbers into his own phone.

"And this one," Belle said, pulling up Miranda's entry. "She knows the whole story and more about me than anyone else in the world. If you—or the cops—have any more questions after you talk to Ezra and Miranda, you can ask me. But right now, can I please go back to bed?"

Hours later, Belle awoke, sensing she'd just had the weirdest dream ever: police pounding on her door, a jail cell, Roscoe coming to the rescue. Then the dawning realization it was no dream; it all really happened. Panic jolted through her like a current. Then another reality check. Roscoe had told her not to worry; if Ezra and Miranda corroborated Belle's sketchy story and provided more exculpatory details, he was sure he could convince his police pals it was all a misunderstanding. Of course, they'd want to talk to Ezra and Miranda and see the buried figure for themselves, but he'd make sure they didn't "mess things up too bad."

Belle got up, dressed in work clothes, made coffee, and took a cup with her to the front yard. She surveyed her creation—still surrounded by crime scene tape—and the mound of bare earth covering the burial site.

Now what? Her first impulse was to build something over the effigy's grave. Not a memorial to Jamison—no way! More of a glorious and exultant celebration of her release—partial, at least—from the shadow of his subjection. But that would have to wait until the police finished their investigation and cleared her, as she had to believe they would.

As she looked over *Belle Jardin*, a swelling sensation in the middle of her chest took her by surprise. It was like her heart was expanding to fill the whole cavity. *Am I having a heart attack? Is my heart about to explode?* She dropped to the ground. The swelling didn't subside; it continued to spread. That's when she realized it was no medical emergency. That heart-swelling sensation she was experiencing was gratitude.

Yes, in spite of her troubles, Belle had a lot to be grateful for. For starters, there was Roscoe, who'd just sprung her from jail and promised to straighten things out with the police. There was the whole Soulstice gang—Reba, Mae, DeShawn, Jax, Lakshmi, Olive Pickle, and all the rest, who each, in their own way, had offered assistance and support and enriched her life in ways that went beyond bailouts.

Up to now *Belle Jardin* had been a vehicle for healing old wounds and cultivating her creativity; from now on it would also be a monument to gratitude.

She scanned the space for a starting point. So few empty spots now, but one stood out, right next to her last aboveground addition. Without realizing it, she'd already started her tribute with the likeness of Queen Aquamaureen. As she looked upon it now, its turquoise and aqua embellishments sparkled in the sun like gems in a jewelry store window, luring her in—not to splurge on a luxury but to luxuriate in the act of creation.

Belle rounded up her supplies and threw herself into crafting the biggest and grandest addition yet. So what if she had to duck under crime scene tape to do the work?

Heaping up concrete, she shaped the hassock-sized mound into a half-sphere that appeared to rise from the ground. Next, she collected a stack of plates, and instead of smashing them into shards, carefully broke them in half and then into rough quarters. She stuck the pieces into the top of the rounded mound, their sharp ends pointing outward. Then she set to decorating the half-orb with the brightest, most glittery bits of crockery and cast-off jewelry in her collection.

As she worked, she visualized the final result: a resplendent rising sun, a worthy homage to those dear Soulstice souls.

After an hour or so of concentrated work, a voice silvery as a stream of water spoke three words: "This is it." And then: "You have found it. You have found *me*."

Belle didn't bother looking to see who was speaking. She knew.

Belle Jardin had found its voice.

– 24 –
THE MUSE

Belle sat cross-legged in a bare spot in the middle of *Belle Jardin*, sketchbook balanced on one knee, listening. A neighbor's lawnmower droned; blue jays scolded squirrels, squirrels chattered back. In the distance, a garbage truck clanked and whirred as it emptied the dumpster behind Johnny's tavern.

She listened harder, intent on receiving the next message. Scrawling doodles in her sketchbook, she tried to empty her mind of any thoughts that might cloud her reception.

There it was. A word, not exactly spoken, but transmitted into her consciousness. A single word: "Box."

She drew a box on the page and stared at it. *Huh?*

"I don't get it," she said. "What are you trying to tell me?"

Silence.

Belle mulled over the word. With her mission redefined and messages coming straight from her own creation, she'd expected inspiration to flow unimpeded, like the ideas for the rising sun and Queen Aquamaureen.

But a box? What kind of box was she grateful for? Care packages from her dad had stopped coming once she graduated from college. And sure, she was always happy when her latest Amazon purchase arrived, but that was hardly worth memorializing in concrete.

She stared harder at the box she'd drawn, doodled the letters B-o-x inside.

Ohhhhh. It finally hit her. That day she and Reba had driven past Roscoe's driveway. The name Box painted in red on the side of the striped mailbox. *Roscoe Box.* Of course. He deserved his own place in Belle Jardin.

Over the next few hours, Belle built a boxy framework, sheathed it in concrete, and sculpted a roguish face peeking out from the top. With a straightedge and the point of a leftover broken plate, she inscribed stripes on the side of the box, leaving a blank square on the front, where she printed "Box."

"There you go, my friend. Thanks to you, I'm out here, free to celebrate my gratitude, instead of moldering in that jailhouse box." Well, not moldering, exactly. The cell was actually quite accommodating, and she hadn't been locked up all that long. But still . . .

Belle stood and bowed deeply. "Roscoe Box, I thank you." Then, shifting her position to take in all of *Belle Jardin*—from that first tentative slab to the defiant walladog to the winged woman and the babies, the vision-corrected Mrs. Glick, and the loving tributes to Miranda, Mae, the rest of the Soulstice gang in general, and now Roscoe in particular—she dropped to her knees, and assuming something like a child's pose in yoga, murmured, "And I thank *you.*"

Day in, day out, Belle communed with her creation. With her deepest hurts assuaged—if not fully healed—she still felt driven to keep working, adding more and more elements to *Belle Jardin* before the city's judgment day. Though the deadline had been extended and she now had more than a month's reprieve, the pressure was even greater now in a way: She had to convince not just the zoning department and Mrs. Dumas, but the "community at large" that *Belle Jardin* had "artistic merit." What did that even mean?

What's more, the police investigation was still underway. They'd excavated a neat seam along the burial site—enough to confirm the concreteness and nonhumanity of the body buried there. They'd asked Belle perturbing questions, like where she got the glass eyeball and how many other bodies she'd buried. They'd snooped around the neighborhood, talking at length to Mrs. Pruitt, but also, *thank goodness*, to Mitchell. Luckily, they hadn't (yet, at least) confiscated her laptop, with its search history of bomb-making. She'd been too discombobulated to delete it sooner and now feared any attempts to cover her tracks might somehow be detectable. Who knew what snoopy computer geniuses could unearth these days?

It was enough to keep a person awake at night, mind racing, heart pounding. Thoughts ricocheted around Belle's brain like pinballs—drifting at first in a slow arc, then being flipped into random trajectories, triggering a flash of light in one patch of neurons, a clanging sound in another, but ultimately falling down some hole to lie still and impotent until launched on another crazy circuit. When sleep did come, it was peppered with nightmares so violent they woke her like a thunderclap and set her pulse pounding in her ears.

Disconcerting as everything was, Roscoe kept assuring Belle things would turn out fine and encouraging her to keep working. So work she did.

As she worked, one thing became clear. *Clear as a bell*, she thought with a smile. *Clear as a Belle*. She'd been wrong to think event planning was her calling. Maybe it was, once. Now, it was obvious her true calling was art. Why else would she wake every morning so eager to continue creating, prickly with something between imaginative energy and anxiety? What else could account for her total absorption as she worked for hours at a time, guided at every turn by subtle signs she was sure were coming from the assemblage itself?

Continuing with the theme of gratitude, she thought again about her father's care packages. Those were just small drops in the deluge of things he'd done for her. She'd somehow let those memories fade in the years since his marriage to Shelley. Convinced herself that he'd always been as preoccupied and unavailable as he now seemed, wrapped up in his new life. But that wasn't true.

It all came back to her as she set to work on this mid-July morning, prompted by one vivid memory from sixth grade. That year, Belle's passion was volleyball. She practiced every day after school, made the team, and had a blast riding the school bus with Miranda and the rest of their team to out-of-town games, singing silly songs to pass the time and pump themselves up. Her mom and dad attended all the home games, cheering her on and hosting victory parties for her team.

When the team made the state playoffs, Belle rushed home breathless to spill the news. The crucial games were in two weeks in downtown Chicago. Blocks of hotel rooms had been reserved for the competing teams, their coaches, and chaperones.

"You'll chaperone, right?" She didn't inflect it like a question.

Her father's face clouded. He shot a look at her mother.

"That's the weekend of Dad's annual company meeting in New York," her mother said. "He's scheduled to give a presentation that could help him move ahead. It's something he's been working toward for a long time."

Belle understood working toward something. That's how these playoffs felt. "It's okay, Dad," she said. "I get it." Inside, she deflated like a forlorn balloon left over from a birthday party.

Later that evening, doing homework in her room, she overheard her dad on the phone. She couldn't make out all the words, but she heard "daughter," "tournament," "substitute," and "thanks a million." Was he asking her coach to put someone in her place? To take her off the team and make her miss the whole tournament, just to avoid a conflict with his schedule? Would he do that? Belle wanted to storm downstairs and plead her case, but she knew it wouldn't do any good.

Once Greg Marsden made up his mind about something, he wasn't likely to change it.

After a mostly sleepless night, she dragged herself down for breakfast and skulked into the kitchen.

Her mother, spooning oatmeal into Belle's bowl, met her daughter's glower with a smile. "You can sign us up."

"Us? Meaning both of you?"

Her dad lowered the newspaper he was reading and nodded. "Priorities, Belle. You're mine."

Now, crouching in one of the few remaining spaces in *Belle Jardin*, admiring the play of morning sunlight on her own concrete garden, Belle pondered how to enshrine her father's unselfish act and all the others over the years. How to encapsulate his goodness? His steadiness? His gentle humor? She could fill another whole yard with gratitude memorials to that one man.

Instead, she opted for one small symbol. She hopped into her car, drove to Dick's Sporting Goods in the endless stretch of strip malls and chain retailers on Iowa Street, and came home with a brand-new volleyball.

She decided against encasing the ball in concrete, fearing that would obliterate its ball-ness. From memory, she drew a striking likeness of her dad's face—complete with the tiny scar on his chin—on the front of the ball with one of the chisel-tip Sharpies Reba had given her because "they're good to have on hand." She added a clump of dried grass for his unruly hair and called it done.

"Thanks for everything, Dad," she said. "I really mean that. Guess I should tell you in person sometime, huh?"

Another day, another inspiration. Sitting in a bare spot she'd come to think of as her vision position—a throw pillow–sized spot in the middle of *Belle Jardin* that she'd kept clear for just this purpose—she waited, sketchbook open, pencil poised, for the morning's message. The messages didn't always come as words; sometimes directives came as other sounds or even visual cues.

A bumblebee whirred by, nearly grazing her shoulder on its way to Mitchell's flowers. How quiet his yard seemed now, without the hammering and sawing sounds of Ezra's industry.

Ezra! How could I leave him out?

Belle tossed her notebook and pencil aside and got busy with the day's project. She fashioned a tower of books, stacked every which way, topped with a man's head, his features a Picasso-esque study in asymmetry.

Picasso, she'd once read, painted faces with misplaced features in an attempt to portray the subject from all angles at once and to convey the entirety of that person's emotions and struggles in a single painting. Was that what Belle was trying to do? Or was she just depicting the actual lopsidedness of Ezra's features? A little of both, she guessed.

To interject a touch of whimsy, she added an Aussie hat atop the head. Then, on the cover of the top book, she inscribed, "To Ezzy, with gratitude, from Izzy and Ozzy."

When she read it back to herself, the inscription sounded stiff and formal and didn't really match the feeling she was trying to express. She tried out different words in her mind but couldn't find a substitute. At least not one she was willing to commit to something as permanent as concrete.

Ten days into Belle's creative frenzy, Reba swooped in with Wallace in tow. Wallace immediately scampered away to visit Ozzy; Reba circled *Belle Jardin*, exclaiming over the latest additions.

"You're on a real streak here." She continued around the assemblage. "The crime scene tape adds a snazzy touch." Fingering a loose end of the plastic ribbon, she held it up to her throat like a necktie.

Belle looked at her with mock disdain. "Believe me, as soon as I'm cleared—which should be soon—that's coming off. It's an affront to my artistry."

"Really?" Reba stroked the tape as if it were a silk cravat. "Can I have it then? I could use it in one of my pieces."

Belle kept stirring the concrete she'd just mixed. "Be my guest."

Moving on, Reba came to the likeness of Belle's father, stopped short, and burst out laughing.

"What's so funny?" Indignation tinged Belle's voice.

"Wilson! Great job of capturing him, Belle. I knew those Sharpies would come in handy someday. Tom Hanks would be impressed."

"I have no idea what you're talking about."

"Wilson? The volleyball from *Cast Away*?"

"Never saw it. And for your information, that's my dad you're looking at."

Reba rocked back and forth, still highly amused. "Well, then, your dad bears a striking resemblance to Tom Hanks's volleyball friend in *Cast Away*. Watch it on Netflix. You'll see."

"Mmmmmm." Belle nodded and continued stirring concrete. Enough water, or should she add more?

Reba crouched to Belle's eye level. "So, just to bring you up to speed, the pressure is on to make the exhibit and gala pay off. Lakshmi says Coogan's been talking to real estate developers."

"Hmmmmm." Belle lifted her stir stick to check the mixture's consistency. Goopy. Goopy was good.

Reba shrugged and continued. "See, he's come up with a scheme to move to a trailer park in Florida and get work as a python bounty hunter. But to do that, he's got to unload the property A-S-A-P. Just so happens developers are itching to get their hands on that land—prime subdivision potential."

Preoccupied with concrete consistency and still on the alert for messages from her muse, Belle gave her a blank look.

"The *animals*, Belle. What's going to happen to them?"

Belle stared at Reba for a long minute, comprehension flickering in and out. She nodded. "Right."

"Lakshmi's been hinting to Coogan that an anonymous buyer is prepared to match or beat the developers' offers. At this point, it's all a bluff, but we're hoping she can convince him to hold off on the sale until we raise the money to buy the whole kit and caboodle: land, menagerie, and all."

"Sounds good," Belle said, turning her attention back to the concrete, which was reaching peanut-butter thickness—just about ready for spreading and sculpting.

"Yeah, but we're in a bit of a panic, see, because we don't know what the hell we're doing. I mean, we've had art openings before—little gatherings in some café or gallery—but nothing on this scale." Reba stood and paced around the periphery of *Belle Jardin*. Wallace, back from his visit, bopped along behind her.

"It'll be fine," Belle said, her voice floaty. "Just follow the directions I gave you."

Reba stopped pacing and planted her hands on her hips. "We *are*, Belle. But I just need to know we can count on you to help out if push comes to shove."

"Mmmmmm," Belle said, looking past Reba into some faraway place. "That's up to *Belle*. I just do what *Belle* tells me to do."

Reba squatted again to Belle's level and spoke in that talking-down-from-a-ledge voice. "*You* are Belle. No one else is telling you what to do."

Another bumblebee buzzed by. Or was it the same one as before—a designated messenger? Belle watched it pass and waited for a sign. Receiving nothing, she turned back to Reba.

"You don't understand." Her tone mirrored Reba's, slow and

patient, as if explaining something obvious to a slow-witted person. "There are two Belles. There's Belle . . ." She laid a hand on her chest. ". . . and there's *Belle*." She lifted the hand and swept her arm in a great arc, taking in all of *Belle Jardin*. "Belle and *Belle* are on the same wavelength. We communicate, and *Belle* is my spirit guide."

Her forehead wrinkled, and she poked at the concrete mixture. "Now, if you don't mind, *Belle* says I need to get back to work."

– 25 –
THE PAINTER

Lucky for Ozzy, Belle's spirit guide had his interests at heart. Guided by the mystical muse, Belle roused from her art-induced trances to visit and feed the fox at the appropriate times every day. She didn't view the visits as disruptions but more as pauses that recharged her imagination.

After each feeding, she sat in Ozzy's pen, discussing the day's work or simply appreciating the presence of another living being.

Mitchell often joined them, pulling up a lawn chair and easing himself into it. Hungry for companionship since Ezra left, he talked a blue streak. Stories of his youth, his years as a janitor at "the college up yonder," the satisfaction he got from planting and tending flowers. His was an uncomplicated life, and a good one. For once, Belle's life felt that way too.

One steamy day about a week after Belle had crafted the Ezra tribute, Mitchell brought news along with the iced tea he always offered Belle.

"Welp. Ursula's out of the picture." He took a long swig of tea but kept an eye on Belle's face, gauging her reaction.

"Ursula." Who was he talking about? In his ramblings, he was always dropping names as if Belle should recognize people from his past. She sifted through what she remembered of his stories, trying to recall where she'd heard that name.

"Don't tell me you forgot already." Mitchell half chuckled, half clucked in a scolding way. "You know. *Ursula*. That woman."

Belle shook her head. "Sorry, I don't . . ."

"For Pete's sake, girl! I do believe that thingamabob you're all the time working on has scrambled your brain. *Ursula*. Ezra's ex. She's a double-ex now—and I don't mean that in a dirty way. Anyhoo, she took off again—this time to dig for dinosaur bones or old pots or whatever. Good riddance, I say."

The veil clouding Belle's comprehension lifted momentarily, and she zeroed in on Mitchell's words. "What does Ezra say?"

"You'd have to ask him yourself, Miss Belle. He don't tell me all he's thinking. But I reckon he knows it's for the best."

"What about the library? Has he made up his mind about the job?"

Mitchell lifted his cap and scratched at a balding patch. "Don't know that either," he said. "Guess time will tell."

Day by day, *Belle Jardin* consumed more and more of Belle's time, energy, and front yard. When nearly every inch of lawn was covered with sculpted and scavenged miscellany, Belle built upward, dragging a rickety stepladder from Mitchell's garage and teetering atop it to add spires and intertwining branches, all adorned with bric-a-brac and symbols only she understood.

By late July, the police investigation had wrapped up, clearing Belle just as Roscoe had predicted. Sure, Detective Stone, who'd led the investigation, still looked at Belle like she was a lunatic when he delivered the news, but what he thought didn't matter now. She was free from suspicion and free to create. Still, the pressure to create something *worthy* interrupted her sleep, leaving her alternately foggy, frenzied, and panicky during waking hours.

Reba and Wallace stopped by almost every day now, "so Wallace can visit Ozzy," Reba claimed. Sometimes Roscoe, Mae, DeShawn, or Jax came along. Belle didn't mind their company, as long as they didn't expect her to entertain them.

Sometimes the visitors inspected and commented on her progress. She would stop working only long enough to respond in monosyllables, and they would leave her alone. Sometimes they poked around inside her house. Later, Belle would find the refrigerator—bare that morning—stocked with cheese cubes, fruit, yogurt cups, and protein drinks and her countertop laden with bags of nuts. All nourishment in forms that required no preparation. Had Belle mentioned that her muse insisted cooking was a waste of time that could be used more constructively?

Other times the visitors stood off to the side observing Belle as if she were an animal in Coogan's collection. They talked among themselves in low voices. Belle heard words like "unhinged," "delusional," and "intervention," but she was far too engrossed in her work to have any inkling they applied to her. All she was attuned to were *Belle*'s messages transmitted directly into her skull.

One morning, as Belle hastened to throw on her work clothes and get an early start on the day's artistry, she caught a glimpse of herself in the mirror and did not know who she was looking at. Her face had taken on an otherworldly expression. Her hair, never well-behaved, had a feral look about it. (Hair care and other personal grooming tasks were a waste of creative energy. *Belle* had told her that.) When she realized she was looking at herself, she had a sudden impulse to shave her head, not only to be rid of the hair, but to consecrate herself, monk-like, to her mission. But she let go of that urge when it dawned on her that keeping her head shaved would be one more unnecessary chore. Everything now must be pared down, stripped down. Everything except expanding and exalting *Belle Jardin*.

After feeding and communing with Ozzy, she went prospecting

in Mitchell's garage, where she made a beeline for the tower of old paint cans. One by one, she lifted and shook the cans, some hopelessly dead, but others sloshing with promise.

Her latest message from *Belle*, received on the last day of July, had been the single word "paint," and though Belle didn't know what, exactly, she was being bidden to paint, she intended to be ready when the instructions came through. Grubbing around beside the pile of cans, she unearthed a tool for prying them open, stir sticks coated with multiple layers of color, and a couple of usable brushes.

Bonanza! She smiled, not even sure what she was smiling about. As she maneuvered the loaded wheelbarrow through the yard, she puzzled over what she might be instructed to paint. The figures in *Belle Jardin*? Possibly. Dinsmoor had added touches of color to some of his: Eve's rosy cheeks and red apple; a fluttering American flag in red, white, and blue; trickles of blood on one particularly gory vignette. But she was sure *Belle* had something grander in mind.

When she reached the side stoop, Belle set the wheelbarrow down and dashed into the house to retrieve her sketchbook from the living room. She scooped the tablet from the side table where she'd left it and turned to leave, but something stopped her in her tracks. On the blank wall directly across from where she stood, a word appeared, as if projected onto the white surface:

Here

Belle stared at the word until it disappeared, then closed her eyes and saw it again as an afterimage imprinted on her retina.

Okay, here. But what goes here? In an instant, a flood of images replaced the single word in her visual field, and she knew the answer, or at least enough of it to get a start. She toted all the paint cans into the living room and began prying off lids and stirring the contents, astonished at the array of colors. Fuchsia, vermilion, lavender, goldenrod, mango, cobalt, teal. Had Mitchell tried to duplicate his garden's splendor on the walls of his outwardly colorless house? Belle never had been inside, but she had assumed his interior walls were the same featureless white as hers.

As hers *had been* until now, that is. Taking up a broad brush, Belle began slapping color onto the living room wall. She grabbed a second brush and applied swipes of a different color. Some of the paint had separated with age, leaving thick sludge in the bottom of the can, but Belle didn't even bother stirring it to a uniform consistency. She rather liked the gloppy texture of the bottom goo. It added an extra dimension of artfulness.

Had she seen a drop cloth beside the paint cans in the garage? Should she have laid one down before she set to work? She briefly considered the questions, but as she watched flecks and drops spatter and drizzle onto the bare wood floor, she gloried in the Jackson Pollock–like patterns they made.

"I'm painting, *Belle*!" she shouted. "Just like you told me to."

Even with the windows open, the paint fumes made Belle lightheaded. Or was it just the act of creation that made her head swim?

When she'd covered the whole wall with swaths and stripes of every color in her serendipitous palette, Belle took a break to let the paint dry. She washed the brushes, careful to clean off every speck of latex. This wouldn't be her only painting project, she was sure.

Returning to Mitchell's garage, Belle rooted around until she found more brushes—smaller ones this time, some never used and still in their plastic sleeves. Back inside the house, she cozied up on the futon with her sketchbook, alternately admiring the morning's work and doodling dreamy images. When at last the wall's background colors were dry to the touch, she popped open the cans again and began daubing, stippling, and stroking, creating a fantastical mural. Winged women with fox faces fluttered across a lavender sky; trees sprouted from fuchsia soil, their leaves where roots should be, their roots where branches should be, their trunks bearing unearthly fruits and flowers. Monsters cavorted with babies, monkeys, hummingbirds, and bumblebees. Aphids and ants marched in formation.

Exhausted, Belle barely managed to close the lids and clean the brushes before collapsing into a deep sleep on the futon. When she woke a few hours later, she wandered through the house, thrilled to discover blank wall after blank wall. How had she always seen these as mere walls and not canvases awaiting her touch?

The next few days and nights blurred: painting to the point of exhaustion, sleeping, waking, and painting some more. Belle kept to no schedule but somehow remembered to pop next door twice a day to care for Ozzy and give Mitchell the attention he craved, if he wandered out while she was there.

Reba and Wallace still visited most days. If Reba found Belle crashed on the futon, she didn't wake her but left a note:

REMEMBER TO EAT! CHECK THE FRIDGE. YOUR FRIENDS LOVE YOU.

If Reba found Belle wide awake and caught up in creation, she offered praise for the new direction Belle's artistry was taking her.

"Fabulous use of color, Belle! And so imaginative," she gushed one late July afternoon when she saw the fox-faced winged women, upside-down trees, monsters, monkeys, babies, bumblebees, and all the rest.

"Mmmm," Belle responded, preoccupied not only with her work, but also with the thoughts that kept coursing through her mind in her painting mania. Would the "community at large" see the artistic merit of her painting, or would this new work be seen as another atrocity to be wiped out along with *Belle Jardin*? Would Mrs. Dumas finally appreciate Belle's improvements (as Belle saw them) to the property or see them as further cause for eviction?

Whatever. Belle was not about to let what-ifs derail her. Fortified by snacks and Mitchell's iced tea, she covered every wall in the house with her wild imaginings. When she ran out of indoor surfaces, she started on the exterior, painting individual stones in the house's outer walls different colors like polka dots. As she painted, she felt a kinship with Detroit artist Tyree Guyton, whose Heidelberg Project she'd read about in the *Fantasy Worlds* book and on the artist's website. More than thirty years before, Guyton had transformed a rundown neighborhood into an art environment, painting polka dots on houses and filling vacant lots with assemblages of found objects: broken dolls, shoes, telephones, hubcaps, and vacuum cleaners, as well as his own paintings.

Guyton's work was controversial—an eyesore to some—but eventually it gained respect and support and came to be recognized as one of the most important art environments in the world. All along, Guyton viewed art as "medicine"—sometimes a bitter pill to swallow but healing all the same.

Belle could relate to that. Also to the message printed on the bumper sticker she'd ordered from the shop on Guyton's website. Her Chevy Spark now sported the slogan: "Life without art is stupid."

Absorbed in rock-painting, careful to keep each stone's color from intruding on its neighbors, Belle failed to hear the car pull up, the door open and slam shut. Only when the tremulous shriek reached her ears did she realize she had company.

"Now what have you done, you lunatic! I knew I should have kicked you out as soon as you started this insanity." Striding toward Belle, a red-faced Mrs. Dumas ranted on. "Where are the flowers you were going to plant? And don't tell me this is what they're doing in Chicago. I asked my cousin in Forest Glen, and she'd never heard of any such thing. You're not only a lunatic, Miss Marsden, you're a liar!"

Belle dropped her brush and wiped her hands on her jeans. "Mrs. Dumas!" she said, maneuvering her landlady away from the windows so she wouldn't see the muraled walls inside. "*Belle Jardin* needs no flowers. This art environment might be unacceptable to *some people—*" she punctuated those two words with a narrowing of her eyes, "—but so was the Heidelberg project. It's not, you know, a painting to hang over your sofa."

Just as she had in Steve Schwann's office, Belle felt she was making a highly cogent argument, yet Mrs. Dumas's color deepened from rose to a shade like sangria. Her landlady peered at the polka-dot rocks and circled the shapes and spires of *Belle Jardin*. "Thank god the city is going to demolish this atrocity," she squawked. "Yes, that's right, I've heard about the demolition notice. And once this abomination is demolished, you damn well better clean up the mess before you vacate the premises. And scrub that paint off the rock walls—pronto! I have half a mind to fine you the several thousand dollars it'll cost me to clean it up, just in case you don't follow through. In fact, I think I'll call my lawyer as soon as I get home to put some teeth into it."

The threats rattled Belle, but the word "pronto" almost made her giggle. (What *was* it with her emotions these days—cartwheeling without warning from distress to hysterics?) She composed herself as best she could and looked Mrs. Dumas in the eye, hoping her expression was appropriately serious.

"Perhaps you're not aware that the original demolition deadline has come and gone, Mrs. Dumas. The city postponed demolition due to the artistic value of my creation. I promise you, plenty of art aficionados admire this kind of work. As a matter of fact, there's a major exhibition being organized right here in Lawrence that's expected to draw fans from far and wide." Belle impressed herself with how quickly she segued from preoccupied painter to public relations ambassador. Perhaps her old skills were not as alien to her nature as she'd come to believe.

"You do have a knack for sculpture," Mrs. Dumas allowed, pausing before the trio of babies. "But my property is *not* your studio. You'll be hearing from my lawyer."

Her property? *Her* property? No, no. This was Belle's house, Belle's garden, *Belle Jardin*. Mrs. Dumas might hold title to the property, but she couldn't feel the attachment to it that Belle felt. The sense of belonging, the rightness of being in this place, doing this work. And she knew *Belle* felt that too.

– 26 –
THE CONSPIRATORS

"We're abducting you, Darlin'." Roscoe's grin was playful, but his tone was no-nonsense. Reba nodded. Even Wallace signaled agreement with a steady gaze.

"What?? No!" Belle protested. She reflexively tightened every muscle and gripped the ground where she sat in her vision position.

"What, yes!" Reba countered.

When the trio had piled out of Roscoe's truck moments before, they'd found Belle sitting there, sketchbook open to a blank page, staring into the distance with a look of intense concentration. Or concern. Or agony. Some forehead-furrowing state of mind.

Reba glanced at Belle's car, parked in the same spot in the driveway it had occupied for more than two weeks. "When's the last time you went to Lucas? Or anywhere, for that matter?"

Belle squinted as if trying to bring some far-off scene into focus. "I'm . . . not . . . really sure." Then she shook her head and quickly added, "But there's been no reason to go anywhere. I'm getting all I need from *Belle*."

Roscoe leaned in, trying to make eye contact with Belle. "Uh-huh. And what are you getting from her today?"

Belle kept staring into the distance. "Well, so far, nothing. But I'm waiting."

"Looks like you've been waiting more than just this morning," Reba said, looking around the assemblage and beyond to the painted rock walls. "From what I can tell, you haven't done anything since I was here a few days ago and saw the polka-dot rocks."

Belle considered the site as if seeing it through Reba's eyes.

"Huh. Well," Belle replied, careful to choose the most agreeable words, "maybe you're right. *Belle* hasn't told me what to do next. Do you think she's mad at me? Did I do something wrong?" Steamy air notwithstanding, a cold sensation settled over her.

Roscoe and Reba exchanged looks and subtle nods. "No, hon," Roscoe said. "I think she's telling you to take an inspiration break. All artists need that sometimes. You can't work nonstop forever—you have to refill the well. I know I do. When I get stuck on a poem, I take a walk or feed the chickens or check in with Reba to see what new uses she's found for roadkill. Hell, even muses need a break. Maybe *Belle*'s taking time off too."

Belle relaxed her grip on the ground but didn't budge from her position.

Roscoe held out a hand to her. "Here's what I want you to do—go put your notebook away, grab your purse, and come with us. We've got something to show you that'll get those juices flowing again—or at least get your butt off that spot. Believe me, *Belle* would agree it's for the best."

Riding through the countryside in Roscoe's truck, Belle felt transported to a place that was only vaguely familiar. Where had those fields of ready-to-burst-into-bloom sunflowers come from? How had the corn grown so tall? Since when did a new dance hall replace the Chevy dealer? (And come to think of it, wasn't her Spark due for an oil change last month? Or the month before?)

The driveway to Roscoe's farm, with its prison-striped mailbox, was unchanged. So was the poet-painted pole barn with a cluster of cars and trucks parked every which way beside it, the boxers dozing in a shady spot, and chickens clucking and flapping all around.

Inside, the scene was as bustling as it had been during float construction, but considerably more chaotic.

"I think this goes here," Olive Pickle said, holding a roughly carved leg against a similarly fashioned torso.

Peering at a crude sketch of the figure they were trying to assemble, Zebulon shook his head. "Nope. That's where the arm goes. I *think*."

Around the barn's perimeter, other sculptures and triptychs lay in pieces or partially put together as teams of similarly bewildered Soulstice folks tried to figure out how to reassemble them.

Piles of papers and photographs littered a large table in the middle of the room, with camera memory cards sprinkled like confetti atop the whole mess.

"So this is what we've got so far," Reba said as Wallace bounced off to investigate the assortment of colors and shapes. "Great response, huh?"

Belle's eyes widened. She pivoted slowly to take in the whole scene. "Wellllll, yes. But *when* is the gala again?"

"A month from now. Yeah, I know, there's a lot to do between now and then."

Belle's brain shifted, just as it had in her latest encounter with Mrs. Dumas, and she clicked into a well-worn groove.

"More than you know," she said. "Have invitations been sent to potential donors? Press releases to all the local media? Posters printed for store windows? Have you hired the caterer and selected the menu? Written the script for the program?"

Reba clapped a hand to her chest and dropped her head. "Oh. Well, see, Lakshmi was going to do some of those things, but her aunt—the one who lives in Wichita—got really sick and she had to go over and take care of her. We don't know how long she'll be gone."

Belle raised her eyes to the ceiling and said nothing for a full minute, shaking her head and then nodding from time to time.

Reba gave Roscoe a sideways look; he shot her a grin as if they were conspiring on a clever scheme.

Belle noticed none of that.

"Can you take me home now?" she said. "I need to talk to *Belle*."

Belle gripped the door handle when Roscoe veered unexpectedly into the parking lot of Riverfront Park. "Why are we stopping here? I thought you were taking me home."

"Relax, Darlin'." Roscoe grinned over his shoulder. "Just a little more Roscoe and Reba R&R before we turn you loose on your creation again." In a flash, he and Reba slid out of the front seat and opened both backseat doors. Roscoe crawled in one side and nudged Belle from behind as Reba tugged her arms from the other side.

"C'mon now, Belllllle," Reba cooed. "Just a little walk along the river to stretch our legs. It's the best thing for creative refueling, and it'll do wonders for your sleep—which I know has suffered lately."

Belle eyed her friends as if they were cops rousing her from bed to haul her off to jail. She anchored herself to the seat as best she could, given the muscle Roscoe and Reba were applying to dislodge her.

"Trust me, *Belle* will still be there when you get home," Roscoe said.

Belle let the "trust me" remark slide and went limp, not exactly giving in, but no longer resisting with all her might.

Once they all took to the trail that ran beside the river, Belle couldn't deny there was something soothing about just walking and taking in the scenery. How long had it been since she'd even strolled around her neighborhood?

A family of quail skittered across the path ahead of them, comical in their lickety-split scurry. Yet it was the languid river that captured Belle's attention. Though this river was bathed in sunshine, not shrouded in mist, it reminded her of the river in the dream about her mother. So serene and comforting.

Back home, Belle spent the rest of the afternoon and evening glued in her vision position.

"You wouldn't believe it, *Belle*," she told her silent muse. "They've made a horrible mess, and it'll take every spare minute for the next month to set things straight and keep the gala from failing. And it *can't* fail, *Belle*. For the sake of the animals, it *can't*. They need me, *Belle*. I can save the gala, save the animals. But I need to be here, working to save you. So I'm asking you, what should I do? What do you want me to do?"

Hour after hour, no answer came. Mrs. Pruitt ventured out to sprinkle her petunias and cast her usual disparaging glare in Belle's direction. The nighthawks swooped and whirred. Mosquitoes attacked; Belle slapped.

A whimper from Mitchell's yard reminded Belle that Ozzy was still waiting for supper.

"I'm coming, I'm coming," she called.

Was that a doleful look Ozzy gave her when she set his food bowl in front of him? Or did she read that emotion onto his expression? Either way, she could hardly bear to return his gaze.

"I know," she said. "It's not looking good for your friends at the zoo."

Ozzy trotted closer and stuck his nose through the wire, close enough for Belle to touch, but she held back. She wasn't sure she deserved his trust.

With no clear guidance, there was nothing for Belle to do but keep returning to her vision position until she received *Belle*'s directives. Days were different now, though. Reba and Roscoe took turns stopping by to coax Belle away from her work and take her for a walk, venturing a little farther into the neighborhood each time, past the grain elevator, through the local park, and around the old train depot, now a visitors' center. They sent her links to sleep-inducing music and meditations and called her every evening to remind her it was time to stop sketching, have a cup of warm milk, and plug in her earbuds. Of course they made sure there was always milk in the fridge, and Reba kept Belle supplied with zucchini-jalapeño cookies.

She took their advice. After all, they were artists too. Still, every evening before milk and music, Belle implored *Belle* to tell her what to do. Save the animals or save *Belle Jardin*? But either *Belle* wasn't talking or she was speaking in a language Belle didn't understand.

Sitting by Ozzy's pen after another feeding, Belle put the question to him. "*Belle* won't tell me, and the gala is only a month away. Maybe you'll tell me what to do." They locked eyes, and she remembered the words that seemed to come from Grandpa Jake when she agonized over pawning his ruby ring: *Go ahead, girl. Do whatcha gotta do.*

"You're right, Ozzy," she said. "I've been asking the wrong question."

With a last long look at the fox, Belle slipped away and returned to *Belle Jardin*. Instead of hunkering down in her vision position, she stood tall and addressed her muse in a clear, steady voice.

"I *know* what I should do," she said. "What I'm asking is your permission."

The dream came the moment Belle closed her eyes. No Garden of Eden figures, no showdown with Jamison. This dream was all about Lakshmi—not the evolutionary biologist, animal- and aunt-caretaker, but the four-armed Hindu goddess for whom she was named. Literally translated as "She who leads to one's goal," Lakshmi is believed to bestow power, wealth, and fulfillment. All things that could come in mighty handy in the Soulstice gang's fundraising efforts.

In the dream, Lakshmi held out gifts to Belle in each of her hands: a candle glowing in an amber glass holder, a book with jeweled cover, a peacock-blue butterfly, and a cupcake. When Belle reached for them, Lakshmi pulled away, smiling.

"You already have received," she said. "It's your turn to give. *Seva*, Belle. Selfless service."

No more dreams intruded. Belle sank deeper and deeper into the dark, muffled world of slumber. She woke long after sunup, slowly, groggily at first, then prickly with anticipation. Cracking the blinds, she looked out at *Belle Jardin*. The gleam of glass shards, the glint of mirror fragments, the fit of all the pieces—all more intense and pleasing than ever before—relayed the message she'd been waiting for.

She had *Belle*'s blessing.

– 27 –

THE ORGANIZER

Heads swiveled and chatter stopped when Belle strode into Roscoe's pole barn later that morning, wearing khakis and a polo shirt—clean and only moderately rumpled from being crammed in the back of her closet. Her phone peeked from the shirt's breast pocket; her laptop, secure in one hand, swung in time with each step. Clamped under her other arm: a brand-new accordion folder, picked up at Office Depot on her way to Roscoe's.

She cleared a space on the cluttered table and arranged her things: laptop in the middle, phone to its right, folder to its left. She squared the bottom edge of the folder to line up precisely with the bottom edge of the laptop and centered the phone halfway between the laptop's top and bottom edges.

Must organize. Must organize. Must organize.

With a quick nod to herself, she flipped open the laptop cover. Only then did she notice the stares and silence.

She searched the sea of faces. "What??"

Reba took a tentative step toward her, as if approaching a strange animal.

"Yoooooou look . . . different. I mean, you look the same. I mean, you look like *yourself* again. It's like you've come back from that far-away place you've been for so long—that place none of us could get to."

Belle pulled a pen and a pad of sticky notes from her purse and laid them beside her phone. “What are you talking about? I’ve been right at home. You’ve been there almost every day. You’re talking crazy, Reba.” She waved a dismissive hand.

Crazy. Everyone’s acting crazy. Except me. Crazy is one thing I am definitely not.

“Yeah, crazy.” Reba shot a look at Roscoe, who raised his eyebrows. A wave of whispers and murmurs spread around the room. “Well, you’re here now, thank god.”

“Actually, thank Lakshmi,” Belle mumbled as she rummaged in her purse for more office supplies.

“Did you say, ‘Thank Lakshmi’?” Reba took a few more steps in Belle’s direction, less hesitantly now. “You’ve talked to her? How’s her aunt?”

Belle straightened, deposited a fistful of paperclips on the table, and looked Reba squarely in the eye. *Do I have to explain every damn thing? Who has time for that?* “Not *that* Lakshmi. The other one—with four hands. Which we could all use right now. Now can we please get to work? We’ve got a lot to get done and not much time to do it.”

Within a matter of hours, Belle had created spreadsheets, entered contact information for potential donors, downloaded photos, ordered supersized prints on foamcore backing, and made the rounds of the room several times to check on the workers’ progress and offer encouragement or guidance.

“I think you’ve got that one upside down, Mae. Try it like this. There you go!”

“Coming right along, Olive!” Belle pulled the glass eyeball from her pants pocket and held it against her forehead as she inspected Olive’s work. Olive tittered and winked at her husband’s approving eye.

"Good work, Zebulon," Belle said. "Now we're getting somewhere. Love the outfits, by the way." Zebulon had taken to improvising costumes for himself and Olive to match whatever outsider art piece they were preparing that day. Today it was giant, cardboard arrow-through-the-head hats and spangled shirts to complement an Ed Root mosaic sculpture.

Wrapping up the latest inspection round, Belle returned to her folding chair at the work table and busied herself drafting a press release. Intent on finding just the right words, she barely noticed Roscoe watching her from across the table.

"We knew the professional organizer could save the day," he said, a wry smile in his voice. "If we could just get her back."

It took a minute for his words to sink in. When they did, an involuntary twitch took control of Belle's right eye, and she hiccupped three times.

"Professional organizer?" *Hic!* "Who told you that?" *Hic! Hic!* She'd been so careful not to let that detail slip out. That part of her life was in the past. Wasn't it? Sure, she was pulling out some old tricks now to help her friends, but this was just a temporary detour on her new path. "I'm not an organizer, Roscoe; I'm an *artist*."

Aren't I?

"Of course you are, Darlin'. And it was to save your art that you gave me your friend Miranda's phone number. Remember? You said she could tell me your whole story. Well, she didn't leave anything out." He reached out and turned Belle's accordion folder sideways, just to watch her compulsively straighten it. "Couldn't resist, could you?" Roscoe chuckled; Belle tucked her hands under the table. "Anyway," he continued, "artist, organizer, whatever you are, you're saving our skin. Or our animals' skins."

The animals. Yes, that's what this was all about, and the enormity of that responsibility hit Belle full force now. Nothing she had ever organized in Chicago—the anniversary parties, the awards banquets, even the museum fundraisers—had mattered so much. The success or failure of this exhibit and gala was literally a matter of life or death. And though she had the whole Soulstice gang working their asses off, it was Belle who had to pull it all together and make it succeed.

On her own.

– 28 –
THE BENEFACTOR

A tingle rippled through Belle's torso, and her head filled with sparkles as she walked through the two-story limestone columns of Spencer Museum of Art on the University of Kansas campus. Was this venerable institution really to be the setting for their cobbled-together exhibit and gala?

Reba waited in the lobby, Wallace tucked into her backpack.

"Soooooo, ready to check out the space?" She grabbed Belle's hand and pulled her toward the central court. A guard rushed over, chest puffed out, eyebrows squinched in a V. He jabbed a finger toward Wallace.

"No animals, ma'am."

Reba feinted right and breezed past him.

"Therapy animal. Thank yoooou!" Then in a stage whisper to Belle, "He doesn't have to know Wallace is the one getting therapy."

They entered the soaring, light-filled central court, and Belle's head sparkles swirled again like glitter in a snow globe. When Reba had told her they'd snagged an exhibit space in the Spencer, Belle had assumed it would be a smaller, out-of-the-way area, perhaps not even big enough for the event they hoped to pull off. But this grand gallery was beyond anything she could've hoped for.

She whipped out a tape measure and began checking dimensions and scrawling numbers in a notebook. Reba and Wallace wandered around, Reba looking gaga, Wallace looking restless, the guard keeping a close watch from a few feet away. Museum patrons drifted in, gave Reba, Wallace, and the guard puzzled glances, then saw Belle measuring and scrawling and ducked out so as not to interrupt her clearly important work. Or so Belle interpreted their avoidant behavior.

"Hmmmmmm." Belle checked the measurements again, and a cold, stony sensation hit her in the gut. "I'm not sure this . . ."

Reba emerged from her daze and scurried over. "Not sure what?"

"Well," Belle sighed heavily. "According to my calculations, we've assembled more pieces and blown-up photos than we have room to display. I'm just not sure this is going to work. But it *has* to work." Her palms began to sweat, and the cold stoniness progressed to heart quavers.

Reba pivoted in place, her expression now more grim than gaga. "This space looked so big when I reserved it. I was sure it would . . ." She glanced at the figures in Belle's notebook, then threw up her hands. "Never was any good with numbers. Shit, Belle, what do we do?"

Belle mirrored Reba's pivot, but with a look of keen concentration, tinged with alarm. She tapped her temple with her index finger.

"This, Reba."

With phone calls and emails to return, not to mention constant interruptions from Soulstice workers and an overexuberant wallaby, Roscoe's pole barn was hardly the environment for concentrated problem-solving. Every time Belle took out her pad, calculator, and measuring tape, there was an "Oh, hey, Belle, would you mind looking at . . ." or an earnest "What do you think we should do about . . ." to scramble the numbers she was just starting to untangle. On top of all that, Reba and Jax reported hourly their mounting concerns about Coogan selling the zoo property out from under them.

"He's gotten wind of our plan," Jax told Belle two weeks before the gala, chartreuse hair flopping in a way that belied the gravity of the message. "'Course it'd be hard not to with all the posters we've been plastering around town."

Belle's stomach, already a gurgling, roiling jumble, took an extra somersault and swan dive. "So he wants to stop us, just to be a jerk."

Jax held up a hand in a "hold on" gesture accented by lime green nail polish. "Not really. He just thinks we're too flaky to pull off the gala and raise the kind of money he's asking. So he's still negotiating with developers, and from what I can glean, they're getting close to a deal. Lakshmi keeps calling him from her aunt's house, begging him to hold off on signing anything until after the gala. but if we don't have every last cent to beat the developers' offer by then, we're screwed and so are the animals."

Belle's mouth went dry and she groped for a place to sit down. Great. So now she'd have to double down on fundraising efforts by day and tackle the exhibit arrangement problem at home by night. Okay. Sleep could wait until after the gala. She could go without sleep for two weeks, right?

Sleep was all Belle could think of when, exhausted from the day's work, she pulled into her driveway that evening. On her way into the house, she paused to survey *Belle Jardin*. Had she done enough to prove its artistic worth, or would the city demolish it after all, clearing the way for Mrs. Dumas to make good on her eviction threat?

Had Belle really made the right decision to abandon that project and devote herself to the save-the-zoo gala? It was too late for second-guessing. She was all in now, and she had to see it through, no matter the cost to herself.

Seva, she reminded herself. Selfless service.

On sleepless nights, she replayed that reminder. Night after night, she puzzled over the space problem, drawing diagrams on her sketch pad, ripping them out, wadding them up, starting over. Some evenings she sketched by lantern light in Ozzy's pen—for inspiration, if nothing else.

Ozzy cast curious squints and head-tilts her way.

"Yes, my friend, we're in a bit of a jam here," Belle told him one night, less than a week from the gala. "And I've got to use my noggin' to get us out." She rapped the side of her head, prompting a new round of tilts and squints.

And then, just like that, dawn was breaking over the fox pen, where Belle lay with Ozzy's furry chin resting on her head and Mitchell holding out a mug of coffee.

"Omigod, I've got to get going!" Belle scrambled to get up, but a thought overtook her. Or was it a sensation? Or a memory? Whatever it was, it exerted such a powerful hold, she found it impossible even to shift her position.

"I had . . . I had . . . I had a dream!" The words came out in an astonished murmur.

"Well, yeah, silly girl," Mitchell said, leaning closer with the coffee cup. "That's what happens when you go to sleep."

Belle raised herself from the ground and shook her head. "But it's been weeks since I've had a dream—not since I started working on the gala. My brain has been so overloaded with details and tasks and numbers, there hasn't been room for fantasies. Now all of a sudden I see that the solution to this problem is just a matter of fitting pieces together, like a *Belle Jardin* mosaic, one piece at a time."

Mitchell nodded and set down the mug. Ozzy stuck his nose into it, but Belle paid no mind, having no need for stimulants now. She reached for her drawing pad and pencil. In minutes, she'd designed a staggered arrangement with tall pedestals to display some pieces behind others and oversized photos mounted on every available wall and hung from the balconies that overlooked the court from the upper-floor galleries.

The effect was totally unconventional and a bit slapdash—just like outsider art.

Belle stared at what she'd just designed. *Who did this? Who* did *this?*

The answer came to her from who knows where: *You did, Belle.*

And with that answer, a startling thought: *Maybe I haven't abandoned my artistic side; maybe I'm* integrating *it with my organizing side. Maybe my authentic self isn't one or the other, but a salmagundi mashup of both—and possibly other pieces I've yet to discover.*

The parking lot and sign hadn't changed since the first time she'd sat there.

SUNFLOWER PAWN & JEWELRY

$$ MONEY TO LOAN $$

That time, though, she'd been reluctant to open the car door and go inside, heartbroken to be pawning Grandpa Jake's ruby ring, yet knowing it was the only way to save Ozzy. Now, on the eve of an event that might—and *might* was still the operative word—save his cronies in the zoo, she'd come to retrieve the ring before heading to the art museum to check on the installation. A $500 advance on her credit card would get the ring out of hock. How she'd pay back the advance was another matter, but one she was not concerned with just now. All she knew was, she *had* to wear that ring to the gala. She needed Grandpa Jake's presence to steady her.

Belle marched into the pawn shop, where the same clerk greeted her with the smile that gleamed like jewelry on display. She pulled the claim ticket from her wallet, proud of herself for finding it exactly where she'd put it two months earlier, and plunked it on the glass countertop with five one-hundred-dollar bills. She scanned the shelves below, half expecting to see the ruby ring with a price tag attached, but it was nowhere in sight. She hoped that meant it was safe in a vault or at least a secure back room.

"Where is it?" Belle tried not to let panic inflect her voice. "You said it would be safe here. You said I could *trust* you."

The young man scrutinized the ticket. "Oh, sure, I remember. The ruby ring. A family heirloom, right?"

How could he be so cavalier, knowing what the ring meant to her? Where *was* it?

"I was just about to call you," the young fellow said.

Call her? *Why*? Had the ring been stolen? Had he sold it by mistake? Just when she was finally about to reclaim it?

"Yeah, someone came in less than an hour ago and paid for it."

"But you said I had ninety days." Belle couldn't contain the panic now. The fluorescent lights overhead flashed; the wall display of guitars became a psychedelic swirl and disappeared into a tunnel. She clutched the counter to steady herself. "I think I'm going to . . ."

The young man gripped her shoulders with both hands and gave her a gentle shake. "Whoa, there, ma'am, everything's okay. The person who came in didn't *buy* the ring, they just repaid your debt. The ring is yours now, free and clear."

Another swoon almost overtook Belle, but she recovered and simply shook her head, astonished. *Who could've done such a thing?* Faces of her Soulstice friends flashed through her mind. Not one seemed capable of coming up with that kind of money. And anyway, who would've known how much the ring meant to her?

"Did you get the person's name?"

"Nope. It was somebody I've seen around, though," he said over his shoulder as he ducked into a back room to fetch the ring.

"What'd this person look like?" Belle called after him. "Male? Female? Nonbinary? Young? Old? Black? White? Brown?"

The pawnbroker returned with the ring and handed it to Belle with his broadest, brightest smile yet. "That I can't tell you," he said. "I'm sworn to secrecy. But they did leave this envelope for you."

Belle slipped the ring onto her finger, took the envelope from the broker, and thanked him, but waited until she was back in her car to open it.

Inside she found a crumpled scrap of newspaper—a crossword puzzle with a single word circled in peacock-blue ink: *Salmagundi.*

– 29 –
THE GALA

Spotlights shone on art displays; balloons and streamers festooned refreshment stands; mosaic vases filled with sprawling bouquets of summer flowers decorated cocktail tables. Yes, everything was exactly as Belle had specified. Now, if the program proceeded as she'd planned it, this event might just come off.

If anyone showed up.

Every time she'd asked DeShawn, the designated ticket master, how sales were going, he'd answered with a vague superlative: "Great!" "Fantastic!" "Awesome!" Who knew what those words meant to him. When Belle asked for specifics, like actual amounts of money raised, he'd hem and haw and promise to get back to her. Which he somehow never managed to do.

On her way to the museum that evening, she'd steeled herself for an empty gallery, despite DeShawn's assurances. Outsider art was so—well, *outside* the mainstream. Who really appreciated it besides the grassroots art association folks? And they'd already seen most of these pieces elsewhere.

To Belle's astonishment, though, guests began trickling into the central court shortly after she arrived a full forty-five minutes before the designated hour. Then more . . . and more . . . until the place was teeming. Even more bewildering, everyone stared and whispered as they passed. Had she forgotten to comb her hair? Was there a rip in her dress—the slinky number she'd bought in a last-minute trip to the secondhand store after the pawn shop visit? She stole a glance at her reflection in a mirrored wall. Nothing amiss that she could see. Even her hair was styled—or at least combed for a change. Then all of a sudden, strangers were thrusting out hands to shake hers. "Congratulations! Amazing work!"

Well, she'd never had *that* kind of reaction to organizing an event before! But this *was* Kansas, she reminded herself. Lots of things were different here.

Still more guests poured in. Familiar faces—Reba, Mae, DeShawn, Lakshmi, Olive Pickle, Jax, Roscoe—as well as many Belle had never seen before. And some she'd seen nearly every day but didn't recognize in their cleaned-up, dressed-up forms. Like the elderly gent shuffling through the double doors, decked out in a wide-lapelled, pin-striped suit from another era. Could it be? Sure enough, it was Belle's neighbor Mitchell, thinning hair slicked back, stubbly chin shaved clean. And beside him—Ezra? What was he doing here? Wasn't he still in Nebraska? And that large-eared woman with the messy bun chatting with Ezra. Could that be . . . *Miranda*? Belle had been texting her boiled-down summaries of her gala travails, knowing Miranda and Nick were deep in wedding details, hardly expecting a reply, much less attendance at the event. Now here was her lifelong bestie, Nick-less and beaming as she mimicked the dance moves their volleyball team used to execute before matches.

Belle tried to make her way through the crowd to Miranda, Ezra, Mitchell, and the others, but with all the hand-shaking and congratulating, she was stuck in place—cemented like a piece in one of the sculptures.

"Thank you, thank you so much, thank you." Belle didn't know what else to say.

Roscoe hopped onto the stage to emcee the proceedings. The

crowd's din decrescendoed to a murmur and then a hush. Reba and Miranda materialized on either side of Belle and hugged her in a three-way embrace. (Four, if you counted Wallace, who peeked out from Reba's Snugli.) As they all turned to face the stage, Reba and Miranda each grabbed a hand and squeezed it so tightly Belle almost yelped. Odd in its intensity. Yet so comforting to have her longtime bestie and new sidekick beside her for this event that had so consumed her for the past month.

Before Belle could further analyze the strange behavior of everyone around her, Roscoe tapped the microphone. "Greetings, folks, and welcome to 'Outside In,' this indoor installation of outsider art. Thank you all for coming. As you probably know, donations from this evening's event will benefit the Zoology Project, a noble endeavor to turn the controversial roadside zoo on the outskirts of town into a sanctuary where our furry, feathered, and scaly friends—no, not you, Zebulon—can live out their lives in natural settings."

Belle let out the breath she'd been holding. *So far, so good. He's following the script.* With Roscoe, you never knew. He could be acting normal as apple pandowdy and then, without warning, go off the rails.

"Very shortly, you'll have a chance to look at all the art we've assembled here and enjoy some refreshments, solid and liquid. But first, we want to share a short video to introduce you to some of the artists whose work we're celebrating."

Roscoe ducked out of the way as the room darkened and the screen behind him filled with a rapid-fire montage of faces and names, interspersed with video clips of some of the artists talking about their work. Even with everything she'd read about outsider art, all the images she'd seen, and the assemblages she'd visited in Lucas, Belle was blown away by the variety of works and the equally colorful personalities of their creators.

The clips concluded; the house lights came up.

So that was it. Now all Roscoe needed to do was declare the

exhibit and refreshment stations open, and guests could start milling around. He popped up behind the lectern and spoke into the mic.

"And now, one more thing. Well, two or three, actually."

Wait . . . what? There's not one more thing. Or two or three. That's the end of the script. Please don't let him start reciting poetry or some damn thing. Belle tried to catch Roscoe's eye to communicate telepathically or pantomime throat-slitting—anything to get him to wrap it up.

Roscoe continued unabated. "Thanks to the generosity of all you folks, we raised a whole bunch of money. And it woulda been plenty if some greedy developers hadn't started a bidding war for the zoo property. When they outbid our top number, we thought we were sunk. But at the last minute, we were blessed by a benefactor who offered a two-for-one match for every donation. That took us over the top. So let's all give a rousing round of applause for our fairy godparent, Salvatore McGundy."

All around the room, looks of *Who???* crossed faces as a pitter-patter of applause swelled into a deluge. Belle, still stuck on *Who???*, was too preoccupied to clap.

Salvatore McGundy. Sal McGundy. Salmagundi?

Before she could finish processing that thought, Roscoe was on to the next announcement.

"With that magnanimous gift, added to all of yours, we've been able to seal the deal. The former roadside zoo will henceforth be known as the Audrey Coogan Memorial Animal Rescue Center. We won't seek out additional animals, but we'll care for any critters that come our way, with the idea of eventually transitioning the property into a nature preserve."

This time, Belle joined in the applause and beamed along with the rest of the crowd. As she scanned the room, she thought she saw a red-bearded man swipe a finger beneath an eye and slip out the back.

"And finally," Roscoe said as the applause died down, "this whole thing started as a project to save the animals, but along the way it turned into a different kind of rescue mission."

Still more? Come on, man, wrap this thing up. Belle's ears buzzed, her head pounded, and she felt woozy, the way she always did when something she'd so carefully planned didn't go according to plan. She could hardly make out what Roscoe was saying until she heard, ". . . Belle Marsden . . ."

What was he saying about her? Miranda and Reba squeezed her hands again.

"He wants you up on stage, Belle," Miranda said.

"What on earth for?" Belle scowled and shook her head.

Reba and Miranda looked at each other and, in unison, nudged Belle forward. "Get up there, woman," Reba said. Belle balked. They shoved; she stumbled. Then someone took her arm—Ezra!—and guided her to the stage.

"What's this all about?" Belle stage-whispered to Roscoe when she joined him at the podium. "This wasn't in the script."

Another image flashed on the screen behind Roscoe. *Belle Jardin*, the caption read. Belle's face flushed. Her "eyesore" on display for everyone to see. The "atrocity" that was still threatened with demolition three days from now and would likely get her evicted.

A rustling in the crowd alerted Belle to movement. Someone else was striding toward the stage.

Oh god, no. Not the city manager! Don't tell me he's going to announce the demolition. As if I haven't been through enough.

City manager Roger Morton was buddy-buddy with Steve Schwann—Belle's nemesis in the zoning department. She'd seen the two of them tooling around town in Morton's Camaro convertible. Same model as Jamison's—the one he once gave her a late-night ride home in.

Smiling broadly, Morton bounded up the steps and took the mic from Roscoe.

Maybe he's just commandeering our event to call attention to himself and gain supporters for his reelection bid. How crass. Belle crossed her fingers and sidled toward the edge of the platform. Roscoe reached out both arms and wrapped her in a bear hug too tight to escape.

"Isn't this a terrific event?" Morton said, still beaming.

Seriously? He's saying those words?

"They say outsider art is influenced by inner vision," Morton continued. "By revelations, you might say. Well, I've recently had a revelation." He turned and fixed his eyes on Belle's, then turned back to address the audience. "Thanks to the behind-the-scenes efforts of the Soulstice Foundation, the other city officials and I have come to recognize the value of outsider art. They've been educating us over the past few weeks, and now we're downright proud to have a fine example right here in Lawrence in the work of Isabelle Marsden, better known as Belle."

Then turning again to Belle: "Normally it would take months to approve what I'm about to announce, but due to the special circumstances, we've expedited the process. I'm proud to reveal that we are designating *Belle Jardin* as a municipal art installation and honoring its creator, Belle, with this award."

From a shelf in the lectern, Morton brought forth a gleaming medal on a wide ribbon—the kind draped around the necks of Olympic winners. Roscoe released Belle from his grip. Dazed, she ducked her head as Morton slipped the medal over it.

"I'll let Belle say a few words in a moment, but first I want to announce that at the conclusion of this opening, the Soulstice Foundation and I will lead a parade to North Lawrence, where I'll install a plaque on Belle's creation. You're all invited to come along and see her fantastic work for yourselves."

Morton handed Belle the mic. Her ears buzzed again; glittery waves danced before her eyes; the room spun; she hiccupped. *Am I about to faint?* She gripped the lectern and forced herself to take slow, deep breaths. The walls stopped moving, and the audience came into focus. Miranda nodded encouragement. Reba pumped a fist. Mae clapped her hands like a four-year-old. Ezra grinned sideways. Jax and DeShawn held up a sign: "We Love You, Belle!!! You're One of Us."

At last, Belle composed herself. "Mmmmm . . . my friends. To say I'm astonished at this turn of events would be a colossal understatement. Just now, Mr. Morton spoke about revelations. Well, I've had a revelation too."

Around the room, every head turned toward the stage, every face expectant.

Belle sucked in another breath and let it out in a whoosh. "When I moved here three and a half months ago, wounded and confused, I was looking for a hideaway. I thought the only way to heal was to retreat from life, to remain detached, to cloister myself in a sanctuary where I was in control." She paused. "Boy, did I pick the wrong place for that!"

Laughter rippled around the room. Appreciative laughter, not the derisive kind she'd endured from city workers gawking at *Belle Jardin*.

Belle smiled and went on: "But even as I was pulled into interactions with other people, I held back, still believing I needed to be in control to heal myself. And I thought the only path to putting myself back together was through this crazy whatever-it-is." She swept an arm toward the image on the screen behind her, simultaneously trying to process this whole amazing turn of events and collect her thoughts enough to continue.

Another deep breath. *Grounding, grounding.* She scanned the crowd for Ezra, easy enough to find with the way he towered over most heads. He nodded encouragement so enthusiastically his sweep of black hair obscured his eyes.

Belle went on: "But now I see that, while working on this piece under the guidance of my muse helped me heal, what really has made me whole again is being embraced and supported by the eclectic bunch of folks who make up the Soulstice Foundation and its associates." She held out her arms toward Reba and the rest of the gang, all clumped together now, and then directed a you-too finger point toward Ezra and Mitchell. "In all of you, I've found a family—something I thought I'd lost forever—and in that family, a place where I don't have to be in control to be safe."

A trickle of applause leaked from the audience. Belle held up both hands, palms facing forward.

"One more thing. By helping to organize this event and seeing how the Soulstice Foundation pulled together, not only to make this happen but also to save my sculptures from demolition and me from the brink of, well, *lunacy*, I understand now that artistry and organization can coexist. You don't have to choose one over the other."

A voice rose from the crowd. "Bravo for that!" Mae was on her feet, baby-clapping her hands again. The rest of the audience sprang from their seats as one, applauding, cheering, whistling, and stomping.

For me? Belle shook her head and handed the mic back to Roscoe, who tried to close with a quip. For once, the poet was without words, and that was just as well. Who could've heard him over all that hoo-ha and hullabaloo?

And anyway, what more was there to say?

Perched on the back of Roger Morton's convertible, Belle rode through town, regal as Queen Aquamaureen. By the time the Camaro pulled up to her house, the yard was swarming with fans admiring *Belle Jardin*. In the midst of them stood none other than Mrs. Dumas.

"Why yes, I guess you could call me a patron of the arts," Belle heard her landlady say. "Benefactor? Well, that's a bit of a stretch, but if you say so." She laughed a tinkly laugh that didn't seem at all suited to her personality, and she beckoned to Belle as if she were a favorite niece.

"Oh, Belle, darling, I was just telling everyone how much I adore your artistry and how pleased I've been to provide a creative milieu for your work."

Belle pasted on a smile every bit as phony as Mrs. Dumas's and in her most saccharine voice replied, "I couldn't have done it without you, Mrs. Dumas, dear."

Which was true, she realized, thinking back to the day Mrs. Dumas called *Belle Jardin* an "atrocity," and Belle, fired up with fresh inspiration, vowed, "We'll show her atrocity."

So here it was, the utterly unacceptable atrocity of Isabelle Marsden, now destined not for demolition, but for distinction. And here was Belle, accepting so many handshakes, hugs, and pats on the back she finally had to slip next door to Ozzy's pen to catch her breath.

"We did it, Oz." She reached out to stroke an ear. The fox moved ever so slightly closer and finally, they connected. "You and your friends can breathe easy now, too."

"Well done, Sister," came a familiar voice. "Reba told me I'd probably find you here." Miranda let herself into the pen and sat on the ground beside Belle, oblivious to the Kansas dirt smudging the floaty skirt she'd bought for the occasion. "Guess we can consider this experiment a success, even if your six-month stint isn't quite over."

"And even if it turned out nothing like I expected."

"Which is good."

"Which is very good."

Miranda dragged a finger through a bare patch of dust. "I have to ask—have you given any thought to calling that attorney Nick recommended? He's having good outcomes on assault cases like yours."

Belle grimaced. "Did you have to bring that up? Let's just say I've given it some thought and leave it at that for now. Okay?" She turned her face back to Ozzy and ignored Miranda's hand on her shoulder.

"Of course. It was stupid of me to even mention it." Miranda rose to her knees, brushed off her skirt, and held out a hand again. "Let's get back to the party. Your public awaits."

The celebration was in full Soulstice swing when they returned to Belle's yard. Roscoe stood on the front porch reciting poetry; DeShawn dispensed champagne like a human fountain; Jax passed around questionable-looking snacks; Wallace bounded from group to group, begging for handouts; Reba half-heartedly pursued him, cooing nonsensically and pausing to chat with anyone open to meandering conversation. Belle stopped to give Reba a hug so extra-affectionate Reba looked at her in surprise, then hugged back even tighter.

Was it fate that brought them together at that quilt show? How differently the summer would have passed if not for that chance encounter. Belle couldn't even imagine the past months without this unconventional, artsy, cooing woman and her coterie of colorful characters. And without the trips to Lucas, the inspiration for her own unacceptable atrocity.

Belle searched the crowd for Mae, then realized it was well past seven. She'd be tucked in with a book by now.

A glimpse of an aqua silk frock and a coil of silver braids (streaked today with aqua hair color, courtesy of Jax) told her Aquamaureen's curfew was being violated. Mae sat on Belle's back stoop, crumpled crossword on her knee, turquoise pen in hand.

"Eleven-letter word for generous, starts with M," she muttered to herself as Belle approached. Her eyes traveled from Belle's face to the hand dangling at her side.

"Nice ring," Mae said, turning back to her crossword.

"Indeed," Belle said. "It was a gift. Twice over. And by the way, the eleven-letter word is 'magnanimous.' One I should think you would know."

A noise from the kitchen startled them both. "Don't tell me Wallace is on the loose in there," Belle said. "I'd better go check it out."

Wallace was nowhere in sight, but Ezra was clanking bottles as he loaded a case of Stormchaser into the fridge. He held out a bottle to Belle, took one for himself, and clinked it against hers.

"To the artistry of atrocities. Didn't I always say you were a true artist? About time you were recognized for it."

Belle shook her head and looked down the neck of her bottle.

"Looking for your fortune down there? What *is* next for you, anyway?" Ezra raised an eyebrow that was already higher than the other.

Belle took a long pull on the bottle and gazed out the window. "Now that the threats of demolition and eviction are behind me, and I'm no longer wanted for murder, I guess I can head back to Chicago."

Ezra's eyebrow sank into a furrow. "You're moving back? Before your six months are over?"

Belle kept staring out at the darkening sky. "Not moving. Just going back to do something I couldn't do before. Kind of like when the King of the Wild Things had to go back to Nebraska to tend to business. When that's squared away maybe I'll even swing through Phoenix for an overdue visit." She turned back into the room, set her bottle down, and patted the kitchen table. "But once that's all done, I'm coming back here. I know now where home is."

Ezra gave her a long look. For once his features arranged themselves in a way that was oddly appealing.

"Yeah," he said. "Me too."

CREDITS

Walking On Sunshine

Words and Music by Kimberley Rew

Copyright © 1983 Kyboside Ltd.

All Rights Administered by BMG Rights Management (US) LLC

All Rights Reserved Used by Permission

Reprinted by Permission of Hal Leonard LLC

Your Feet

By Pablo Neruda, from THE CAPTAIN'S VERSES

Copyright © 1972 by Pablo Neruda and Donald D. Walsh

Reprinted by Permission of New Directions Publishing Co.

Tus Pies, from LOS VERSOS DEL CAPITAN

© Pablo Neruda, 1952 and Fundación Pablo Neruda

Reprinted by Permission

Making Concrete Garden Ornaments

By Sherri Warner Hunter

Published by Lark Books, a division of Sterling Publishing Co., Inc.

Text Reprinted by Permission, Sherri Warner Hunter © 2001

BOOK CLUB DISCUSSION QUESTIONS

1. Why does Belle feel the need to retreat, regroup, and reassess when she moves to Kansas?

2. What is the first indication that Belle's plans may go awry?

3. Has a chance encounter with a stranger ever led you in an unexpected direction? Looking back, are you glad you were sidetracked?

4. How would you describe the relationship between Belle and Ezra? Does it change over the course of the story?

5. What does *Belle Jardin* represent to Belle?

6. How does the author use dreams and imagery to enhance the story?

7. If you were in charge of casting for a film version of this book, who would you cast as Belle? Reba? Mae? Ezra? Do you have ideas for any of the other characters?

8. Did this story change any of your perceptions of eccentric artists? Of Kansas?

ACKNOWLEDGMENTS

Given enough concrete, ceramic fragments, and sparkly bibelots and baubles, I would construct my own creation like Belle's, paying tribute to all the colorful characters who contributed in so many ways to the making of this book.

I would devote a prominent place in my assemblage to the incomparable Brooke Warner, whose energy and expertise I've long admired. I had benefited from Brooke's editorial savvy when I hired her for a whole-manuscript evaluation of my 2019 memoir *Mango Rash* and again when I sought her input on an earlier draft of this novel. I'm delighted to work with her in a different capacity and to be a She Writes Press author.

Megan Milton also deserves a glittery star for guiding this project through the many steps from acceptance to publication and promptly answering questions that came up along the way.

I'd add a ruby-studded red pen to show my appreciation for Anne Durette's skillful edits—conscientious without being heavy-handed. *Merci beaucoup*!

Fellow authors in my She Writes Press Spring 2026 cohort have offered encouragement and support through monthly Zoom meetings and a private Facebook group. For them, I'd create a towering stack of books with the smiling authors peeking out from behind as they celebrate their own publications and glowing reviews.

A gateway would represent Phillip Sterling and Elizabeth Stolarek (aka Rebecca Thaddeus), whose writing retreats at Three Ponds Farm gave me—an entrenched nonfiction writer—the confidence to try writing fiction. A writing exercise at one of those retreats made Isabelle and her wheelbarrow take shape in my mind and sparked my imagination to keep filling in details.

Extra recognition in the form of a bottle of Stormchaser beer goes to Phillip for his ongoing support of this and other writing efforts over the years. His input on an earlier draft of this story was invaluable.

If I could find a glass eyeball like the one Olive Pickle gave Belle, I'd incorporate it to represent the Artworks writers group, whose first looks at pages helped me clarify my vision of the story and its characters.

A jewel-encrusted polishing cloth would express my gratitude to beta readers Sally Kane, Janet Glaser, Kathy Misak, Margaret Hrencher, Laura Bailey, and Tonya Howe for their insights.

I'm fortunate to have my own Soulstice gang in the form of the Monday morning yoginis. To show my appreciation for their friendship and interest in this book, I would craft a dazzling figure doing sun salutations.

A fanciful power cord would represent Jenni Laidman, who helped me connect with contacts in the outsider art world.

For their support of local authors and artists, I would create a multifaceted gem in honor of the vibrant arts and literary community in my part of the world, particularly Newaygo County Council for the Arts—Artsplace, Artworks, and Flying Bear Books & Creperie.

An oversized megaphone would announce my special shoutout to Erika Nelson and Lynn Schneider of S. P. Dinsmoor's Garden of Eden for enthusiastically embracing and endorsing this novel.

I'd sculpt a giant pair of arms wrapped in an embrace as a tribute to the many creative, eccentric, and goodhearted friends who have enriched my life and inspired my imagination over the years.

I envision a magnificent budding blossom to honor my parents, Harold and Neva, and my older brother, Ron, who nurtured my creativity from childhood. By appreciating the artistic work of others and setting examples with their own, they raised me in an environment where artistry was valued.

And for Ray, my love, cheerleader, helpmate, inspiration, traveling companion on whatever road we find ourselves, and so much more, I would save an elevated spot in the very center of my creation on which to craft two enormous linked hearts.

To help keep S. P. Dinsmoor's Garden growing, please visit www.gardenofedenlucas.org and scroll down to the Donate button in the CONTACT *section at the bottom.*

ABOUT THE AUTHOR

photo courtesy of the author

After a rewarding career writing about science, medicine, and healthful living for the *Detroit Free Press*, the University of Michigan, and numerous other newspapers, magazines, and online publications (under the byline Nancy Ross-Flanigan), Nan now focuses on memoir, fiction, and photography.

Her memoir *Mango Rash: Coming of Age in the Land of Frangipani and Fanta* (Behler Publications, 2019) won first place in the memoir/nonfiction category of the 2018 Pacific Northwest Writers Association literary awards and was featured in the "Breaking In" section of *Writer's Digest* magazine.

A lifelong admirer of visionary art and all things quirky and unconventional, Nan has visited and photographed outsider art sites around the United States. Those visits and her graduate student years in Lawrence, Kansas, inspired *The Utterly Unacceptable Atrocity of Isabelle Marsden.*

In addition to writing, Nan takes award-winning photographs, creates collages, and wanders the woods around the West Michigan home she shares with her husband, Ray Pokerwinski. Her blog HeartWood (www.nanpokerwinski.com/blog) focuses on cultivating creativity, connection, and contentment.

VISIT THE AUTHOR AT:
www.nanpokerwinski.com
www.facebook.com/MangoRash
www.linktr.ee/nansanpo